THE MERIWELL LEGACY

THE CASEBOOK OF BARNABY ADAIR: VOLUME 8

STEPHANIE LAURENS

ABOUT THE MERIWELL LEGACY

THE EIGHTH VOLUME IN THE CASEBOOK OF BARNABY ADAIR NOVELS

#1 NYT-bestselling author Stephanie Laurens returns with her favorite sleuths to unravel a tangled web of family secrets and expose a murderer.

When Lord Meriwell collapses and dies at his dining table, Barnaby and Penelope Adair are summoned, along with Inspector Basil Stokes, to discover who, how, and most importantly why someone very close to his lordship saw fit to poison him.

Well-born rakehell and head of an ancient family, Alaric, Lord Carradale, has finally acknowledged reality and is preparing to find a bride. But loyalty to his childhood friend, Percy Mandeville, necessitates attending Percy's annual house party, held at neighboring Mandeville Hall. Yet despite deploying his legendary languid charm, by the second evening of the week-long event, Alaric is bored and restless.

Escaping from the soirée and the Hall, Alaric decides that as soon as he's free, he'll hie to London and find the mild-mannered, biddable lady he believes will ensure a peaceful life. But the following morning, on walking through the Mandeville Hall shrubbery on his way to join the other guests, he comes upon the corpse of a young lady-guest.

Constance Whittaker accepts that no gentleman will ever offer for her —she's too old, too tall, too buxom, too headstrong…too much in myriad ways. Now acting as her grandfather's agent, she arrives at Mandeville

Hall to extricate her young cousin, Glynis, who unwisely accepted an invitation to the reputedly licentious house party.

But Glynis cannot be found.

A search is instituted. Venturing into the shrubbery, Constance discovers an outrageously handsome aristocrat crouched beside Glynis's lifeless form. Unsurprisingly, Constance leaps to the obvious conclusion.

Luckily, once the gentleman explains that he'd only just arrived, commonsense reasserts itself. More, as matters unfold and she and Carradale have to battle to get Glynis's death properly investigated, Constance discovers Alaric to be a worthy ally.

Yet even after Inspector Stokes of Scotland Yard arrives and takes charge of the case, along with his consultants, the Honorable Barnaby Adair and his wife, Penelope, the murderer's identity remains shrouded in mystery, and learning why Glynis was killed—all in the few days before the house party's guests will insist on leaving—tests the resolve of all concerned. Flung into each other's company, fiercely independent though Constance is, unsusceptible though Alaric is, neither can deny the connection that grows between them.

Then Constance vanishes.

Can Alaric unearth the one fact that will point to the murderer before the villain rips from the world the lady Alaric now craves for his own?

A historical novel of 75,000 words interweaving romance, mystery, and murder.

PRAISE FOR THE WORKS OF
STEPHANIE LAURENS

"Stephanie Laurens' heroines are marvelous tributes to Georgette Heyer: feisty and strong." *Cathy Kelly*

"Stephanie Laurens never fails to entertain and charm her readers with vibrant plots, snappy dialogue, and unforgettable characters." *Historical Romance Reviews*

"Stephanie Laurens plays into readers' fantasies like a master and claims their hearts time and again." *Romantic Times Magazine*

Praise for The Meriwell Legacy

"A mystery's afoot when Lord Meriwell collapses at dinner, poisoned. Which one of his family members or esteemed dinner guests has means and motive to want the wealthy man dead? Investigator wife-and-husband team Penelope and Barnaby Adair are on the case, assisting Scotland Yard in catching the killer. Fans of historical fiction and murder mystery aficionados will enjoy this well-plotted and suspenseful story." *Brittany M., Proofreader, Red Adept Editing*

"An MP and his family are enjoying a house party at Meriwell Hall when Lord Meriwell dies by poisoning at dinner one night, and many of those who gathered around the table that evening stand to gain from their host's demise. When some talented aristocratic sleuths are summoned to help solve the murder, the unmasking of the culprit is simply a matter of time. More mystery than romance, this new tale from Stephanie Laurens features a barrelful of red herrings and is a delight to read." *Angela M., Copy Editor, Red Adept Editing*

"Penelope and Barnaby Adair have solved several mysteries for the social elite of Regency London. So when Lord Meriwell dies under suspicious circumstances at his country estate, it's natural for Inspector Basil Stokes to enlist their help in clarifying matters. Did Meriwell succumb to old age, or was he felled by a cash-strapped descendent desperate for an inheritance? In genteel but relentless fashion, the investigators untangle a web of family intrigue—and a few romantic matches."

Kim H., Proofreader, Red Adept Editing

OTHER TITLES BY STEPHANIE LAURENS

Desire's Prize

Novellas

Melting Ice – from the anthologies *Rough Around the Edges* and *Scandalous Brides*

Rose in Bloom – from the anthology *Scottish Brides*

Scandalous Lord Dere – from the anthology *Secrets of a Perfect Night*

Lost and Found – from the anthology *Hero, Come Back*

The Fall of Rogue Gerrard – from the anthology *It Happened One Night*

The Seduction of Sebastian Trantor – from the anthology *It Happened One Season*

Short Stories

The Wedding Planner – from the anthology *Royal Weddings*

A Return Engagement – from the anthology *Royal Bridesmaids*

UK-Style Regency Romances

Tangled Reins

Four in Hand

Impetuous Innocent

Fair Juno

The Reasons for Marriage

A Lady of Expectations An Unwilling Conquest

A Comfortable Wife

THE MERIWELL LEGACY

THE MERIWELL LEGACY

Copyright © 2024 by Savdek Management Proprietary Limited

ISBN: 978-1-925559-60-2

Cover design by Savdek Management Pty. Ltd.

Cover couple photography by Period Images © 2024

First print publication: March, 2024

Savdek Management Proprietary Limited, Melbourne, Australia.

www.stephanielaurens.com

Email: admin@stephanielaurens.com

The names Stephanie Laurens and the Cynsters and the SL Logo are registered trademarks of Savdek Management Proprietary Ltd.

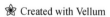 Created with Vellum

CHAPTER 1

MAY 4, 1840. MERIWELL HALL, SURREY.

"*D*amn!" Veronica Haskell muttered as she halted—was forced to halt—in the shadows of the gallery around the main staircase of Meriwell Hall.

From the front hall below, from just inside the front door and therefore out of her sight, came "Busselton! Good man! Welcome to Meriwell Hall."

The words were uttered by Veronica's employer, Lord Meriwell, in what, to her, sounded like teeth-gritted geniality, while the subsequent noises informed her that the guests expected for a weeklong stay had arrived.

"Thank you, my lord. Thank you" was offered in response, presumably by Mr. George Busselton, Member of Parliament for the local area. "It's a great pleasure to be here. Allow me to introduce my wife."

Veronica listened as greetings were exchanged.

If she continued around the gallery to her younger charge's room, she would be seen by the guests, and she wasn't at all sure that his lordship wished to advertise the presence of a nurse in his household, and in her neat uniform, she was readily identifiable as one of that species. Consequently, she loitered, waiting while the MP's children, Persimone and Peregrine, were introduced. Veronica was struck by an impulse to inch forward until she could peek into the hall, but reluctantly reined in her curiosity.

The purpose of the Busseltons' visit was to advance the cause of a potential liaison between Persimone Busselton, a young lady of some twenty-three summers, and Mr. Stephen Meriwell, his lordship's oldest nephew. Stephen was patently keen to impress the Busseltons with his connection to the Meriwell title and estate, and courtesy of the staff grapevine as well as her own observations, Veronica had learned that his lordship regarded the prospective alliance with great favor and was eager to support Stephen's suit.

Stephen's voice drifted up from below. Apparently, he'd escorted the Busseltons to the Hall.

Surely the company would go into the drawing room now? Veronica knew that Lady Meriwell and Lord Iffey, a close friend of the Meriwells, were waiting in the reception room to meet the much-anticipated guests.

Veronica shifted impatiently. She was on her way to check on Miss Sophie Meriwell, his lordship's only grandchild, primarily to assess just how Sophie thought to react to the Busseltons and their visit. Sophie was given to indulging in histrionics, to acting in overly dramatic ways in order—or so Veronica firmly believed—to draw, focus, and hold the attention of everyone within earshot.

Sophie lived to be the center of attention. Always.

Although ostensibly, Veronica had been hired by his lordship to oversee his and his wife's health, her true purpose over the nine weeks since she'd joined the household had been to observe and assess Sophie's predisposition to dramatics to determine whether the young lady, now eighteen years old, was a true hysteric.

That diagnosis came with significant negative connotations and adverse impacts, especially for a young lady yet to make her come-out, and Lord Meriwell had been sufficiently concerned by the possibility to veto Sophie having a London Season this year. Apparently, the notion that she would behave hysterically while under the ton's censorious gaze and, thus, reflect badly on the Meriwell family wasn't a risk he'd been willing to court.

At twenty-five years old, Veronica had completed four years of training and had more than six years' experience on which to call, all of it spent nursing ladies, young and old. She'd been temporarily between engagements when Dr. David Sanderson, the physician of her most recent patient, old Lady Ardlington, sadly now deceased, had asked Veronica to undertake this short-term assignment.

After dealing with Sophie for nine weeks, Veronica was ready to make her report and move on. Despite their advanced ages, the elder

Meriwells were not in need of her services, and Sophie would benefit more from a strong-willed companion, one who would act as a common-sense anchor. In reality, all Sophie needed to live an entirely normal life was to have someone make her think through the consequences of her actions before she embarked on her latest dramatic flight.

At last, Veronica heard shuffling and footsteps indicating the guests were filing into the drawing room.

She drew breath and was poised to continue on her way when she heard his lordship furiously whisper, "I want to see you later. After dinner, in the library."

Suppressed rage vibrated beneath his lordship's rigidly civil phrasing.

With the same contained anger and still speaking in a forceful whisper, he added, "It's about the business in Seven Dials."

Seven Dials? Veronica was amazed that any Meriwell would have any interest whatsoever in that seediest and most dangerous of London slums.

Stephen's tone as he answered, "Yes, of course," suggested he was as surprised as she, and both men walked into the drawing room.

"Finally!" Veronica murmured and set off for Sophie's room. As she passed the head of the stairs, she looked down and saw the butler, Jensen, and the two footmen, Thomas and Jeremy, busily sorting luggage.

As she continued along the corridor to Sophie's room, Veronica mulled over what she'd overheard. Judging from the staff's views of the members of the Meriwell family, it seemed likely that any link with a presumably unsavory business in Seven Dials would be via one of Stephen's younger brothers, Arthur or Peter Meriwell. Both younger nephews frequently tried his lordship's temper, the terms "wastrel" and "profligate" being habitually applied. In contrast, Stephen was regarded as the golden-haired future of the family, and from all Veronica had seen of the man, he was a steady, sensible, solidly respectable gentleman, who managed his affairs sufficiently well never to have applied to his lordship for financial relief, something Arthur and Peter did with distressing regu-larity. Over just the past nine weeks, she'd seen Arthur and Peter on several occasions when they'd arrived to try to pry more funds from Lord Meriwell.

Concluding that the cause of his lordship's ire would lie with either Arthur or Peter—both of whom were expected to arrive within the next hours and remain for several days, putting on a show of familial solidarity for the Busseltons in support of Stephen's cause—Veronica foresaw family fireworks in the immediate future.

~

That evening, Veronica sat at the long table in the servants' hall and, over the remains of their dinner, chatted with various members of the staff. Only Jensen, Thomas, Jeremy, Cook, and Maddie, her assistant, were absent. They'd eaten earlier, before Jensen and the footmen left to set the dining table and Cook and Maddie returned to the kitchen to ready the dishes for the family and guests above stairs.

Veronica turned to Sally, Sophie's maid, who was sitting on Veronica's right. "How did Sophie seem when she left for the drawing room? I hope she went down in good time."

"Oh yes, miss." Sally bobbed her head. "She went down right after you'd gone." Sally grinned. "That was a clever notion of yours, telling her about the young gentleman who's come. Made her forget her idea of ignoring the visitors, that did, and your suggestion she use the opportunity to show his lordship she can be trusted in company gave her a new direction. She went off in a much more agreeable frame of mind. If anything, she was curious to meet the young lady and her brother."

"Good." Across the table, Veronica met the eyes of the housekeeper, Mrs. Hutchinson. "With luck, Sophie might learn something from observing Miss Busselton."

"We can only hope!" Mrs. Hutchinson declared.

From deep within the house, a sound like a scream—abruptly cut off —reached them.

The staff looked at each other, mystified, wondering. Had Sophie decided she needed more attention?

A minute of pregnant silence ensued, then footsteps pounded down the corridor toward them.

The swinging door to the servants' hall flew open, crashing against the wall.

Everyone jerked and shifted to stare—at Thomas. Wide-eyed and white-faced, the young footman stood gasping in the doorway.

"It's his lordship," Thomas blurted. "He's collapsed at table." Thomas's gaze raked the gathering and locked on Veronica. "They've asked for you to come and see to him, miss."

She was already rising. "Yes, of course."

Thomas spun about and led the way.

Veronica rushed after him, and Gorton, his lordship's valet, followed at her heels.

They ran into the hall and around to the open dining room door. Veronica stepped into the room and paused.

Chaos reigned. Voices—mostly male—were exclaiming and arguing.

The room was long and narrow and, with four heavy sideboards hemming in the large dining table, was perpetually cramped. With one comprehensive glance, Veronica took in the four Busseltons, who had risen and gathered in a tight knot around the far end of the table, behind the small carver in which Clementina, Lady Meriwell, sat, her expression one of shock and stunned dismay. She seemed frozen in place, while Wallace, Lord Iffey, equally stunned, remained seated on her left.

Halfway down the table on the opposite side, Sophie Meriwell looked shocked speechless. She remained in her chair and stared uncomprehendingly at the melee surrounding her grandfather.

As for his lordship...

At the head of the table, nearer Veronica, a bevy of men were clustered around the large carver, presumably attempting to assist Lord Meriwell. Stephen, Arthur, and Peter were there, along with Jensen, while Thomas and Jeremy hovered, ready to help if required.

Her lips tightening, Veronica stepped forward, only to have Gorton dart around her and join the crowd around his lordship.

Gorton pushed Jensen aside to reach his master, and Jensen glanced up and saw Veronica. "Miss Haskell!" His expression one of incipient panic, the butler beckoned. "Please." To the men, he said, "We should make way for Nurse Haskell. Perhaps..."

Veronica followed Gorton and attempted to get close enough to see her patient.

Lord Meriwell lay slumped forward, his face pinning the empty soup plate to the plates beneath it. The fingers of his right hand were curled about the base of his wine glass, and his left arm, partially extended, lay on the white tablecloth.

His silver hair—despite his eighty years, still thick—and a small slice of his profile were all Veronica could see. She couldn't even judge his complexion from that.

Before she could demand to be given space to examine her patient, Arthur, his features harsh and his expression hard, cast her a sharp glance. "Stand back," he ordered. "Let us get him upstairs."

With that, Jeremy and Thomas drew back the large carver, and Stephen—on his lordship's other side—and Arthur hauled his lordship's limp arms over their shoulders and hoisted him up.

Veronica tried to peer at his lordship's face, but was blocked by Arthur as he and Stephen turned their uncle—suspended between them, slumped and apparently unresponsive—toward the doorway. When she pushed nearer, trying to see, Stephen snapped at her, "Wait until we get him to his bed. You can examine him there."

She gritted her teeth. She didn't need her patient stretched out to diagnose a faint or a seizure, but she had no authority to overrule them. Swallowing her professional ire, she followed as, assisted by Jensen, Gorton, and Jeremy, Stephen and Arthur maneuvered his lordship into the corridor.

Stephen glanced at Peter, who had been hovering ineffectually at Stephen's side. "See to the guests and Aunt Clementina, Iffey, and Sophie. Take them to the drawing room—I seriously doubt anyone feels hungry at the moment. Tell them we'll come down and report as soon as we know more."

Jensen sent Thomas to help Peter escort the guests to the drawing room, and Stephen and Arthur lurched forward, half dragging his lordship toward the stairs. Jensen and Jeremy rushed to get ahead of them, while Gorton fussed behind.

Veronica was about to follow when a thought impinged, and she briskly stepped back into the dining room.

Supported by Thomas, Peter was diffidently suggesting to the group clustered about the far end of the table that they repair to the drawing room to await further word.

Meanwhile, Sophie Meriwell remained seated at the table, her expression curiously blank.

Veronica recognized the look; Sophie was considering indulging in a massive display of hysterics.

Small wonder, but...

Catching the younger woman's eyes, Veronica brutally advised, "Not now."

She held Sophie's gaze until she saw acceptance bloom, then turned and grimly hurried after the men.

They hadn't even allowed her to check his lordship's pulse!

Veronica was forced to stand back and watch as, between them, Stephen, Arthur, Jensen, and Gorton laid Lord Meriwell on his bed.

By then, she'd seen enough to entertain the gravest fears. His lordship did not appear to be breathing, and there was a worrying bluish tint to his lips.

When the men finally straightened and stepped back, Stephen brusquely waved her to the bed.

Quickly, she went to the bed's side, picked up his lordship's wrist, and searched for a pulse.

As she'd feared, she could find no hint of one.

She released his wrist, leaned over him, and inserted her fingers behind his cravat, feeling for a pulse in the great vessels of the neck.

Nothing.

She breathed in, and the faint scent of bitter almonds teased her senses.

Frowning, she straightened and looked down at his lordship. "He's passed." That much was certain.

Arthur softly swore and ran a hand down his face. He looked haggard.

Somewhat shakily, Stephen said, "No doubt his heart gave out."

Arthur sighed. "He was old—his heart had to be weak."

Increasingly puzzled, Veronica said nothing. Yes, his lordship's heart had ultimately failed, but he'd been in the care of one of the country's foremost physicians, and this was the first she'd heard of any weakness of the heart.

That didn't mean the cause of his death hadn't been his heart giving out, yet what she was seeing didn't entirely fit.

Granite-faced, Stephen stirred. "I'll go down and break the news."

Arthur nodded. "I'll come, too." After a last lingering glance at the bed, he turned away. "Nothing more we can do here."

Veronica waited until the door shut behind them, then looked at Jensen and Jeremy. "What happened?"

Jensen drew in a huge breath, then, his gaze resting on his dead master, said, "I'd just filled his glass with wine. He took a gulp of it, swallowed…and then he had some sort of seizure."

"He couldn't seem to catch his breath," Jeremy said. "He gasped like a landed fish, then he tried to raise his hand—the left one—as if he wanted to point down the table."

Jensen nodded. "But he collapsed before he managed it."

Veronica didn't like the sound of any of that. "He didn't clutch at his chest?"

"No," Jensen replied, and Jeremy shook his head.

She beckoned the pair, and Gorton, too, to come to the bed. "I need you to sniff just above his lips. Don't think about it—just do it. Then once you've all sniffed, you can tell me what you smelled."

They cast her wary looks, but her standing in the household was high enough that they did as she'd asked.

Each sniffed, then frowned as they straightened.

Once all three had had a moment to think, she asked, "All right. What did you smell?"

"Almonds," Gorton promptly replied. "The bitter kind."

Jensen was nodding. "Definitely like almonds."

"Like in Cook's marzipan icing on his lordship's birthday cake," Jeremy supplied.

Increasingly grim, Veronica said, "That's what I smelled, too." She pointed at his lordship's lips. "See the bluishness there? That indicates difficulty breathing. So it wasn't his heart but his lungs—they seized."

Gorton, who'd worked for Lord Meriwell for more than forty years and had been deeply attached to his late master, was watching her closely. "And the smell of bitter almonds?"

Veronica swallowed a sigh and stated, "That means he was poisoned."

The discombobulating shock the realization provoked had already coursed through her. Now, she watched it wash over the three men's features. But as she'd expected, as she waited, their expressions hardened.

Before they could speak, she took charge. "The first thing we need to do is for you two"—she tipped her head at Jensen and Jeremy—"to tell me and Gorton *everything* you can remember about what happened leading up to and immediately following his lordship's collapse."

Jensen and Jeremy exchanged a glance, then Jensen drew in a bolstering breath and commenced, "Everything was going along in the usual way. Once the table was set and all was ready for the first course, I sent Jeremy to fetch the soup tureen, and I went to summon the company from the drawing room. They followed me back to the dining room and filed in and found their seats. Jeremy returned with the tureen and set it on the sideboard nearest the door. I picked up the wine decanter and unstoppered it." Jensen paused, frowning slightly as he revisited the moment in his memory. "His lordship was glaring down the table at Miss Sophie or Mr. Stephen—I couldn't tell which one. I stepped up to the table and, as usual, filled his lordship's glass first. He was still glaring down the table, and as I straightened, he reached out, picked up the glass, and took a large mouthful. He swallowed—still glaring—and I stepped around Mr. Busselton, who was seated on his lordship's right, to fill his glass. That was when his lordship choked and gasped. He tried to breathe —to haul in a breath—but couldn't seem to manage it."

Jensen glanced at Jeremy, and the footman nodded.

"I was standing on the other side of Jensen." Jeremy swallowed. "It was just as he says. His lordship couldn't get any air, and then he tried to lift his left hand and point, it seemed in the same direction he'd been glaring. Then he slumped, and his hand fell to the table, and his head hit the plate." Jeremy swallowed again. "That was it."

Veronica nodded. "So his lordship took one mouthful of wine, swallowed, and almost immediately, he couldn't breathe and died." She glanced at Gorton. "At the table, you got closer than I did. As far as you could tell, was his lordship already dead?"

Gorton held her gaze for several seconds, then sighed. "From the moment I first saw him slumped at the table, I detected no sign of life."

Veronica looked at Jensen. "We'll need to notify the authorities, but first, one thing I know we'll be asked about is the seating at the table. Most people had moved by the time I got there, so who was sitting where?"

Jensen drew breath and recited, "Starting from her ladyship's right, that was Miss Busselton. Then came Mr. Stephen, and Miss Sophie, and beside her was Master Busselton. On his lordship's left was Mrs. Busselton. Then down the other side, on his lordship's right was Mr. Busselton, followed by Mr. Arthur and Mr. Peter, then Lord Iffey beside her ladyship."

"Very well." Veronica looked from Jensen to Jeremy. "You mentioned his lordship was glaring down the table."

Jeremy nodded. "At either Mr. Stephen or Miss Sophie. Like Jensen, because of the angle, I couldn't tell which."

Veronica grimaced. "Given the usual issues, I suppose it was at Sophie."

"Most likely," Gorton agreed. "Mr. Stephen rarely if ever gave his lordship cause for worry."

Jensen had been staring at the body on the bed. Now, he shook himself and looked at Veronica. "So who do we send for? The local doctor? His lordship was never happy with him."

"No, indeed. We have to send for his lordship's current physician—to Dr. Sanderson in Harley Street. He'll organize everything—all that needs to happen."

"Will you write a note, miss?" Jensen asked. "Best it comes from you, don't you think?"

Veronica nodded. "Yes, I'll write a brief account, and we'll need to send it by rider." She looked at Gorton and Jeremy. "I suggest you two remain here on watch while Jensen and I go down and set matters in train."

All agreed, and Veronica and Jensen made their way downstairs.

At the base of the stairs, Veronica paused. "One moment." She beckoned Jensen to follow as she diverted toward the dining room. As they neared the door, she murmured, "We should secure his lordship's glass, with the rest of the wine in it, as well as the decanter."

"You think the poison was in the wine?" Jensen asked.

Veronica glanced at him. "Don't you?"

He grimaced as they reached the still-open dining room door.

Pausing in the doorway, they looked at the table.

His lordship's wine glass was gone.

Moving into the room, Veronica surveyed the rest of the table. "Do my eyes deceive me, or is everything else exactly as it was when we left?"

Jensen, following her, was also examining the scene. "All the cutlery and plates are still in place and all the other glasses." Beside Veronica, he halted by the large carver. "The only thing missing is his lordship's glass."

"Along with the wine it contained." Veronica tipped her head at the sideboard. "Best take the decanter and put it somewhere safe."

Jensen crossed to the sideboard, picked up the decanter, and returned to Veronica's side.

"Just a second." She lifted the stopper and sniffed. Her features hardening, she replaced the stopper. "There's no scent of bitter almonds."

Jensen frowned, then glanced at the table. "So the poison was in his glass?"

"Yes." Veronica stared at where the glass should have been. "And it vanishing confirms beyond doubt that we have a murderer in the house."

~

Jensen went to put the decanter in his pantry, and Veronica tiptoed past the drawing room door, helpfully closed, and slipped into the library.

She sat at the desk, found paper, pen, and ink, and swiftly wrote an account of the critical points that David Sanderson needed to know.

After signing and sealing the missive, she rose and, taking the note, went downstairs. She found Jensen sitting, looking lost, in his pantry. He accepted the letter and summoned his lordship's groom, who was waiting, and she and Jensen went out to the back step and saw groom and note off on their journey to the capital.

With the thud of hooves receding, Veronica remained on the step and, with the gentle night breeze wafting over her face, fervently prayed that David Sanderson was at home when her missive arrived and not out attending some aristocratic client's confinement, a duty that might keep him away for hours if not days.

With a sigh, she turned in to the house and, with Jensen, returned to the servants' hall, now empty and shrouded in a pall of quiet gloom. She paused and, after a moment's thought, murmured, "I believe our best way forward is to not mention what we believe to have occurred and, instead, wait for Dr. Sanderson to confirm it officially."

Jensen readily acquiesced. "No sense in us causing a furor." His lips twisted. "And the arguments and outrage don't bear thinking about."

"Exactly." She accepted that they weren't in a position to make such judgments and expect to be supported by their betters. Betters who would almost certainly prefer such unsavory prospects as murder, murderers, and poison to be swept under a convenient rug.

"I'll warn Jeremy and Gorton," Jensen said, "so they don't accidentally start any hares."

Veronica thought that wise and said so, and she and Jensen returned to the front hall, Jensen intending to go up to his lordship's room while she went to check on Sophie and her ladyship.

Veronica had to admit that her feet felt leaden, and Jensen seemed equally plodding.

They were nearing the bottom of the stairs when Stephen Meriwell came out of the drawing room and spotted them.

"Jensen. Miss Haskell."

They halted and waited as Stephen closed the drawing room door and strode up.

He glanced briefly at them, then stated, "I believe the correct procedure is to inform the local doctor that his lordship has passed away. It's Dr. Grimshaw in Thames Ditton, isn't it?"

Veronica pressed her palms together and raised her chin. "Dr.

Grimshaw is in Thames Ditton, but he can't and won't pronounce on a patient under the care of an eminent Harley Street physician. We need to send for his lordship's physician—Dr. Sanderson."

Grimshaw was an old-fashioned quack exceedingly set in his ways. He and David Sanderson had clashed over his lordship's health and even more about the treatment Grimshaw had prescribed for Sophie's supposed hysteria. More, Grimshaw was easily influenced by those of higher social standing; if Stephen and Arthur said his lordship died of a heart attack, that was what Grimshaw would obligingly put on the death certificate.

That said, it wasn't surprising that Stephen had suggested Grimshaw be called. Having spent many of his formative years at the Hall, Stephen was acquainted with Grimshaw but not, as far as Veronica knew, with David Sanderson.

Stephen was frowning. Thinking to head off any further argument, she added, "We've already sent a rider to summon Dr. Sanderson." As a nurse, she had that right. "I'm sure he'll respond as soon as he can."

Stephen grimaced, but reluctantly nodded. "Very well. Let's hope he gets here soon."

With that, he turned and walked back to the drawing room.

When the door closed behind him, Veronica exchanged a relieved look with Jensen.

"Miss Haskell?"

Veronica turned to look up the stairs, to the gallery where Sally was peering over the balustrade.

"Can you come up, miss? Miss Sophie says as she needs to see you."

"Of course she does," Veronica murmured.

After a last glance at the drawing room door, she started up the stairs beside Jensen.

CHAPTER 2

*P*enelope Adair, sitting alone at her breakfast table in the dining room of her marital home in Albemarle Street, crunched and munched a slice of toast slathered with marmalade and debated what her next—indeed, first—step in re-establishing her life should be.

"My life as I wish it to be." She reached for her teacup. "That's what I need to focus on. I need to find the right balance again." Supporting the teacup with both hands, she tipped her head. "Well, the right balance for as we are now."

Since the birth of her second child, Phillip—Pip—a brother for Oliver, now a rambunctious three-year-old toddler, she'd spent more time at home than she ever had. During the recent Season, she'd attended a smattering of balls and family events, but—much to the relief of her husband, Barnaby—had taken her re-emergence into society slowly.

The truth was she'd used the lack of social expectation Pip's birth had afforded her as an opportunity to re-evaluate the true importance of each aspect of her normally very busy life. Spending time with Oliver and Pip would always take precedence—she saw guiding them into their futures as her life's principal duty—and given her and Barnaby's families and their social and political prominence, there would always be demands from those spheres, yet still…she needed more.

Admittedly, she remained on the board of the Foundling House, along with her sisters and several cousins and connections, but that work, too, she took in her stride. Dealing with business required little effort from her naturally organized mind.

She needed intellectual challenge. Indeed, she couldn't remember when she had not, and given her background and experience, navigating the social and political arenas was rarely difficult enough to tax her brain, and although working on deciphering ancient manuscripts was a challenge of sorts, it was hardly exciting.

"Hmm." She narrowed her eyes. Where might she find her next exciting challenge? She really needed to get out and about and use those mental muscles that childbearing and the immediate aftermath had left underexercised.

Footsteps approached, and Barnaby strolled in. He'd been out for a morning walk with Oliver.

Barnaby came up behind her chair, closed his hands about her shoulders and, when she obligingly lifted her face, bent his head and dropped a light kiss on her lips. She smiled at him as he straightened, and he smiled back. "The children are happily ensconced in the nursery. Oliver spotted a baby bird, and I had to explain that he couldn't catch it and bring it home to care for."

"Ah." She arched her brows. "Perhaps it's time to actually get a puppy rather than just discussing it."

Barnaby's smile didn't dim as he ambled around the table. "Very likely. If you like, I can ask Papa if any of his bitches will soon have pups."

She nodded. "Oliver would like that. He loves visiting your father's kennels."

She watched as Barnaby drew out his chair and sat. To her eyes, he was still the most handsome man in the ton, with his golden curls and intelligent blue eyes. While Pip had inherited her dark hair, she was waiting to see if he might have inherited Barnaby's cerulean-blue eyes. A devastating combination, if it proved to be so.

Mostyn, their majordomo, bustled in with the coffeepot. He deftly filled Barnaby's cup, then paused to hunt in a pocket.

He drew out a missive. "This was slipped under the door at first light, sir."

Penelope perked up. In her experience, missives slipped under doors at dawn usually heralded something unexpected.

Possibly exciting.

Certainly interesting.

She waited with what patience she could muster as Barnaby accepted the ivory packet, frowned at the inscription, then turned it over and broke the seal. She watched as he scanned the first lines, then he glanced at her.

"It was addressed to me, but is actually to both of us."

"From?"

"Sanderson, of all people."

"David?" Penelope blinked. David Sanderson was the family's physician. It was he who had delivered Pip; she'd seen David only a week ago for her last check-up after the birth.

Barnaby nodded as he quickly read the note. "He writes that one of his patients, Lord Meriwell of Alderly, died at Meriwell Hall in Thames Ditton, Surrey, yesterday evening. As it happened, for a different reason, David had placed a nurse—Miss Veronica Haskell—in the household, and it was she who wrote to summon him. Apparently, Miss Haskell believes Lord Meriwell was poisoned with cyanide administered via his wine. David accepts her observations and conclusions, which means his lordship was murdered."

"Good gracious!" Penelope didn't have to feign being intrigued.

"David notes that he examined his lordship in London only a few weeks ago, and although the man was eighty years old, he was in fine shape, and David fully expected he would live to see ninety. He—David —goes on to say that by the time we read this, he'll be on his way to Thames Ditton. He's given directions and ends with a plea to the effect that he would greatly appreciate our presence there and our opinions on the situation if we are able to attend."

Barnaby met Penelope's eyes. "Are we able?"

His wife's expression was all the answer he needed. Her dark-chocolate eyes gleamed, and her expression all but glowed. "We are not just able," she declared, "but this is precisely what I need! A nice mystery to get back into the swing of investigations."

Setting down her teacup, she smiled into his eyes. "I truly have missed the mental stimulation. As much as I love our two imps, dealing with them doesn't exercise that part of my brain."

Barnaby grinned. "You don't have to explain that, not to me." He glanced at the letter. "If ever murder could be considered opportune…"

"Exactly! And Pip is now old enough to be left with his nursemaid for a few days, and Oliver is an old hand at us going off, which will help Pip understand that us being elsewhere for a few days is normal."

The doorbell pealed, and they paused to listen as Mostyn crossed the hall and opened the door.

The rumble of a familiar voice reached them.

Barnaby caught Penelope's eyes as they widened in delighted comprehension, and he arched an amused brow.

Two seconds later, Inspector Basil Stokes walked in. He greeted them, waited while Mostyn efficiently set another place, then Stokes sat and accepted a cup of coffee with a grateful sigh.

Plainly agog, they waited as he sipped and swallowed, then he grunted and said, "I was summoned to the Yard at first light. A new case, an aristocrat murdered by poison, down in Surrey, with the added complication that the murder happened at a house party being attended by an MP and his family. Before heading down there, I've been instructed to inquire whether the pair of you are available to accompany me officially, as consultants to Scotland Yard, to assist in the investigation."

Penelope beamed at him. "We're definitely available."

Barnaby frowned. "I didn't think the boundaries of the Metropolitan Police district stretched that far."

Stokes reached for the platter of eggs and bacon. "Not into Surrey per se, but by some quirk of long-ago fate, our boundaries encompass Thames Ditton. Possibly because it's just barely over the county border and also directly across the river from Hampton Court." Stokes sat up and lifted his cutlery. "I don't know exactly why, but it is under our direct jurisdiction."

Barnaby waved Sanderson's letter. "We'd just heard about the murder." At Stokes's astonished look, he explained, "David Sanderson"—Stokes knew who Sanderson was—"was Lord Meriwell's physician. He's already on his way down there and wrote to ask for our help."

Chewing, Stokes nodded, then swallowed and said, "Wise man. He also informed the commissioner. Did Sanderson mention that, presumably in addition to others, the household is presently hosting Mr. George Busselton, MP for Surrey, plus his wife and children?"

"No, he didn't." Penelope pushed her glasses farther up the bridge of her nose. "But doubtless that was part of his motivation for requesting our presence."

"As I said," Stokes mumbled, "wise man. I can confirm that the presence of Busselton and his family contributed significantly to the commissioner's motivation. He wants this handled quickly and discreetly. Hence,

I was dispatched to ask for your aid." Pausing, he looked from Barnaby to Penelope. "So are you in?"

Penelope's smile was full of determined intent. She tossed down her napkin and rose, waving at the men to continue their breakfasts. "Give me half an hour. I'll be ready to leave by then."

Barnaby smiled. "I'll follow you up to say goodbye to the scamps."

Stokes reached for the toast rack. "I'll wait here. Just call when you're ready."

David Sanderson drew his curricle to a halt in the gravel forecourt before Meriwell Hall.

He'd visited several times before and barely spared a glance for the Palladian façade. He climbed down, hearing the gravel crunch beneath his boots, and handed the reins to the stable lad who came running to take them. David paused only to lift his black bag from the curricle's seat before striding for the front steps.

A figure clad in the neat blue of a nurse's uniform came hurrying out to meet him.

As Veronica Haskell paused on the top step, David scanned her features and saw only steady determination and a mirroring of his own relief. The nature of that relief he pushed to the farthest reaches of his mind. He'd tried to tell himself that the unnerving, distracting terror he'd felt on learning that Veronica—whom he'd arranged to send to Meriwell Hall to observe the behavior of Lord Meriwell's problematical grand-daughter—was in a household that harbored a murderer was purely due to the implied responsibility of being the reason she was there.

Nonsense, of course, but he—and he suspected she, too—didn't have time, just at that moment, to dwell on such emotional complications.

Nevertheless, as he climbed the steps, the first words out of his mouth were "Veronica. How are you?"

Her hands, clasped before her waist, gripped a fraction tighter. "I'm... as well as can be expected, given the situation."

"Indeed." He halted beside her and studied her face, drinking in her features.

She colored faintly and lowered her voice. "Thank God you're here. I was worried you wouldn't be able to get away."

"I came as quickly as I could. Luckily, none of my ladies are nearing their time. They and London can do without me for as long as this takes. Abercrombie will step in if there's any emergency."

"That's…a relief." She glanced at the open front door and shook her head. "Even now, I can barely believe it." Returning her gaze to his face, she met his eyes. "But I am very sure that it was cyanide that did for Lord Meriwell."

David nodded. "First things first. Take me to the body."

Veronica waved toward the door. "They've put the corpse in the basement, in the laundry. It's the coolest spot and, apparently, has been used for laying out before."

Side by side, they headed for the house.

"How have her ladyship and Sophie taken it?"

"So far, better than I'd hoped. Sophie hasn't enacted any hysterical scenes yet, and her ladyship is, I think, so stunned and shocked that she's barely taken in how irrevocable this change is."

"That's to be expected." He slowed and shot Veronica a sharp glance. "You mentioned the Busseltons, whom I've never met. Who else is here?"

"The nephews, all three of them—Stephen, Arthur, and Peter. And Lord Iffey, of course."

He frowned. "Lord Iffey?"

Seeing his puzzlement, Veronica halted and elaborated, "Wallace, Lord Iffey, a very old friend of his lordship. From school days, I believe. He's a bachelor and is often here, keeping the elder Meriwells company."

"Right, and what of the Busseltons. How many of them?"

"Mr. George Busselton, his wife, Hermione, their daughter, Persimone, and her younger brother, Peregrine."

"Any idea why the local MP is visiting with his family in tow?"

"Stephen Meriwell hopes to marry Persimone Busselton. His lordship approved—highly—of the match, and I believe the idea behind this visit was to impress the Busseltons with Stephen's background and his family." Veronica paused, then added, "Apropos of that, Arthur and Peter were told they were expected to attend and warned to be on their best behavior."

"I see."

They walked on, crossing the threshold into the cool shadows of the front hall.

Veronica tipped her head closer and whispered, "You're about to meet Mr. Busselton."

David's vision adjusted, and he saw two men plainly waiting to intercept them. Or more accurately, given the focus of their gazes, to intercept him.

He knew perfectly well what they were seeing—not some quack but a gentleman who exuded that indefinable aura of inhabiting a higher social stratum than either of them—and was wryly amused at the sudden uncertainty that assailed the pair.

The unexpectedness of his background was often useful.

The butler knew him from his previous visits and came forward to take his hat and overcoat. David surrendered both, then nodded coolly to the men. "Gentlemen."

The younger man—of similar age to David, in his early thirties, well-dressed, hair neat, clothes expensive but not ostentatious, with pleasant features that David recognized as indicative of the Meriwell family—shifted and held out his hand. "Stephen Meriwell."

David grasped the offered hand. "David Sanderson."

Meriwell gestured to the other, older man. "This is Mr. George Busselton, MP for the local area."

Busselton was in his fifties, with a decided paunch he tried to hide behind a tartan waistcoat. With thinning brown hair, brown eyes beneath shaggy brows, and a neatly trimmed beard, he looked the archetype of a staunch, well-to-do parliamentarian; David had met many of such ilk.

He returned Busselton's nod, and they shook hands.

Before either man could attempt to take charge, David stated, "In a situation such as this, my first task must be to examine the body and that without delay. If you'll excuse me."

It wasn't a question. David turned to Veronica and the butler, but Busselton rushed into speech. "I say, but you will tell us your conclusions, won't you?"

David glanced his way and inclined his head. "Once I have conclusions, I will inform the family."

Veronica looked down to hide her smile. He would tell the family, by which he meant Lady Meriwell. The instant she had her features under control, she raised her head and waved toward the rear of the hall. "This way, Doctor."

With another graceful inclination of his head, David fell in beside her, and they made for the kitchen and the door to the basement stairs.

She led David to the spartan room in the basement, stone floored and stone walled, with the deep laundry troughs to one side and the racks for hanging washing suspended overhead. Long windows set high in the walls along one side allowed morning light to slant inside, dispelling the gloom and, at this hour, rendering the space incongruously bright. One of the high deal tables usually used for folding linens played host to the silent form of the late master of the house, decently covered with a plain white sheet.

David set his bag on the counter beside the door, then crossed directly to the shrouded body. He folded back the sheet, revealing the harsh, patrician features of Lord Meriwell, set in uncompromising lines even in death.

Veronica watched as David's gaze sharpened. He spent several minutes examining the face, paying particular attention to the mouth and eyes, patently visually cataloguing all he saw, then he moved the sheet aside and checked his lordship's hands and fingers.

Still studying the fingernails, he said, "Tell me what you saw and smelled."

Veronica explained that she hadn't been able to get a decent look at his lordship's face until he was stretched out on his bed. "At that time, his lips were still distinctly bluish, and when I leaned close, I could smell the scent of bitter almonds."

"Did anyone else notice the smell?"

"I asked the butler, Jensen, and his lordship's valet, and one of the footmen to sniff and then tell me what they smelled. They all said almonds—bitter almonds."

David smiled and glanced at her. "That was quick thinking. The scent's long gone, of course, but I can see the signs well enough." He looked at the still figure on the table. "He was definitely poisoned, and everything points to it being with cyanide."

She felt as if a weight poised to press down on her shoulders released and slid away.

David turned to the stoppered decanter left on the counter. "Is this the wine that was served?"

"Yes. Jensen retrieved the decanter from the dining room and kept it in his pantry. He must have brought it down here for you to examine."

David nodded and did just that, unstoppering the decanter and taking a good sniff, then he swirled the wine, sniffed again, then held the decanter up to the windows and the morning light. After studying the liquid, he said, "I can't detect any sign that the wine itself was poisoned." He lowered the decanter and turned to his bag. "I'll take a sample for later analysis if needed. But otherwise, I believe it would be safest to discard this."

"Indeed. I can't imagine anyone wanting to drink it." Veronica waited until David had poured a small amount into a vial. Leaving him stoppering the vial, she carried the decanter to the trough and poured the contents out. She used water from a jug to rinse the last of the wine from the decanter and sluice all traces down the drain.

She carried the decanter back to the counter and left it for Jensen to fetch later.

David looked up from repacking his bag and fixed his gaze on her. "In your note, you mentioned that the glass his lordship drank from went missing from the table."

She nodded and recounted how she and Jensen had returned to fetch the glass. "But it wasn't there. Everything else was exactly as Jensen and I remembered leaving it, but his lordship's glass had vanished."

David observed, "I can't think of any more definite confirmation. The poison—most likely concentrated prussic acid—must have been in the glass." He paused, then added, "Prussic acid is not something anyone would knowingly take, and I certainly can't imagine Lord Meriwell doing such a thing, much less at that time and place."

"No, indeed." She pressed her palms together. "It's definitely not suicide."

David nodded. "This was murder."

He hoisted his bag and looked at her. "I need to speak with Lady Meriwell."

"I'll take you to her. She'll be in her sitting room upstairs." Veronica caught David's eye. "We can go up via the servants' stair."

His lips curved in a wry smile. "Thank you. That might be best. My patience is already a trifle thin."

Veronica led David directly to Lady Meriwell's private sitting room on the first floor.

It was, Veronica would be the first to admit, a huge relief to have a man of David's unquestioned authority calmly taking the reins. She had every confidence he knew exactly how matters should proceed.

After tapping on the sitting room door and hearing a faint "Come," she opened the door and led the way inside.

Her ladyship was sitting in her favorite armchair beside one of the large windows that looked out over the rose garden. Clementina, Lady Meriwell, still looked rather lost, but judging by the way her gaze strengthened as it locked on Veronica and David, the older woman had started to come to grips with the situation. The wrinkled, liver-spotted hand that was closed over the head of her cane tightened as if she was steeling herself for the conversation to come.

Veronica was unsurprised to see Wallace, Lord Iffey, seated in a second armchair drawn close beside her ladyship's. His lordship had rarely been absent from her ladyship's side since Lord Meriwell's death. He was holding Lady Meriwell's other hand and gently patting it. A large bear of a man, with white hair and a hefty frame garbed in the clothes of a generation past, Iffey barely spared Veronica and David a glance before his attention returned to Lady Meriwell.

Veronica halted a little to one side, allowing David to step past her.

He went forward and took the hand her ladyship removed from Iffey's grasp and waveringly extended, lightly gripping her fingers as he bowed. "I am so very sorry, Clementina. This was not a death any of us would have wished for Angus."

Her ladyship's chins quivered. "No, indeed." Her fingers tightened on David's. "Was it a heart attack, as the others are saying?"

David looked into her ladyship's mild blue eyes, which were imploring him to say he knew not what. "Sadly, no. His lordship was poisoned, apparently via his wine glass."

"Oh my!" Lady Meriwell's voice quavered, and withdrawing her hand, she shrank back into the chair.

"There, there, my dear." Lord Iffey—David assumed it was he— clumsily patted her arm. "We thought it must be something like that. Never knew old Angus to take such a turn before."

Iffey looked up at David from beneath beetling eyebrows. "Wallace, Lord Iffey, sir. I don't believe we've met."

David half bowed. "David Sanderson, of Harley Street."

"Goodness, where are my manners?" Her ladyship fluttered and roused herself to sit upright and gestured at Iffey. "Wallace here is a dear and very old friend, David. An old school chum of Angus's and a very valued friend of the family as a whole."

David inclined his head in acknowledgment, noting how close and comfortable with each other Iffey and her ladyship appeared. "It will be helpful to have the support of someone like his lordship through the coming days." Grateful that her ladyship had refocused, gently, he went on, "Given the situation, meaning that Lord Meriwell's death was not a natural one, then the authorities have to be informed."

Her ladyship's soft gaze steadied on his face, then her chin firmed. "Tell me, David, without any roundaboutation. Was Angus murdered?"

To that, there was only one answer. "Yes," he said. "He was."

The shock on Lady Meriwell's face was echoed in Iffey's more florid countenance.

"Here! I say!" he blustered. "Are you sure it wasn't some sort of accident?"

Calmly, David stated, "I'm quite certain."

A frown overtook Lady Meriwell's features. "Are you saying that someone put poison into the wine?" She met David's eyes. "But you said 'glass.' Did someone put poison in Angus's wine glass?"

He inclined his head. "So it appears."

"Well!" Iffey blew out a noisy breath. "Bless me."

David waited, but both her ladyship and his lordship appeared stunned and rather stupefied. After a moment more, in an even tone, he went on, "As this is inarguably murder, I'm required to notify Scotland Yard and have done so. I understand that they have jurisdiction in this area, and given the household's standing, I'm sure they'll send down one of their best investigators with all speed. Until that person arrives, everyone who was present at the Hall yesterday evening must remain."

At that, her ladyship sucked in a breath and directed a look of near panic at Iffey. "Oh, heavens! Not only do we have a murder to contend with but…" She looked helplessly at David. "What about the Busseltons? What will they think?" Her eyes widened even further. "What will *everyone* think?"

Her wail jerked Iffey from his abstraction. "Now, now, Clemmie— that's hardly something you need worry about." He recommenced patting her arm. "It'll be all right, trust me. Scotland Yard will send down their finest, and it will all be taken care of. You'll see."

To David's relief, the anodyne reassurances had the desired effect. Her ladyship calmed sufficiently to direct a pleading look at him.

Interpreting it with ease, he half bowed. "I will, of course, remain for the next several days in case you or Miss Meriwell require my attention."

Her ladyship appeared relieved, then she looked past him at Veronica. "You will stay, too, dear, won't you? I know how much you've influenced

Sophie, and all for the good. I dread to think of how she might behave were you not here to give her direction."

Veronica nodded. "I'll stay until the household is past this difficult patch."

Her ladyship put a hand to her chest. "That's such a relief. Thank you both."

David stepped closer and took her ladyship's wrist between his fingers. Her pulse was a touch fluttery, but strong enough. Releasing her hand, he said, "I'll come and check on you later, and if necessary, I can give you a sleeping draft for tonight."

"Thank you, David." Then her brow crinkled, and she glanced at Iffey. "But the guests…"

"Are hale and hearty enough to take care of themselves for the nonce," Iffey declared. "You should rest quietly until you feel strong enough to go downstairs."

David agreed. He caught his lordship's eye. "If you feel up to it later, a turn in the garden to get some air would do you good."

Iffey nodded in instant accord. "We'll see how it goes, heh, m'dear?"

Veronica added, "The household will cope—you have everything so well organized, there's no reason to fret on that score."

Her ladyship seemed to accept their assurances and relaxed a trifle. "At least Stephen is here. He'll see that the right steps are taken and that everything is done as it ought to be, especially with regard to the Busseltons."

Iffey patted her hand. "Just so. We can leave it to Stephen, and if he needs our assistance, we'll still be here, old thing. The Busseltons seem reasonable people. I'm sure they'll understand. This is hardly your fault, m'dear."

Her ladyship appeared more settled.

David hesitated, then ventured, "It might help speed up the process, ma'am, if the household has your permission to do whatever is necessary to assist the police with their inquiries into Lord Meriwell's murder."

Lady Meriwell blinked at him. "Yes, of course." Her chin firmed, and meeting his gaze directly, she added, "Angus and I might not, of late, have been as close as we once were, but he was my husband for over fifty years, and I definitely want his murderer hung."

There was unexpected steel behind those words. David acknowledged it with an abbreviated bow.

Iffey patted her ladyship's hand. "Quite right, old thing. I'm sure the detectives from Scotland Yard will oblige."

On that note, David and Veronica took their leave and quit the sitting room.

Once in the corridor and heading toward the stairs, David glanced back at the sitting room door, then looked at Veronica. "Am I right in supposing there's some…more personal connection between her ladyship and Iffey?"

Veronica's lips twisted in a wry smile. She met his eyes and admitted, "Within the household, it's no secret. The pair have had a long-standing affair, one going back more than a decade to the time when Robert Meriwell was alive."

Robert Meriwell, Lord and Lady Meriwell's only child, had died in Africa about twelve years ago. David raised his brows. "That long?" When Veronica nodded, he asked, "Did Lord Meriwell know?"

"As to that"—Veronica faced forward—"I gather no one has ever been sure. The general consensus, including the opinion of Gorton, his lordship's valet, is that his lordship was and remained oblivious." She paused, then added, "Lord Meriwell was decidedly self-centered—self-focused—and truly, I suspect that he never noticed what was going on under his very nose. His wife and his best friend posed no real threat to him, so they didn't feature in his thoughts."

"Hmm." David wasn't sure what to make of that.

They descended the stairs side by side to find Jensen, Stephen Meriwell, and George Busselton waiting to speak with them.

"I take it," Busselton commenced the instant David stepped onto the hall tiles, "that you will be issuing the death certificate forthwith, and my family and I are free to leave."

David tried not to take pleasure in or at least not acknowledge the pleasure he felt in saying, "I'm afraid not. There's reason to believe that his lordship was poisoned. Scotland Yard have already been notified, and I expect that an investigator is on his way. Until such time as the Yard's representatives have examined the scene and subsequently grant each of us permission to depart, it's necessary for us all to remain."

He put sufficient emphasis on the "all" for them to understand that he included himself in that number.

Busselton looked perturbed. He frowned, then huffed, but after a moment—doubtless after considering how such an action might appear—he decided not to argue.

From Busselton's expression, David surmised that he had already had doubts as to the naturalness of Lord Meriwell's demise.

For his part, Stephen Meriwell was frowning, but it seemed more in a considering way as if working out what such a situation would mean for his guests and the household in general.

Like any good butler, Jensen was standing by the wall, attempting self-effacement.

David turned to him and said, "I understand that his lordship's wine glass from last evening has gone missing. As it seems likely the poison was administered via that glass, I suspect that whoever Scotland Yard sends to investigate will order a search of the house and grounds to locate it. Might I suggest there's no reason to wait for the order. Her ladyship has confirmed that she expects the staff to do everything they can to assist the police with their inquiries, so making a start on that search seems wise."

Jensen bowed. "Indeed, sir. I'll see to it straightaway."

"Doctor?"

David turned and, with the others, looked up to see a maid leaning over the gallery balustrade.

Under their scrutiny, she colored, but continued, "If you have a moment, Doctor, Miss Sophie is asking for you."

Beneath his breath, David murmured, "Of course she is." But he nodded to the maid, then collected Veronica with a glance. "We had better go and see what's brewing there."

With concern flaring in her eyes, Veronica agreed and started up the stairs.

David inclined his head to Busselton and Stephen. "Gentlemen."

Then he turned and followed Veronica.

They found Sophie Meriwell prostrate on her bed—rather Ophelia-like to David's mind. But the instant the door shut, Sophie signaled to the maid to help her with her pillows and wriggled up to sit so she could better speak with them. "Grandpapa died, and it was horrible. What's going on?"

David didn't need to take her pulse to know Sophie was in perfect health. No matter whatever die-away airs she affected, her cheeks bloomed, and even red-rimmed, her eyes all but sparkled.

He drew up a chair to the bed, sat, and described the situation much as he had to her grandmother.

Just the bare bones, with no speculation as to who might have done the deed.

Sophie was genuinely horrified. She was also, plainly, unsure how to react—how she should behave. Hysterics were always an option with her, but in this instance, it seemed the gravity of the crime weighed on her sufficiently to quash her disposition toward drama. Likely there was drama enough in the situation to satisfy even her.

Ultimately, she opted to follow her true emotional inclinations and allowed her puzzlement and curiosity to show; for the first time since he'd known her, she asked questions about someone other than herself.

He answered the first barrage, but he wasn't about to spend the rest of his day pandering to Sophie's inquisitiveness, so at the first opportunity, he explained that an investigator from Scotland Yard would be arriving shortly and that he—David—would look in on her later to see how she did.

Apparently, that information gave Sophie enough to think about, at least for the moment. Absentmindedly, she nodded a farewell in response to his and made no demur when he rose and, with Veronica, left the room.

On the way back to the main stairs, she glanced at him. "Are you truly staying?"

He nodded and met her eyes. "I need to see this through."

I need to stay until the murderer is caught to ensure that you remain unharmed.

They reached the stairs, and he looked down as they started their descent. Given that she could probably guess the demands of his busy Harley Street practice, to better excuse his determination to stay, he added, "The investigators will want to speak with me, and I should watch over her ladyship for at least a few days. I've also asked two friends who have helped with investigations in the past if they can come down here and assist the police. They've done that before, in other cases. I'm not sure if they'll be able to oblige, but if they do, I should be here."

There. That sounded convincing.

He added, "I'll ask Jensen to organize a room."

Veronica nodded. "Her ladyship—and Sophie—will appreciate you being here."

"Speaking of Sophie, I note that while she asked about her grandfather, she didn't inquire after her grandmother."

Veronica tipped her head. "They're not particularly close. I understand they never have been. But then, Sophie isn't truly close to anyone, really. She rather takes after her grandfather in that regard—exceedingly self-centered."

"Hmm. Despite having treated his lordship for years, I haven't observed him in company, even among his family. But returning to Sophie and the reason you're here, what's your verdict?" He caught Veronica's gaze. "Is she truly a hysteric?"

That had been the question posed by Lord Meriwell and prosecuted to the point that David had agreed to send an experienced nurse to the Hall to assess Sophie's state of mind.

Veronica huffed, the sound dismissive. "No. She's definitely not a hysteric. She *uses* having hysterics to further her own agenda. She assumes airs and creates dramatic scenes and acts in many ways as a hysteric would, but it's all calculated to draw and hold the attention of all those around her. To Sophie, hysteria is a tool to be used to fix attention on her, and most of the time, more than anything, she craves being the center of attention."

David nodded. "That's what I thought. I suspect her ladyship believes that, too, but his lordship had worked himself into a lather over Sophie being a true hysteric and going into the ton, where her behavior would reflect adversely on the entire family."

"In my opinion, her behavior, if unchecked, will reflect badly, but on her rather than on her family." Veronica met his gaze. "One only needs to watch her for a short time to realize that her outbursts are fabricated and intentional rather than any spontaneous eruption of ungovernable emotion."

As they stepped off the last stair, David concluded, "So after all this is over and the matter of his lordship's murder is addressed, we'll have one piece of better news to brighten the outlook for Lady Meriwell."

CHAPTER 3

*P*enelope peered out of her carriage window at the house at the end of the drive. Sporting two stories with attics above, Meriwell Hall was a relatively newish structure, perhaps fifty or sixty years old. The style was Palladian, with brick walls rendered in cream stucco topped by a sound slate roof. Windows, tall and gleaming, were regimentally arranged across the width of the façade, their stone surrounds and white-painted wood frames in good order.

From an oval-shaped gravel forecourt symmetrically placed before the house, a short flight of stone steps led to the semicircular porch before the tall front door.

To one accustomed to castles and large aristocratic mansions, Meriwell Hall was a modest home whose excellent order nevertheless testified to some degree of pride.

Woods, quite dense, enclosed the house on either side and to the rear, the dark-green canopies lightly rippling courtesy of a playful breeze.

As the carriage turned onto the forecourt and slowed, Penelope felt expectation rise. She looked at Stokes, seated opposite. His men—in this instance, the ever-reliable Sergeant O'Donnell and the baby-faced but experienced Constable Morgan—had traveled in the police coach that had lumbered along behind the Adair carriage. No one had been surprised that Stokes had opted to travel in greater comfort.

She glanced at Barnaby, seated beside her, and as he scanned the house, she saw in his blue eyes signs of the same interest and anticipation rising within her.

The carriage halted. Although she was eager to see what awaited them —to engage with their latest investigation—she refrained from leaping for the door. Both Stokes and Barnaby shot amused glances her way, but at her impatient wave, obligingly descended first, then Barnaby offered her his hand and assisted her down the steps.

As she was on the shorter side, she needed the help; falling down the carriage steps was not the way she would choose to start a new investigation.

She'd barely shaken her skirts straight when footsteps rang on the stone of the porch, and she, Barnaby, and Stokes looked up to see David Sanderson, accompanied by a young lady in a neat blue dress, descending the steps to meet them.

With dark-brown hair and kind brown eyes, David was tall and would have appeared lanky were it not for his broad shoulders. As always, he was exceedingly well if conservatively dressed in a dark suit, subdued waistcoat, and pristine linen.

The young lady was of average height, with shining blond-brown hair swept into a neat coil on the top of her head. The figure beneath the dress of navy-blue twill, which Penelope realized was a uniform of sorts, was curvaceous, and the lady's face and features were gentle and appealing.

Penelope beamed. "David!" She held out her hands, already insatiably curious as to who the young lady was. Was she a nurse or someone else?

"Penelope." David grasped her hands and bent to kiss the cheek she offered. He was a friend even more than he was their physician.

She released him to allow him to greet Barnaby and Stokes. David's and Stokes's professional paths had crossed before.

Then David turned to the young lady. "Allow me to present Miss Veronica Haskell."

After he made the introductions and they and Veronica shook hands, David explained that Veronica had taken a position in the household at his behest.

Immediately, Penelope asked, "Was his lordship or someone else in the family in poor health?"

"No, not at all." David exchanged a look with Miss Haskell—Veronica. "His lordship was in excellent health, and I have few reservations as to her ladyship's well-being. The truth is"—David met Penelope's eyes— "Lord Meriwell was concerned about the behavior of his granddaughter."

"In short," Veronica said, "he suspected she was a hysteric and had vetoed her coming-out this year. My role was to assess whether she was, in fact, suffering from true hysteria." She glanced at David. "Neither Dr. Sanderson nor her ladyship were convinced she was, and after observing Sophie for the past nine weeks, I can report that she merely craves attention. Having hysterics and creating dramatic scenes are simply tools she employs to achieve her goal."

"Ah." Penelope pushed up her spectacles. "I see."

Stokes was already jotting in his notebook. "So Lord Meriwell was Sophie's grandfather?"

David and Veronica agreed. David added, "Sophie is his lordship's only surviving grandchild. He and her ladyship lost their son, Robert, Sophie's father, some years ago."

"Right." Stokes continued scribbling. "And who else is here?" Stokes looked up and fixed David and Veronica with an interrogatory look. "Not the staff, but who else could possibly have murdered Lord Meriwell?"

David shared another look with Veronica, then rattled off a list of names.

"So," Stokes confirmed, "we have three nephews, Sophie, her ladyship, Lord Iffey, and four Busseltons." He closed his notebook and, pocketing it, inclined his head to David. "Thank you. And I can't tell you how grateful I am to have been called in so promptly. I take it you're sure it is, indeed, death by poison?"

David nodded. "No question about that, and the poison employed was almost certainly cyanide." He glanced at Veronica and smiled. "As for the promptness, that was due to Veronica's sharp eyes and experience." He looked back at Stokes. "In her note to me, she included her observations, and it was plain we were dealing with a poisoning."

"The cyanide was in the wine?" Barnaby asked.

"In his wine glass, we now suspect," David replied. "Although I haven't yet definitively tested it, I believe the wine in the decanter wasn't the source of the poison."

Penelope looked duly amazed. "So the poison was put into his glass?"

"It appears so," Veronica said, "especially as the wine glass went missing immediately—well, within half an hour—of his lordship dying."

"That seems a rather pointed clue." Barnaby arched his brows. "Has the glass turned up yet?"

"No," Veronica replied. "The staff have searched, but have yet to find it."

Stokes looked at the house. "Well, I think it's time we got this investigation under way." He glanced to where the police coach had halted. "One moment."

They waited—impatiently on Penelope's part—while Stokes conferred with his men, confirming that they were dealing with a death by poison and that they had a missing wine glass to find, then he dispatched the pair to chat with the staff, in the stables and elsewhere, to see what they could learn.

"Right, then." Stokes returned and waved toward the front door. "Let's have at it."

He led the way up the steps, across the porch, and through the open front door. The butler stood waiting beside the door, and Stokes introduced himself, Barnaby, and Penelope.

Penelope suppressed an understanding smile at the butler's poorly concealed surprise on discovering that two of the investigators dispatched by Scotland Yard were, in fact, aristocrats.

Stokes mentioned his men, then instructed the butler—Jensen—to ask the younger members of the family and the guests to assemble in the drawing room. "We'll address them after we've spoken with Lady Meriwell and viewed the body."

Jensen took the order in his stride. "Her ladyship is waiting in her sitting room, Inspector."

"Excellent." Stokes looked toward the stairs. "Dr. Sanderson and Miss Haskell will accompany us. They can show us the way."

Jensen bowed, and David and Veronica joined Stokes, Barnaby, and Penelope in heading for the stairs.

As they climbed, Penelope could hear the murmur of voices elsewhere in the house, but no one seemed out and about in the corridors.

David glanced at Stokes, then at Barnaby and Penelope. "I broke the news to her ladyship earlier, so she knows her husband was murdered, and I explained the legal process, so she's expecting you."

"Again, thank you," Stokes said. "It helps not to have to deal with the first shock."

"We're likely to find Lord Iffey with her ladyship," Veronica warned. "They're much of an age."

Barnaby frowned. "Iffey is an old friend of the family, I think you said?"

David nodded. "A school friend of Lord Meriwell's. A bachelor who, through the years, has remained close to the Meriwell family. He's very protective of her ladyship and has proved useful in helping her cope."

They reached the sitting room, and David tapped on the door. When a response came, he opened the door, stood back, and gestured for Penelope and the others to enter.

Penelope led the way into what was plainly her ladyship's private domain. The room was comfortably furnished, well lit, and had the feel of a space much used.

After one comprehensive glance taking in both room and occupants— an older lady and an older gentleman seated in armchairs angled beside a window—Penelope advanced with Barnaby beside her.

On reaching the elderly pair, both of whose countenances bore signs of grief, she and Barnaby introduced themselves and explained that they were attending as consultants at the commissioner's request. Barnaby introduced Stokes as the lead investigator whom he and Penelope would be supporting.

Stokes bowed over her ladyship's hand and exchanged a polite nod with his lordship. "In cases such as this, involving the aristocracy, the Yard has found the assistance of Mr. and Mrs. Adair to be invaluable all around."

"Oh yes." Her ladyship looked much relieved. "I can quite see that."

Stokes smiled encouragingly and went through the customary process of confirming that Lord Meriwell was believed to have been poisoned and that the purpose of the investigation was to determine who was responsible for bringing about his lordship's death.

"I do hope you can discover who did it quickly, Inspector." Her ladyship glanced at Lord Iffey, beside her. "I don't know if anyone's mentioned…"

"The Busseltons?" Penelope asked. When her ladyship and Lord Iffey looked at her and nodded, she smiled reassuringly. "We're aware of their presence in the household and will make all due effort not to make anyone's lives more difficult than absolutely necessary."

"Indeed," Stokes affirmed. "And in pursuit of that goal, it would be helpful, your ladyship, if we might say that we have your imprimatur to do whatever might be needful to bring his lordship's murderer to justice."

"Oh, most definitely, Inspector." Her ladyship's features firmed, and her nod included them all. "You may exercise whatever authority you require to catch my husband's murderer."

"Thank you, ma'am. In that case"—Stokes glanced at the others—

"our first step will be to view the body, and Dr. Sanderson will assist us there. Subsequently, we'll speak with the assembled family and guests and arrange to interview them individually, along with all others who were in the house at the time of his lordship's death. That's standard procedure and, for many, will be a mere formality."

Lord Iffey huffed. "Daresay you'll want to speak with us, too."

Stokes inclined his head. "We'll speak with you both as well, most likely early this afternoon." He looked at Lady Meriwell. "It's preferable that we gather information as quickly as possible, while events are fresh in everyone's minds."

"Of course." Her ladyship glanced at Lord Iffey. "We—Iffey and I—will hold ourselves ready to assist as required."

Lord Iffey looked less eager, but dutifully nodded.

Stokes reiterated their thanks, and he, Penelope, and the others withdrew.

In the instant before she stepped out of the room, Penelope glanced back at the elderly pair. Lady Meriwell looked reassured and relieved. Lord Iffey also looked relieved, but in his case, unless Penelope missed her guess, he was relieved because her ladyship was, rather than on his own account.

As she joined the others in the corridor, a niggling suspicion was growing in her mind.

After closing the door behind them, Stokes paused and looked at Penelope, Barnaby, David, and Veronica. "Thoughts?"

Barnaby glanced at the others. "Is it just my antennae malfunctioning, or is there a connection of sorts between Iffey and her ladyship?"

Penelope huffed. "I was wondering the same thing. I would wager they're lovers." She looked at David and Veronica and arched her brows.

David faintly grinned. "I wondered whether you would pick it up." He glanced at Veronica. "I'm reliably informed that their long-standing affair is well known to the entire household."

Veronica nodded. "That said, the widely held opinion is that Lord Meriwell never realized."

Stokes grimaced. "Regardless of the household's belief, there's fodder for a motive there."

Barnaby exchanged a look with Penelope, then mildly suggested, "We need to look at the body." He arched a brow at Veronica. "Which way?"

She hesitated, then offered, "It might be best to take the servants' stair. This way."

With Penelope and Stokes, under the knowledgeable direction of Sanderson, Barnaby took due note of the small signs that remained on the body and indicated death by poison, specifically cyanide.

There really wasn't much to see beyond the bluish tint that barely lingered about the corpse's lips and the odd waxy cast to his skin.

Stokes stepped back from the table on which the body lay. "So Lord Meriwell might have been eighty, but he was hale and in good health and in no danger of succumbing to a heart attack or any other sort of seizure."

David nodded decisively. "Just so."

"And," Barnaby said, staring at the still face, "he was in sound command of his wits."

"Indubitably," David confirmed. "There was nothing whatever amiss with his intelligence and understanding."

Veronica murmured an agreement.

"Tell me again," Stokes said, drawing out his notebook, "why you conclude this death is due to cyanide."

David obliged, running through the telltale signs as Stokes jotted them down. "Most important of all is the distinctive odor of bitter almonds." He nodded at Veronica. "Veronica noted it within minutes of his lordship's death and had the smell confirmed by Jensen, the butler, and his lordship's valet, and one of the footmen."

Stokes nodded approvingly at Veronica. "Good thinking."

She lightly shrugged. "I knew any one of us observing such a thing would be challenged. We needed more witnesses, and there was no time to summon anyone else."

"Those witnesses are quite enough," Penelope assured her. "If the observation is ever questioned, their testimonies will satisfy a court."

"Very well. So we have a death by cyanide poisoning." Stokes looked at David. "Are you willing to act as surrogate for the police surgeon in this case?"

David nodded. "I am."

"Good." Stokes smiled wryly. "On behalf of Pemberton, who would definitely not appreciate being hauled down here to confirm your conclusion, I thank you. Now"—he glanced at his notebook, then looked at Veronica—"who witnessed the death?"

Veronica related what she knew and added what she'd learned of the manner of his lordship's death. "But of course, I wasn't there. That information comes from Jensen and Jeremy, the footman, who I spoke with after his lordship had died."

Barnaby asked, "At what point were you summoned to attend his lordship?"

In an admirably concise fashion, Veronica answered and, without further prompting, described the scene in the dining room as she had found it, then detailed her subsequent actions and those of the others of the household in removing his lordship upstairs. "I didn't get a chance to examine him until he was laid on his bed, and by then, he was dead."

"That was when you had the others confirm the smell?" Stokes asked.

"Yes, but after Stephen and Arthur left to break the news to the family." Veronica went on, "With poison confirmed, to help fix the facts in their minds, I got Jensen and Jeremy to tell Gorton and me everything they remembered of what had gone on. Then Jensen and I went down to send the message to David, but along the way, I thought of the wine glass and the wine decanter, and we went to the dining room, and that was when we discovered the glass had vanished. Jensen took the decanter to keep it safe, and I went on to the library and wrote my message to David, then took it back to Jensen, and we saw it off in the care of a groom."

She paused, clearly revisiting her memories, then continued, "When we got back to the front hall, Stephen stopped us and suggested we send for the doctor. He meant the local man, but I explained that we'd already sent for David, and Stephen accepted that. Then Sally—Sophie's maid—called me to attend her mistress upstairs, and Jensen went up, too, to warn Gorton and Jeremy not to say anything about his lordship being poisoned until David confirmed it."

Veronica looked at Stokes, Barnaby, and Penelope. "That's everything I saw and did during that period."

While Stokes continued scribbling, Penelope was plainly attempting to piece together a picture in her mind. "Did Jensen and Jeremy mention how the people entered the dining room?"

"Specifically," Barnaby amended, "the order in which they filed in."

Veronica thought, then shook her head. "Jensen said he'd summoned them and led the way back to the drawing room, but that's all I know."

"We'll ask Jensen." Stokes made a note in his little black book.

"Hmm. And we also need to know who Lord Meriwell was glaring at," Penelope said.

"Especially as, in gasping his last, he tried to point in the same direction," Barnaby added.

Veronica looked at Stokes, Barnaby, and Penelope. "It might be helpful for you to take a look at the dining room. It's unusually narrow— or rather, the sideboards lining the walls restrict the space around the table. Viewing the layout will help you understand where everyone was in relation to each other and to his lordship's wine glass."

"That's a good idea." Stokes glanced at David. "You're certain the poison wasn't in the wine itself?"

"As certain as I can be without testing the wine," David replied.

"And we do have the vanishing wine glass," Penelope pointed out. "I can't imagine why the murderer would think to spirit the glass away unless they thought to make it harder to be certain poison was used."

Barnaby accepted her reasoning. "If the poison was in the wine, then removing the glass makes no sense."

"Exactly." Penelope smiled at Stokes and David. "I believe we're on sound ground in concluding the poison was in the glass and not in the wine."

"Which," Stokes rumbled, once again busily scribbling in his note-book, "gives us a solid avenue to investigate."

"Namely," Barnaby elaborated, "how the poison got into the glass and who could have put it there."

"Right." Stokes shut his book and looked at the rest of them. "Let's take a quick look at the dining room, then go and meet our suspects."

After they'd examined the dining room and noted the cramped conditions and what that would have meant for prospective diners entering the space and finding their places at the table, Penelope followed Stokes into the drawing room, eager to get her first look at their potential suspects.

Barnaby strolled in behind her, and David and Veronica slipped in last and lingered near the door, observing yet subtly removing themselves from the proceedings.

Their entrance brought all conversations to a halt. As Stokes, Pene-lope, and Barnaby advanced, everyone in the room shifted to face them.

Surprise flared on each and every countenance, and Penelope knew the cause. They'd expected a policeman; the ton's view of policemen was generally rather...lower class. Stokes didn't fit their preconceived notions; although not of the ton, he exuded the confidence of a man better born, grammar school educated, and his assurance had only grown with the years.

As for herself and Barnaby, they were wholly unanticipated. In her fashionable plum carriage dress, with her dark hair plaited and curled in a coronet about her head, even her thick-lensed spectacles could not disguise her quality, that innate attribute that accrued to those born to the nobility. It was a characteristic she and Barnaby shared, and in his subdued yet superbly elegant coat and trousers, it was impossible to mistake his station.

None of them were the "investigators" the company had expected to appear.

Taking advantage of the momentary hiatus, she rapidly counted heads, identifying who was whom as she did. The Meriwell nephews were presumably the three gentlemen with similar features who were standing in various poses about the room—one to each side of the fireplace while the third was poised behind the long sofa.

Each of the three had brown hair, but the hues ranged from almost blond to chestnut. Their builds were similar—solid rather than lean—and all three would qualify as middling tall, so shorter than Barnaby, Stokes, or Sanderson.

Sophie Meriwell had to be the pretty young woman draped languidly over the chaise longue. She had elfin features, and her long dark hair was gathered in a loose arrangement on the top of her head, with numerous tresses artfully bobbing about her ears and the elegant column of her throat. As surprise waned, her expression suggested she was entirely uncertain over what the next minutes might hold.

As per their request, the four Busseltons were also present. Standing in pride of place directly before the hearth, Mr. George Busselton, MP, was a man in his mid-fifties, of average height and build, with thinning brown hair, a neat beard, a developing paunch, and a regrettable liking for plaid waistcoats. His surprise left him frowning slightly, and judging by the anxious tightening about the corners of his lips, Penelope deduced that he was increasingly concerned over how the situation might impinge on his political career.

His wife, Hermione Busselton, was made of sterner stuff. Seated on the sofa, she presented as a formidable matron, large boned with substantial bosom and hips and a determinedly rigid spine. After the first flash of surprise, her face had cleared, and she appeared to be patiently waiting for whatever might occur next, prepared to meet any challenge, an uncompromising expression on her rather plain features. She was dressed in a well-tailored jacket and skirt of brown-and-moss-green tweed, eminently suitable for a country house visit, teamed with a single row of pearls about her throat. Her hair, worn in a bun at the back of her head, had been a rich brown, but was now graying.

Beside her sat a young lady, presumably the Busselton daughter. Physically, Persimone Busselton was a curious cross between her parents. She was as long boned as her mother, but not as hefty, and her features were finer, more like her father's. She was not in the very first blush of youth; Penelope guessed her to be twenty-two or -three. But there was intelligence lurking in her eyes and a quick alertness about her that, to Penelope at least, signaled genuine and significant curiosity.

Penelope noted that one of the Meriwells—most likely Stephen Meriwell—was standing directly behind Miss Busselton in what could be construed as a possessive and protective stance.

The last member of the company was the Busseltons' son. In his very early twenties, he was propped against the arm of the sofa beside his sister in what he no doubt imagined was a graceful pose. With mid-brown hair and pleasant features, he resembled his father in height and general build, but the open curiosity in his face had more in common with the expression in his sister's eyes.

Penelope observed all in mere instants, then Stokes introduced himself, then her and Barnaby, somewhat to the consternation of the company. None of those present had expected to face investigation by such a team, one that could not and would not be cowed by social rank or political consequence.

Stokes was an old hand at pretending not to notice the discomfort they generated, much less acknowledge its cause. In his deep voice, he informed those gathered that they had just come from speaking with Lady Meriwell and Lord Iffey. "We are now in a position to inform you that Lord Meriwell did not die from natural causes. He was murdered, via poison, specifically cyanide administered via his wine glass."

Stokes paused, and Penelope and Barnaby were observing closely, but from the general lack of reaction, the company had suspected something of the sort.

"Consequently," Stokes resumed, "everyone present at Meriwell Hall over the past twenty-four hours must remain until such time as we can justifiably release you as free of all suspicion. To that end, Mr. and Mrs. Adair and I will be conducting individual interviews with each of you, commencing immediately after luncheon." He paused to draw out his little black book. "Now, if each of you will give me your full name."

While one after another, everyone obliged and Stokes wrote down the names, Penelope continued to observe. She was pleased to note that she'd guessed all the identities correctly. The only new information she gleaned was to distinguish Arthur Meriwell as the nephew with mid-brown hair, while the youngest, Peter, had a head of chestnut brown.

Her only additional observation of note was that with the exception of Mrs. Busselton and her children, everyone was, to some extent, uncertain and uneasy over what they—the investigators—might uncover.

In Penelope's eyes, that was interesting.

When Stokes finished his name taking, George Busselton shifted and asked, "How long will we be required to remain here?"

Stokes considered the man for a silent moment, then mildly observed, "I understood that you and your family were expecting to stay for several days, if not a week."

Mrs. Busselton frowned. "Yes, but…" She met Stokes's gaze. "Quite obviously, matters have changed."

Stokes inclined his head. "Indeed. And you may rest assured that we intend to do all possible to resolve this matter expeditiously."

Abruptly, Arthur straightened from his slouch. "Catch the poisoner, you mean?"

Stokes looked at him, then dipped his head. "Yes. That is what I meant."

To say that Arthur looked peevishly uncomfortable would be under-stating the reality.

Curiously, at least to Penelope, the exchange had noticeably height-ened the tension in the room. The junior Busseltons were the only ones who remained untouched by the spreading unease; even their mother had now succumbed.

George Busselton, Peter Meriwell, and Arthur were all frowning, while Stephen Meriwell had remained somewhat stoic throughout, as if he'd accepted that the law would progress in its own way regardless of what he thought and felt and that there was really no benefit in attempting to influence the process. As for Sophie Meriwell, she was plainly attempting to decide how best to react to Stokes, Barnaby, and Penelope; she was seriously unsure as to what tactics would work with them.

Penelope hoped Sophie was clever enough to realize that any descent into hysterics would result in her receiving a slap—from either of the Busselton ladies or from Penelope herself.

When there were no further comments, Stokes turned to Jensen, who had hovered by the door. "Where do you suggest would be most suitable for myself and the Adairs to conduct interviews?"

They settled on the library, then Stokes informed the assembled company that the investigative team would be putting up nearby. "We'll return prior to two o'clock to commence the interviews. Please hold yourselves ready to be called."

With a general nod, Stokes turned for the door. Penelope and Barnaby preceded him from the room, and David and Veronica followed.

Stokes waited until Jensen quit the drawing room and closed the door before fixing his gaze on David and the butler. "It might be wise to keep an eye out in case any of our suspects tries to bolt. I don't expect that, but one never knows."

Jensen nodded. "I'll have a word with the stablemen."

Barnaby looked at Jensen. "Do you have any suggestions of a place nearby where we and also the inspector's men might get rooms?"

Penelope added, "We prefer to put up elsewhere."

Jensen was transparently relieved that the household wouldn't be called on to house them as well as their current guests. "I can recommend the Angel Inn. It's quite close—walking distance if you take the path through the wood—and my widowed cousin is the innkeeper there. Mention my name, and she'll see you right."

Barnaby's smile was entirely sincere. "Thank you. That sounds perfect. We'll try there and see if it suits."

CHAPTER 4

everal hours later, Barnaby walked with Penelope and Stokes through the wood toward Meriwell Hall.

The Angel Inn had proved perfect for their needs, with clean, comfortable rooms and a private parlor Barnaby had hired to give them privacy for later deliberations. Best of all, the woodland path they were currently following led directly from the rear corner of the inn's yard to the side lawn of Meriwell House.

After consuming an excellent luncheon, they were returning to the hall to commence their interview-cum-interrogations.

They reached the edge of the wood and stepped onto well-tended lawn. The side façade of Meriwell House rose before them, with the green grass ending at a terrace that gave access to the side door. The house struck Barnaby as an edifice that was still growing into itself; the sharpness of its elegant lines had yet to be softened by the encroachment of the years.

As they continued toward the terrace, Stokes glanced to their left, at the stable tucked behind the house. "O'Donnell and Morgan will be back at it, seeing what they can winkle from the staff."

The experienced sergeant and constable had joined them at the inn and reported that, to that point, all they'd learned was that the late Lord Meriwell had been generally held to be a fair if occasionally demanding master. None of the staff had said anything to indicate the existence of household ructions.

Barnaby had followed Stokes's gaze. "In this case, I seriously doubt there will be any involvement of staff, not directly."

"But," Penelope stated, as usual effortlessly following his line of thought, "they might know if there's any tensions within the wider community. Busselton, after all, is the MP for the local area. There might be some motive there."

Stokes grunted agreement. "At the very least," he added, "O'Donnell and Morgan should be able to gain some idea of the atmosphere in the house immediately before and after the murder."

"As we've found again and again, staff see far more than their employers imagine," Barnaby said. "However, thus far, I've got the impression that Lord Meriwell dying as he did came as a complete surprise to everyone."

Stokes and Penelope nodded. They reached the terrace, stepped onto the flagstones, and crossed to the side door. Stokes opened it, waved Penelope and Barnaby through, and followed.

They found Jensen hovering in the front hall, waiting to conduct them to the library. "Her ladyship has given orders that the staff should endeavor to provide anything and everything you need."

"Excellent." Penelope smiled and waved him on.

Located down a short corridor leading away from the front hall, the library proved eminently suited to their needs in that, as well as the expected bookshelf-lined walls, the room boasted two separate seating arrangements. At one end of the room, a cozy setting of four large armchairs surrounded a low table before the hearth. In addition, a large mahogany desk was placed more centrally, directly opposite the door, with an admiral's chair behind it and two simple armchairs facing it. A pair of long windows behind the desk admitted steady afternoon light, perfect for illuminating the faces of anyone seated in front of the desk.

Under Penelope's direction, Jensen added two comfortable chairs on either side of the admiral's chair and removed one of the chairs before the desk.

"Perfect." Penelope surveyed the two settings. "One more relaxed, the other more formal. That will do very well."

Jensen inquired, but Stokes assured him they needed nothing more at that point, other than her ladyship's presence.

"We'd like to interview her first," Penelope explained. "Then she can rest for the remainder of the afternoon while we speak with everyone else."

Jensen bowed. "I will fetch her ladyship and, subsequently, will hold myself ready to inform whomever of the party you wish to speak with next."

Stokes nodded, and Jensen departed.

Penelope headed for the armchairs before the small fire. "Comfortable and reassuring for her ladyship, I think."

Barnaby and Stokes followed her lead. They selected seats, leaving vacant one of the chairs nearer the fire for her ladyship.

When the door opened, all three of them rose. Barnaby didn't think any of them were surprised to see Lady Meriwell enter on Lord Iffey's arm. His lordship appeared determined to tenderly escort her ladyship to her allotted seat, and the investigators drew back and allowed him to do so.

Lady Meriwell looked tired and wan, but gamely returned their encouraging smiles. To their collective relief, once Iffey had helped her settle in the commodious armchair, she looked up and patted his arm. "I'll be quite all right, Wallace. There's no need to fuss. These nice people are not going to eat me, and I really must insist that you allow them to speak with me alone. I expect it's a necessary requirement, and I do so want Angus's murderer caught without delay."

The latter half of that statement left Iffey with little choice but to— albeit grumpily—withdraw. With a muted glower at Stokes, he added, "I'll be waiting just outside the door if you need me."

Stokes smiled. "By all means, do wait in the corridor, and we'll interview you next."

Penelope smiled brightly. "That will allow you to remain with and entertain her ladyship for the rest of the afternoon."

Patently unhappy but with no real choice, Iffey left.

Barnaby heard the door shut and resumed his seat, as did Penelope and Stokes.

Stokes began, "Thank you for speaking with us, your ladyship." He drew out his notebook and opened it. "I hope you won't mind if I take notes. It helps avoid having to ask people to repeat things."

"Of course." Her ladyship clasped her hands in her lap. Although her features looked tired and drawn, her gaze was clear as she looked at them expectantly. "I'm ready to help in any way I can."

Stokes nodded encouragingly. "If you could cast your mind back to the moment when Jensen came to summon the company to dinner last night. Can you tell us what you did, and what you saw and heard from that time to the instant when Jensen picked up the wine decanter?"

"Yes, of course." Lady Meriwell composed herself, then began, "I was speaking with Hermione Busselton and Wallace when Jensen arrived to announce that dinner was served. The three of us led the way." Her ladyship switched her gaze to Penelope. "We wished to keep the gathering informal, like a family dinner, you see?"

Penelope nodded. Noting that Stokes was jotting in his book, apparently content to let her lead, she asked, "Who came next?"

"Persimone and Stephen had been conversing with Sophie, and the three of them followed us. Then…" Her ladyship paused, clearly thinking back, then nodded and confidently went on, "The three younger men—Arthur, Peter, and Peregrine—fell in line, and George Busselton and Angus were the last through the dining room door."

"Thank you," Stokes said. "That's very clear."

"Can you tell us the seating around the table?" Barnaby asked.

"Well, starting on Angus's right, it was George, Arthur, Peter, then Wallace on my left. On my right was Persimone, with Stephen beside her, then Sophie, Peregrine, and Hermione on Angus's left."

"Thank you," Penelope said. "That gives us a clear view of who was where around the table."

"Speaking of the table," Barnaby said, "did you notice anything different or unexpected about the glasses?"

Her ladyship clearly thought back, then shook her head. "I can't say that I did. Everything seemed exactly as it should have been." She glanced at Penelope. "I always do a last-minute check as I walk in—it's a habit I got into long ago—so I'm certain that, at that point, nothing was out of place."

Penelope exchanged a swift glance with Stokes, and at his nod, refixed her attention on her ladyship. "We're sorry to ask this of you, Lady Meriwell, but if you could recount what happened after everyone was seated—purely what you saw and heard from your position at the other end of the table."

"I'll try." Lady Meriwell's hands were still clasped in her lap, and her fingers tightened and gripped. "Angus seemed…out of sorts. He was angry, although I have no idea why. He was glaring down the table toward Sophie, then Jensen poured the wine into Angus's glass, and he picked it up and took quite a swallow…"

Her voice faded, and briefly, she closed her eyes in transparent pain, but before they could react, she opened her eyes and said, "Angus choked. He gasped, I think twice, then he tried to reach out along the table, possibly toward Sophie. And then he collapsed."

Her tone made it abundantly clear that she had been deeply fond of her husband, and grief was her dominant emotion.

Stokes stirred, drawing her attention. "You said that Lord Meriwell was angry when he sat down to dinner. When did you become aware of his temper? At that point or earlier?"

"Oh, earlier. He was angry—I would even say furious—and trying to hide it from the moment he walked into the drawing room."

Barnaby asked, "In the drawing room, was his lordship's anger directed at anyone in particular?"

Lady Meriwell frowned. "Not that I saw, but he was doing his best to rein it in, you know, and he and I were chatting in different groups."

Gently, Penelope said, "You mentioned he was glaring down the table at Sophie."

"In her direction, yes." Lady Meriwell lightly grimaced. "I can't imagine what she might have done to occasion his ire this time, yet it seemed very real."

"I understand," Penelope probed, "that there was some tension between his lordship and Sophie regarding her going up to London for the Season."

Her ladyship sighed. "Yes, there was. Sophie was set on going to London and making her come-out, but Angus had taken it into his head that she might be a hysteric and vetoed the plan—which, of course, put Sophie's back up with a vengeance. There were many heated words exchanged on that subject. Sadly, Sophie couldn't see that the way she reacted only piled fuel on the fire of Angus's concern."

"And," Penelope concluded, "that was why Lord Meriwell asked David Sanderson to arrange an evaluation of Sophie's mental state."

Her ladyship nodded. "Exactly."

Penelope glanced at Barnaby and Stokes, then went on, "Dr. Sanderson and Nurse Haskell have given us to understand that, based on their observations, they do not believe Sophie is a true hysteric."

Lady Meriwell shook her head, and a rueful smile curved her lips. "I'm not surprised. I often thought Sophie was more like Angus than he could bear to see. They both insisted on getting their own way—they just used different means. For Angus, it was trenchant argument. For Sophie, it's emotional, often-irrational outbursts. They clashed frequently, yet even so, Angus was fiercely fond of Sophie. She's his only surviving grandchild, and his drive to protect her was behind many of his attempted dictates."

Her ladyship paused, then sighed and went on, "Unfortunately, in the matter of her putative London Season, his protectiveness intertwined with his other great obsession—protecting the family name. He was deeply afraid that if she went into the ton and was seen as a hysteric, that would reflect not merely on her but even more on the family itself. On the Meriwell family as a whole."

Barnaby frowned slightly. "So protecting the family name from any social stigma was an abiding concern of his?"

Her ladyship nodded. "Indeed, it was. I called it an obsession, and it was of that order, but given the family's history, one can hardly be surprised. Angus's younger brother, Claude, was the epitome of the term 'wastrel.' He was a profligate hedonist of the worst sort, a gamester, philanderer, and shyster who constantly expected the family to bail him out of the scrapes he continually landed himself in. Claude died in his forties, and sadly, Arthur and Peter seem intent on following in his footsteps." She paused, once again seemingly captured by memory, then in a quieter voice, continued, "In some respects, it was Angus's obsession with the family's standing that led to our estrangement from Robert, our son, and his wife, Elizabeth. Both felt strongly about improving the lives of others, and when Angus refused to countenance Robert pursuing good works of the kind he was passionate about here, in England, Robert and Eliza decided they would go to Africa and serve in the missions there."

Sadness drew down her features. "They died out there, leaving their children, Jacob and Sophie, to us to raise. Jacob was sixteen and in his last years at Winchester. He wanted—passionately—to work as an engineer, but of course, he was heir to the Meriwell title, and Angus had very different ideas. Sadly, Angus had learned nothing from his dealings with Robert and so drove Robert's son from this place, too. Jacob was determined to establish himself in business in a way that would benefit others, even if that meant becoming a factory owner, something Angus could simply not condone. Jacob left the Hall when he was nineteen, we believe to follow in his parents' footsteps."

When she fell silent, Penelope softly probed, "Where is Jacob now?"

Her ladyship heaved a deep, heartfelt sigh. "Angus told me Jacob had gone to Africa and, like his parents, was now dead."

The silence stretched, redolent with the abiding sorrow of an old woman whose family had, perhaps needlessly, torn itself apart.

Cataloguing her earlier words, Barnaby finally asked, "What of Stephen Meriwell? Was he a concern to Lord Meriwell, too?"

"Oh no." Animation returned to Lady Meriwell's features. "Stephen was the exact opposite of the rest of his branch of the family. Indeed, Stephen was and continues to be everything Angus wanted in a son." Raising her head, she met their gazes. "Stephen was Angus's great hope for the future of the Meriwells. With Robert and Jacob gone, Stephen will inherit the title and the entailed estate and will become the next Lord Meriwell. Angus was quite chuffed by the news of Stephen's intention to offer for Persimone Busselton's hand. Angus considered that an excellent match, as I believe anyone would."

Barnaby nodded. "I see." He glanced at Penelope and faintly arched a brow, but she fractionally shook her head. He glanced at Stokes and met the same response. None of them thought it prudent to ask her ladyship about her affair with Lord Iffey, at least at this point. Despite her determination to help them by providing clear answers to their questions, there was a fragility behind her façade of which they were all aware.

Stokes closed his notebook and rose with a smile. "I believe that's all we need from you for now, ma'am." He half bowed. "Thank you for your assistance. We appreciate that discussing such matters would not have been easy."

Lady Meriwell waved away his thanks and, when Barnaby rose and offered his hand, gripped it and allowed him to help her to her feet. Then she planted her cane, drew herself up to her rather insignificant height, and fixed Stokes, Barnaby, and Penelope with a distinctly fierce look. "The one thing I would ask of you is that, regardless of who they are, you catch whoever did this. For all his faults, Angus was a good, sound man, and he did not deserve to die in the manner in which he did." She tapped her cane on the floor. "I *will* have justice for him. It's the least we can do."

Barnaby smothered a smile. Behind her ladyship's outward softness lay a spine of steel. He half bowed. "Indeed, ma'am. We will do our very best to find his murderer."

Her features eased. "I pray you will succeed."

With a general nod to Penelope and Stokes, she allowed Barnaby to escort her to the door.

Glancing back, he saw Penelope and Stokes confer, then move to the desk.

Barnaby handed Lady Meriwell into the care of her dresser, who had wisely been waiting in the corridor, and at a brisk nod from Stokes, invited Lord Iffey, also loitering in the passageway, to join them, distracting his lordship from hovering over her ladyship.

Iffey clearly felt torn, but at her ladyship's urging, he grudgingly surrendered and, when Barnaby stepped back, stumped into the library.

After shutting the door, Barnaby led his lordship to the armchair before the desk. While his lordship sat, Barnaby rounded the desk and sank into the chair on Stokes's right. Penelope was sitting on Stokes's left, upright and plainly attentive, with her dark gaze fixed on his lordship.

Initially, Stokes led Iffey over the same ground they'd covered with Lady Meriwell regarding the movement of the company into the dining room, the seating, and the actions prior to Lord Meriwell's collapse. His lordship's account did not materially differ from her ladyship's, although Iffey expanded on the conversation he and her ladyship had been having with Hermione Busselton as they'd entered the dining room.

"Very interested in hearing about the family," Iffey said, referring to Mrs. Busselton. "Understandable, I suppose, given the interest Stephen has shown in her gel."

"As to the Meriwells," Stokes said, "we gathered that you enjoyed a very long friendship with the late Lord Meriwell."

Iffey bobbed his white head. "We went back a long way, Angus and I. Winchester, you know. He and I were inseparable while there, and we never really broke the habit, what?"

Penelope somewhat diffidently ventured, "Her ladyship told us something of Meriwell family history by way of explaining his lordship's attitude to preserving the family's reputation in the face of the challenges posed by, among others, his two younger nephews. Can you add any details regarding any recent incidents his late lordship found disturbing?"

"Ah." Iffey nodded sagely. "I suspect you're alluding to Arthur's wanting the horse."

Barnaby blinked. "Horse?"

"Angus's gray hunter, a stallion. Excellent beast. Many have thought so, including, apparently, a long-time creditor of Arthur's. The cent-per-cent was putting the screws on Arthur, has been for months now, not for the money Arthur owed—which he couldn't repay regardless—but for the horse. Seemed that the lender had another client who was willing to pay far over the odds for that particular horse. Presumably to breed him, although who knows? Anyhow, there was no way Angus was going to part with that horse, and the last Angus told me—just two days ago— Arthur was getting desperate."

Barnaby clarified, "Yet regardless of that desperation, Lord Meriwell was not inclined to part with the horse."

"Not in the slightest. Angus might have been eighty, but he still enjoyed riding, and the gray was his favorite mount."

"I see." Stokes was jotting busily. "And what of Peter Meriwell?"

"Oh, that was plain old debts." Iffey waved dismissively. "Peter seems intent on following as diligently as he can in his father's footsteps. Claude's, that is. A bounder, he was, through and through. Died in a stupid curricle race years ago, much to virtually everyone's relief. I mean, what man of forty-plus years wagers his house on a curricle race?" Iffey snorted derisively.

"And Lord Meriwell was disinclined to assist Peter out of the mire?" Barnaby asked.

Iffey nodded. "Exactly. Angus said just the other day that he'd concluded that the only way to force Peter to pull up his socks was to hold firm and let him suffer whatever consequences befell him as a result of his profligacy."

Barnaby caught a pointed look from Penelope and duly ventured, "Her ladyship told us that preserving the family name and reputation was of prime importance to Lord Meriwell."

"Prime importance?" Iffey huffed. "It went much deeper than that. A fixation, certainly. Labeling it an addiction wouldn't be going too far. Indeed, for Angus, after being forced to deal with the ramifications of Claude's behavior for half his life, it became a consuming passion to ensure that absolutely no breath of scandal so much as brushed the Meriwell coattails."

"I see." Stokes fixed his steely gray gaze on Iffey. "And what would —or did—his lordship make of your liaison with Lady Meriwell?"

Iffey blushed painfully. "Here, I say. What... I mean... Dash it all," he blustered, "what sort of question is that?"

"A pertinent one," Stokes countered. "We have it on good authority that you and her ladyship have enjoyed a very close personal relationship for quite some time."

"In short," Penelope said, deeming it time to intervene, "you and she have been lovers for years. More than a decade. What we wish to know is what Lord Meriwell, with his overweening passion about his family's reputation, made of that."

Iffey blinked as if the question made no sense. "But, of course, he never knew."

"Never?" Barnaby arched a cynical brow. "Are you certain of that?"

But Iffey was regaining his composure. "As certain as I—and Clementina, too—can be." He paused, studying their skeptical expressions, then sighed and explained, "Angus never looked our way. He was so busy watching over the lives of everyone else—Sophie, Stephen, Arthur, and Peter, and indeed, even himself—that he'd lost all sight of Clemmie and me. We were merely fixtures in the background of his life —always there, reliable and steady, never any problem."

Iffey paused, looking inward, then more quietly said, "Even if Angus had suspected, to be perfectly frank, I'm not sure he would have cared. He and Clemmie were over long ago—before Robert and his wife left for Africa—and the one thing Angus would have been unswervingly certain of was that, no matter what occurred, neither Clemmie nor I would ever have caused even a whiff of scandal. So our liaison was never any threat to him—we would never have tarnished the family name—and at base, over the past decade and more, that, above all else, was the most important thing of all to Angus."

Barnaby, Penelope, and Stokes studied Iffey, but he was steadfast and sincere, and his demeanor declared that as he saw it, he'd told them nothing but the unvarnished truth.

Accepting that, Stokes slowly nodded. "Very well." He glanced at Barnaby and Penelope, and receiving no sign that either had further questions, Stokes refocused on Iffey. "Thank you for your candor. At this time, we have no further questions to put to you."

Iffey gruffly mumbled, "Good," and pushed to his feet.

With a nod to them all, he turned and stumped to the door, opened it, and left.

"Well," Penelope said, "between them, they've given us a fairly detailed understanding of what drove Angus Meriwell."

"And now, we need to determine what drove his killer." Barnaby looked at Stokes. "Who should we have in next?"

～

They settled on the nephews, commencing with the eldest, Stephen Meriwell.

Penelope watched as, with passable elegance, Stephen sank into the chair before the library desk, behind which she, Stokes, and Barnaby were sitting.

Stephen Meriwell was a pleasantly handsome man, not an Adonis like Barnaby nor as striking as Stokes, yet he was well built, with agreeable features, and exuded an aura of vitality without being overwhelming.

He appeared to be the sort of character who, in normal circumstances, would be easygoing, even charming, and his attire—a fashionable if conservative gray suit teamed with a dark waistcoat and highly polished boots—was expensive yet understated and projected an image that suggested a reliable, practical, steady personality.

As he settled his attention and his hazel gaze on Penelope, Stokes, and Barnaby, she could readily imagine Stephen being the golden-haired nephew, even though his hair was actually a pale light brown.

She glanced at Stokes; with a man like Stephen Meriwell, she preferred to watch and observe rather than question.

Stokes obligingly opened with their now-standard query of Stephen's memories of the company moving from the drawing room to the dining room.

Stephen answered readily, and his account mirrored the information from his aunt and Lord Iffey. When Barnaby asked, Stephen also confirmed the seating around the dining table.

Stokes nodded. "Once the company sat, what happened next? Please take your time and tell us everything you remember from that point on."

Stephen took a moment to think, then with a faint frown forming, ventured, "From the instant he sat, my uncle was glaring down the table." He paused, then transparently reluctantly, added, "I think he was glaring at Sophie, who was seated on my right."

Barnaby asked, "Why do you think Lord Meriwell was glaring at his granddaughter?"

"I really couldn't say," Stephen promptly replied.

"But if you were pressed to guess?" Barnaby persisted.

Stephen hesitated, then sighed and said, "I suppose it was something to do with some action of Sophie's in retaliation for my uncle vetoing her London Season this year. She'd been so looking forward to it, and Sophie doesn't like being thwarted in any way, much less over something she'd set her heart on." He smiled a touch fondly. "She has great ambitions to take the ton by storm."

"I see." Stokes was scribbling in his notebook. Without looking up, he asked, "Do you know of any other irritants in your uncle's life? Any other sources of anger and ire?"

Stephen huffed. "My brothers might not be good for much, but one could always rely on them to get under Uncle Angus's skin."

"How so?" Barnaby inquired.

As if mildly uncomfortable to be telling tales about his brothers, Stephen shifted, but complied. "Arthur's progressed from straightforward debts to somehow needing a horse my uncle owns—a hunter, a stallion— in order to appease some creditor. Arthur's been pestering Uncle Angus for months to let him have the beast, but sadly for Arthur, the stallion is my uncle's favorite mount. Of course, that hasn't stopped Arthur from continuing his campaign to wear Uncle Angus down."

When Stephen fell silent, Stokes prompted, "And your younger brother, Peter?"

Stephen sighed. "Peter is forever in debt. He's been at low ebb for at least a year, and although I haven't heard about any recent pleadings, Peter more or less never appears here without pressuring my uncle for another handout. As Uncle Angus is"—he paused, then amended—"was no fool, he'd decided to cease sending good money after bad."

Stokes scribbled, then raised his gaze to Stephen's face. "To return to the action about the dining table. We have everyone in their chairs, and Lord Meriwell is glaring at Sophie. What happened next?"

Stephen paused, plainly bringing the scene into focus in his mind. "Jensen picked up the decanter from the sideboard, unstoppered it, and poured the wine into Uncle Angus's glass. As Jensen straightened, my uncle picked up the glass and took a good swallow. Then he choked. He gasped and lifted his free hand as if to point down the table, but he never actually did so. He gasped again, quite appallingly, and collapsed, falling forward onto his plate."

"And then?" Barnaby quietly asked.

"There was a stunned silence. I suppose everyone was shocked speechless. Then Jensen whirled and set the decanter back on the side- board, Sophie screamed, and I pushed back my chair, rose, and rushed up the table. Arthur rose, too, and he reached my uncle just before me. Peter followed Arthur, but it was Arthur and me on either side of my uncle, trying to lift him and help him—trying to get some idea of what was wrong." Stephen's expression clouded as his memories rolled on. "But there was nothing—nothing obvious we could do to help."

He paused, then without prompting, went on, "Arthur suggested we move Uncle Angus upstairs so he would be more comfortable, and I agreed. Then Gorton—my uncle's valet—arrived, along with that nurse, Miss Haskell, and we had more than enough people trying to help."

"Was your uncle breathing at that point?" Stokes matter-of-factly asked.

Stephen frowned. "I'm really not sure. I think we all hoped he was in the throes of some seizure or such and would recover if given the chance. But I'm no medic, and I can't actually say if he was alive at that moment."

Stokes nodded in understanding and studied his notes. "So you and your brothers carried his lordship up to his room?"

"Me and Arthur, with Jensen and one of the footmen—Jeremy, if memory serves—and Gorton assisting. Nurse Haskell followed."

"Your brother Peter?" Barnaby asked.

"I told Peter to help my aunt and the guests. I suggested they go to the drawing room, as it was inconceivable that anyone would want to eat after that. I said I would come down and report as soon as we knew more about my uncle's condition."

"So," Stokes said, "you, Arthur, Gorton, Jensen, Jeremy, and Nurse Haskell carried his lordship upstairs to his room and, I assume, laid him on his bed?"

"Yes. That's right. Once we had, we stepped back and let Nurse Haskell examine him." Stephen's expression darkened. "She pronounced him dead."

"I see," Stokes said. "That must have been a shock."

Stephen frowned. "It was, yet he was eighty years old. We—Arthur and I, and I think the rest of the men—assumed it was a heart attack." Stephen's expression didn't lighten. "On that basis, Arthur and I went downstairs and broke the news to my aunt and the guests."

Stephen looked at Stokes, then at Barnaby. "It wasn't until the next day that we heard any mention of poison." His tone suggested some degree of uncertainty as to whether the poisoning was truly real or not.

Stokes evenly said, "Once she was able to examine the body, Nurse Haskell suspected poison, and the others remaining in the room at that time, once the symptoms were pointed out, concurred, but of course, they had to wait for Dr. Sanderson to confirm their suspicions."

When Stephen, looking troubled, merely nodded, Stokes arched a brow at Penelope. She shook her head; she had no further questions for Stephen Meriwell, at least not at that time.

When Barnaby, too, shook his head at Stokes, Stokes informed Stephen, "That's all our questions for you to this point, Mr. Meriwell. You may go, and if you would send in your brother Arthur? I understand he should be waiting in the corridor."

With a ready nod, Stephen rose, walked to the door, and opened it. To someone in the corridor beyond, he said, "You're next."

Holding the door, Stephen stood back, and Arthur came in.

Arthur was fractionally shorter than Stephen and more heavily built. His hair was mid brown, several shades darker than Stephen's, and his features were less fine than his brother's, fleshier, with a larger nose and a more florid complexion. His brown suit was nondescript, passable for a gentleman but neither of top quality nor in the latest style.

Penelope was watching as Arthur paused just inside the doorway, and the look he and Stephen exchanged was nothing short of mutually venomous. Obviously, there was no love lost between the brothers—those two, at least.

Arthur shifted his gaze to her, Barnaby, and Stokes, seated behind the desk, then came forward to take the chair before it as Stephen went out and closed the door.

She listened as Stokes put Arthur through his paces.

Arthur's recollection of the movements of the company as they went into dinner did not differ from those interviewed previously, but his memory was somewhat less complete; he wasn't sure of the movements of others, and it seemed he hadn't paid much attention to anyone bar himself.

While Arthur confirmed that his uncle had been glaring down the table at someone seated on the opposite side, he declined to venture an opinion as to at whom his lordship's glare had been directed.

"But it could have been Sophie?" Stokes pressed.

Arthur shrugged. "Possibly." Then he grimaced and added, "More likely her than the golden boy—meaning Stephen. But as I said, I can't be certain. I was merely glad that my uncle wasn't glaring at me." He shifted. "Or for that matter, at Peter. He was sitting beside me."

"I see." Stokes made a show of consulting his notebook. "We understand that you've been petitioning your uncle for a particular horse." Stokes met Arthur's gaze. "Why do you need that horse?"

Penelope hid a smile. Stokes hadn't asked Arthur whether that was true nor made any sort of mild inquiry. The direct and uncompromising question left Arthur with little option but to tell Stokes what he actually wanted to know.

After a minute of frowning, Arthur reluctantly came to the same conclusion. He shot Stokes a disaffected look. "If you must know, I owe a sum—*not* an insurmountable sum—to a certain man who has an associate with a keen interest in breeding hunters. My uncle owns a stallion that is highly regarded and likely to prove excellent for breeding. Being eighty and no longer riding to hounds, my uncle doesn't actually require the horse—not that particular horse—and I've been attempting to persuade him to give me the beast in lieu of any future inheritance from the Meriwell estate." Arthur raised his hands, palms up. "It would be an excellent deal for all concerned, including my uncle, but he simply wouldn't listen." Arthur subsided, then muttered, "Or at least he hadn't listened yet. I was still hoping to convince him…"

Barnaby asked, "To whom is your creditor hoping to trade the horse?"

Arthur's expression grew almost surly, but eventually, he replied, "Croxton."

Even Penelope knew Croxton was one of the wealthiest ex-moneylenders, one who, they'd heard, was making a bid to turn himself into a legitimate businessman. Croxton lusting after a breeding stallion previously owned by a lord who rode to hounds fitted the picture.

"Croxton." Stokes's tone was disgusted. "You owe a friend of Croxton a 'not-insurmountable' sum?"

"For how long has that debt been hanging over your head?" Barnaby asked.

Arthur clearly wished he didn't have to answer, but again, eventually obliged, "Four years."

"I imagine Croxton and his friend are growing impatient." Stokes's comment hit the mark, and Arthur's glower turned wary.

After a moment, Arthur wet his lips and offered, "Croxton is prepared to wait to get his hands on the horse—on that particular horse."

Stokes sat back and regarded Arthur steadily. "You must realize that having Croxton—and his friend—after you, wanting that horse that, thus far, you've failed to persuade your uncle to make over to you, gives you a viable motive to poison your uncle."

Arthur looked genuinely taken aback. "Why? If he died before giving me the horse, I'd have to fight Stephen tooth and nail to get it…" His expression changed as understanding dawned. "Oh God—that's what's happened."

He looked at Stokes, Penelope, and Barnaby, his expression a strange blend of belligerence and dejection. "Now I'll have to metaphorically wrestle Stephen for the horse. And he damned well knows I need it!" He looked at the ceiling as if praying for some better revelation, then returned his gaze to them. "So that's what Uncle Angus dying has landed me with—a battle with Stephen for the horse. And in case you haven't realized, my older brother and I do not get on. If you think I would rather go up against him than argue with an old man, well, you're wrong. You don't know Stephen. He's a much harder case than my uncle ever was."

Stokes arched a brow at Arthur. "So you didn't poison your uncle?"

"No. I did not." Arthur sat upright and tugged down his waistcoat.

"Yet it's you who's in debt to Croxton's friend," Barnaby mildly observed.

"But Croxton's willing to be patient, and the sum isn't that much—it's not me who's up to my eyeballs in debt!" Immediately he made the statement, he looked as if he wanted to take it back.

"I assume," Stokes purred, "that you're referring to your younger brother, Peter."

But Arthur's lips primmed, and he endeavored to look down his nose. "You may ask Peter about his situation. I'm not saying anything more."

Stokes glanced at Barnaby and Penelope, and when neither made to ask anything else, Stokes returned his gaze to Arthur and inclined his head. "In that case, Mr. Meriwell, you may go. Please send in Peter, who I believe will be waiting outside."

Without another word and with barely a civil nod, Arthur rose and strode rapidly for the door.

Penelope, Stokes, and Barnaby all watched as Arthur opened the door, nodded to someone beyond, then stepped back to allow Peter Meriwell to enter.

Penelope noted that the look this pair of brothers exchanged was more in the nature of a warning, possibly conspiratorial in nature.

Stokes welcomed Peter and directed him to the chair before the desk.

Peter was several years younger than his brothers; Penelope placed him in his late twenties. He was leaner than Stephen and Arthur, although she thought not as tall, and was easily distinguished from the other two by his dark-brown hair, which was almost sable. Peter's features were more saturnine, a trifle pinched, with a longer nose. He appeared more openly dissolute than Arthur, with a rather peevish cast to his features. Peter's eyes were his redeeming feature—a greeny hazel framed by long, dark lashes. His hair was decently styled, and his clothes—a well-cut black jacket worn over dark-brown trousers and boots—matched the current fashion for gentlemen of his age and standing.

As soon as Peter had settled, Stokes moved quickly through the initial questions regarding the company moving into the dining room and the seating arrangements.

For Penelope's money, judging by Peter's vague and incomplete replies, he'd been paying even less attention to those about him than Arthur; all of Peter's observations of others were referenced to himself, to what he'd been doing or thinking at the time.

Hoping to jolt him from his self-absorption and possibly learn something of use, she leaned forward, drawing his attention. "What can you tell us of Miss Sophie Meriwell's relationship with her grandfather, your uncle?"

Peter blinked, then glanced at Stokes and Barnaby. When neither reacted, he returned his gaze to Penelope and replied, "I don't really know that much. Sophie's younger than us—than me and my brothers. I only really saw her when I was staying here during school holidays or, later, when I came to visit. It's not as if she and I—or my brothers—socialized or moved in the same circles or shared friends. We—Stephen, Arthur, and I—were more friendly with Sophie's brother, Jacob, but he left years ago." He paused, then added, "But I can tell you that Sophie was always —*always*—the apple of Uncle Angus's eye. No matter what she did to annoy him, ultimately, she could do no wrong."

Abruptly, Peter met Penelope's eyes. "Uncle Angus had already made it clear to everyone that Sophie would inherit the bulk of the estate. The unentailed part. So there was no huge motive for any of us to kill Uncle Angus, at least not in the expectation of inheriting any large sum."

From the corner of her eye, Penelope saw Stokes's lips cynically lift.

"As to motive," Stokes said, "inheriting even a small amount can be a great relief if a man is under significant pressure to pay off debts."

Peter's pale complexion paled even more.

"We understand," Barnaby said, "that you presently owe a significant amount. How much are your debts?"

Peter looked furtive, but tried to brazen it out. He tipped up his chin. "I can honestly say that I don't know."

"You don't know, but they are substantial." Stokes jotted in his book and nodded sagely. "And likely increasing by the day." He pinned Peter with a penetrating look. "Is that a reasonable statement of the truth?"

Peter swallowed and didn't answer.

Stokes waited several seconds, then leaned forward and, his eyes narrowing on Peter, asked, "Just how desperate are you to pay off your most urgent creditors?"

When Peter just stared, Barnaby murmured, "The question really is are you desperate enough to have murdered your uncle for however little he might have left you?"

"No!" Peter looked horrified that they might think so, but almost immediately, petulance flooded his expression. "If only Uncle Angus had stopped treating me like some juvenile and handed over a few ponies when I first asked him, I wouldn't be in this state! It was never my fault— it was his! And as I'm sure he's left me a mere pittance that will barely scrape the sides of what I need, he was potentially worth more to me alive than dead! I might have been able to persuade him that the scandal would be worth paying to avoid." He flung out a hand. "I can't do that if he's dead!"

It was an unedifying speech, and Penelope, Barnaby, and Stokes let it lie for a moment, seething in the silence.

Peter folded his arms, then hunched and started gnawing on a finger-nail, his gaze darting around and about, avoiding focusing on them.

Eventually, Stokes consulted his notebook, then asked, "You rushed to help with your uncle, but were superfluous to needs there, and Stephen asked you to assist in conducting your aunt, Lord Iffey, and the rest of the company to the drawing room." Stokes raised his gaze and fixed it on Peter's face. "Tell us what happened once the others took your uncle out of the dining room."

Peter's peevishness was on full show, but he stopped biting his nail and said, "I was as shocked as anyone. That's why I rushed to help. When the others left with Uncle Angus, I went to help Aunt Clementina. She's always been kind to me—well, to all of us—and Iffey was as unsteady on his feet as she was." Peter paused, but his thoughts had clearly tracked back to those moments. "The Busseltons milled about a bit, along with Sophie, who looked more stunned than I've ever seen her, then Mrs. Busselton realized they had to go first to allow us—Aunt Clementina with me and Lord Iffey on either side—to move down the table and out of the door. So they went ahead, but waited for us in the hall, and then we went on, and they fell in behind us. By then, Mrs. Busselton and her daughter had Sophie in hand and were towing her along. No hysterics, thank God!"

"Wasn't there a footman about?" Penelope asked.

Transparently still in his memories, Peter nodded. "Thomas. He was shocked, too, but couldn't do much more than open and hold the doors. He did that, seeing us all into the drawing room. He asked if we needed anything, and Aunt Clemmie seemed to gather herself and said not right now. She sat down on the settee, then said that we would all wait to hear about Uncle Angus. So everyone sat and waited. We didn't know what else to do."

Despite his sulky demeanor, Penelope judged that Peter had related what had occurred reasonably accurately; it seemed that the shock of his uncle's seizure had focused his attention more sharply than in the moments prior to the poisoning.

Stokes seemed to think so, too. After an inviting glance at Barnaby and Penelope to which neither responded, Stokes focused on Peter. "Thank you, Mr. Meriwell. For the moment, that's all the questions we have for you."

Peter blinked as if surprised. "So I can go?"

At Stokes's nod, Peter got to his feet rather rapidly. With the barest of nods, he turned and walked quickly to the door.

They watched him leave, then Barnaby asked, "So who should we question next? Sophie Meriwell or the Busseltons?"

The general consensus favored the Busseltons. As Stokes put it, "Better we have them in before Mr. Busselton, MP, gets on his high horse."

Penelope pushed her glasses higher on her nose. "At least the Busseltons shouldn't take that long, and then perhaps we can break for tea and think about our questions for Sophie and, after her, the staff."

They exchanged a glance of agreement, and Barnaby rose and crossed to the bellpull to ring for Jensen.

CHAPTER 5

Naturally, Mr. Busselton was the first of his family they invited to join them in the library; all three of them felt sure that the MP wouldn't have had it any other way.

Yet judging by his manner when he entered, decidedly tentative, almost wary, Mr. Busselton wasn't sure how to behave—how high-handed he could be—given Barnaby, son of an earl who was also one of the governors of the police force, and Penelope, another scion of a noble house with innumerable noble connections, were sitting there, behind the desk, rather obviously supporting Stokes.

Perhaps unsurprisingly, Mr. Busselton had decided to be careful.

As he responded to Stokes's greeting and invitation to take the chair before the desk, Barnaby felt certain that, had he and Penelope not been present, George Busselton, MP, would have been officious and obstructionist, simply on principle.

Consequently, when Stokes, no doubt reading the man equally accurately, arched a brow Barnaby's way, Barnaby shifted slightly, securing Busselton's attention, and led with, "Mr. Busselton, could you describe for us where you were in the procession into the dining room?"

"Indeed, Mr. Adair. I was walking beside his lordship. Lord Meriwell, that is. Our host." Busselton started to frown. "That is…"

"Quite." Their host was now dead. Barnaby rolled on, "When you and his lordship walked into the dining room, do you recall where the other guests were and whether they were standing or sitting?"

Busselton appeared to rack his brains, but eventually conceded, "I know they were all present, but exactly who was doing what or even exactly where they sat, I fear I can't say. Not with any certainty."

Barnaby nodded understandingly. "I believe you were seated at his lordship's right?"

"I was, yes. Very…" Busselton colored faintly. "Er…appropriate, no doubt."

"Temper-wise," Barnaby continued, "how did his lordship seem to you?"

"Well…tense." Busselton nodded to himself. "Yes, that's how I would describe his manner. Somewhat on edge, although over what, I gleaned no insight."

Penelope leaned forward, drawing Busselton's attention. "Others have confirmed that, once his lordship sat, he was glaring down the left side of the table."

Busselton nodded. "I noticed that."

"In your view," Penelope asked, "at whom was his lordship glaring?"

"Well, I suppose it must have been his granddaughter, Miss Meriwell."

Penelope cocked her head. "Why do you believe it must have been her?" Her tone suggested she was merely curious as to Busselton's process, not that she was challenging his assessment.

"Simple deduction, really. His lordship's glare was directed along that side of the table, but at some position beyond my wife. The next along on that side was our son, Peregrine, and as his lordship had only just met Perry, it stands to reason he wouldn't have cause to be glaring at him. Next seat along was Miss Meriwell, and after her sat Mr. Stephen Meriwell, and beside him was our daughter, Persimone. I'm sure his lordship wasn't glaring at Persimone, so his target had to have been either his granddaughter or Stephen, and again, it stands to reason it wouldn't have been Stephen. Ergo, his lordship must have been glaring at his granddaughter, Sophie."

Penelope manufactured a frown. "Why do you believe it couldn't have been Stephen his lordship was glaring at? We've been hearing that Lord Meriwell had frequent difficulties with his nephews."

Busselton nodded readily. "Indeed, indeed, but the difficulties, I have heard, were with Mr. Arthur Meriwell and Mr. Peter Meriwell, the younger nephews, not—indeed, never—with Stephen Meriwell. My understanding is that Stephen rides high in his lordship's esteem and always has."

"We understand," she ventured, "that your family's visit to Meriwell Hall was, at least in part, to assess Stephen Meriwell's suitability as an aspirant for your daughter's hand." She smiled encouragingly. "From that, I assume you've had occasion to interact with Stephen in London, and in that, you have the advantage of us. How have you found Stephen thus far —both here and in town?"

Busselton's face lit. "I must admit, Mrs. Adair, that as a father and given the office I hold, I've been wary of any approaches to secure Persimone's hand. But in all I've seen and learned of Stephen Meriwell, I have been favorably impressed. Extremely favorably impressed. The gentleman is all he purports to be. He is a charming conversationalist and has a ready store of unexceptionable tales with which to entertain the ladies. He has an excellent sense of what is right and proper and is always attentive and protective of those in his care. He is patently well-to-do and manages a sound business that clearly provides a more than acceptable income."

Busselton paused in his paean to consider and, after studying Penelope for an instant, confessed, "While we—my wife and I—would prefer Persimone married a title and a man with a decent estate, I believe it's no secret that, as matters stand, Stephen Meriwell will inherit the title and entailed estate of the late Lord Meriwell." He grimaced. "Of course, one would prefer that such an inheritance came without murder being the cause, but as I cannot imagine Stephen was in any way involved, ultimately, the alliance remains an excellent prospect." He paused, then added in a quieter tone, "Especially as Persimone is...well, rather finicky. My wife and I have grown concerned—Persimone is already twenty-three —but she was willing to entertain Stephen Meriwell's suit, and now that he will be Lord Meriwell, I expect the engagement to go forward in time."

He glanced at Barnaby and confided, "It never hurts to have a son-in-law in the Other Place."

Barnaby smiled easily. "Thank you for sharing your opinions. Having the view of someone from outside the Meriwell family greatly assists us in our investigation. Now, as to what occurred when Lord Meriwell picked up his wine glass..." Barnaby outlined the sequence of events they'd compiled from their previous interviewees to the point of the guests returning to the drawing room to await word on their host's condition. "Do you have anything to add to that account?"

Busselton frowned in thought, then slowly shook his head. "I believe that covers everything that occurred." He looked at Barnaby, then at Penelope, then somewhat reluctantly settled his gaze on Stokes. "Inspector, given all you have now gleaned, what are your next steps?"

Stokes mildly replied, "We will need to speak briefly to your wife and children, purely to confirm what they saw, before interviewing those of the company with whom we've yet to speak, and then move on to the staff in case there is something pertinent of which they are aware. After that, we'll be in a better position to know what will need to come next." Stokes concluded, "At this point, I suggest we move on to speaking with the other members of your family so we don't keep them waiting any longer than need be."

Barnaby hid a grin at Stokes's deft handling of the MP's wish to know more and, possibly, to have some influence on the conduct of the investigation.

Of course, Busselton wasn't enamored of Stokes's suggestion. "I really can't see why you must question my family. They saw no more than I did, so can hardly tell you anything more."

Penelope smiled confidingly at Busselton and rose, forcing Busselton to get to his feet. She rounded the desk and reached for his arm. "You'd be amazed," she advised him, gently but inexorably steering him toward the door, "by how often the very last person you expect to have noticed the vital clue actually has and remembers it when asked."

On reaching the door, she opened it and released Busselton. "So we really do need to speak with Mrs. Busselton next. I believe she'll be waiting in the drawing room. Would you please ask her to join us?"

There was no way in the world that Busselton could refuse a request from Penelope at her most aristocratically gracious.

Mutely, he nodded, then directed a more distant nod at Barnaby and Stokes and left.

Penelope closed the door, then smiled widely and returned to the desk. As she sat, she beamed at Barnaby and Stokes. "What an excellent team we three make."

~

In her late forties, Mrs. Hermione Busselton was a large, solid-boned matron, plain faced but, from her manner, equally plainly well bred. Calm, unflappable, and, Barnaby judged, highly competent, she was the perfect partner for a minor politician with aspirations to higher office.

She also proved to be just such a witness as Penelope had mentioned; she was observant, shrewd, insightful, and possessed an excellent recall of events.

Barnaby did the honors, taking Mrs. Busselton rapidly through their now-standard questions regarding the movement into the dining room and the actions that followed. To their delight, Mrs. Busselton replied concisely and accurately, confirming what they'd already learned, but with an absolute confidence that was reassuring.

Even more telling, Mrs. Busselton did not speculate over things she did not, in fact, know; when Penelope asked at whom she'd thought Lord Meriwell had been glaring, Hermione Busselton crisply explained that given her position on his lordship's left, she had not been in a position to identify his lordship's target. "All I could say was that it wasn't Peregrine, who was seated beside me, but someone farther along our side of the table."

Relieved to have such a reliable witness, Barnaby asked what had happened next.

Mrs. Busselton related how the butler had filled his lordship's wine glass, then stepped back. "To my complete and utter surprise, his lordship picked up the glass and took a...well, it was almost a swig. A large swallow. I was instantly struck by the oddity of him taking such a gulp before anyone else's glass had even been filled."

Penelope's eyes widened, and she sat straighter. "You're right. That was...quite a faux pas."

Mrs. Busselton's lips primmed censoriously. "Indeed. It surprised me because, until then, his lordship had behaved with all due propriety."

Penelope searched Mrs. Busselton's face. "Why do you think he broke with polite practice?" That was veering into speculation, yet it seemed Penelope had been correct in sensing that Mrs. Busselton might have some observation to share.

"If I had to guess," Mrs. Busselton said, "he was attempting to swallow his anger. The action had that feel to it."

Penelope arched her brows. "Was he—Lord Meriwell—angry prior to coming into the dining room?"

Mrs. Busselton's tight lips told them that she was debating whether or not to share her opinion, but then she looked at Penelope and made up her mind. "He was doing his level best to hide his temper, doubtless on Stephen's and our accounts, but yes. I felt that his lordship was…well, saying he was consumed with rage, suppressed rage, would not be over-stating the matter. He was fairly vibrating with the emotion."

Penelope seized the tangent and ran with it. "You mention Stephen Meriwell. We understand that the impetus behind this visit is to further your knowledge of Stephen and his family given he has indicated a wish to offer for your daughter's hand."

Mrs. Busselton met Penelope's eyes and nodded. "Indeed."

When Mrs. Busselton volunteered no more, Barnaby said, "Your husband seems very taken with the prospect of your daughter becoming Mrs. Stephen Meriwell."

Hermione Busselton compressed her lips, plainly considered for several seconds, then stated, "My husband is deeply impressed by Stephen Meriwell."

Penelope leaned forward. "And you? What do you think of Stephen as a future son-in-law?"

Mrs. Busselton regarded Penelope's wide eyes and, as if accepting that she wouldn't be put off, sighed and admitted, "My husband may prove correct in his reading of Stephen. For myself, I'm waiting to learn more of the man himself. I had hoped to do so on this visit." She paused, then added, "Although it might seem insensitive to say so, his lordship's death and the tension that will inevitably generate will likely provide a revealing testing ground for measuring the mettle of Stephen's character."

With a dip of her head, Penelope agreed.

Barnaby caught Penelope's eye and arched a brow, but she shook her head, indicating she had no more questions for Mrs. Busselton, and after Stokes indicated the same, Barnaby rose and thanked Mrs. Busselton for her assistance and escorted her from the room.

After closing the door, Barnaby turned to his co-investigators only to have Stokes raise a staying hand. "Before we discuss Mrs. Busselton's insights, I suggest we have the younger Busseltons in, just in case they take after their mother rather than their father and can add more detail to our picture of Stephen Meriwell and also Lord Meriwell and his anger."

Penelope concurred, and Barnaby crossed to the bellpull to summon Jensen and send him to fetch their next interviewees.

Miss Persimone Busselton duly arrived and gracefully sat in the chair before the desk. Her father had mentioned she was twenty-three, and like her mother, she was tallish for a female and large boned. Her features were pleasant albeit a trifle plain, but there was intelligence in her hazel gaze, and using their standard questions to open proceedings, Stokes quickly established that Persimone was every bit as observant as her mother and possibly more intelligent as well; she seemed quick to notice, assess, and weigh the importance of what she observed.

For a future politician's or minor lordling's wife, that was quite a recommendation. Barnaby had no difficulty understanding what had attracted Stephen Meriwell's attention.

On the question of the target of Lord Meriwell's glare, Persimone informed them, "From my position on Lady Meriwell's right, I could tell that Lord Meriwell was glaring at either Stephen or Sophie. I can't be certain which."

Stokes sent a wordless invitation to Penelope, and she leaned forward and said, "Lady Meriwell and your mother both mentioned they thought that Lord Meriwell was furious but attempting to hide it during the conversation in the drawing room." Penelope tipped her head. "Can you add anything to that?"

Persimone frowned. After a moment, she shook her head. "That might be so—I would trust Mama's judgment on the point—but I was speaking with Sophie and Stephen and wasn't in a position to notice his lordship's mood."

Penelope nodded, impressed that the younger woman hadn't sought to comment regardless of any factual knowledge. "Moving back into the dining room, once the butler started pouring the wine…what are your thoughts on what followed?"

"Well," Persimone replied, "I was astonished that Lord Meriwell couldn't seem to wait for the rest of the table—not even Papa—to be served but immediately picked up his glass and took a healthy swallow." Persimone's sharply intelligent gaze flitted from Stokes to Barnaby before settling on Penelope. "That seemed decidedly odd, but if the poison was in the wine, then I suppose we must be grateful that in acting as he did— however boorish that might have been—Lord Meriwell spared everyone else from potentially being poisoned."

Penelope nearly laughed. Persimone was clearly angling for information. Rather than give it to her, Penelope said, "You and the others returned to the drawing room to await news of his lordship's state. Who else was there, in the drawing room?"

Persimone took the rebuff in her stride. "At the beginning, there was Peter, Lady Meriwell, and Lord Iffey, and Mama, Papa, myself, and my brother, Perry, and Sophie. It was Peter who urged us to retreat there, and given the situation, everyone complied."

"And everyone remained there until Stephen and Arthur returned bearing the news of Lord Meriwell's death." Stokes made the words a statement, that being what the three of them believed.

But Persimone shook her head. "No. At first, we all stayed there, but then Peter excused himself, saying he would go up and learn what was going on, but we didn't see him again that night. And shortly after Peter had left, Sophie said she was feeling poorly—hardly a surprise—and took herself off to her room."

Barnaby frowned. "So when Stephen and Arthur returned—" He broke off because Persimone was shaking her head again.

"Not Arthur—not at first. Stephen came in, and he was about to speak when Arthur arrived." Persimone paused, clearly replaying the moment in her mind. "I got the impression that Arthur had been somewhere else. He hadn't been with Stephen, at least not just before Stephen walked into the drawing room."

"I see." Stokes was busily scribbling. He paused, read over what he'd written, then looked at Persimone. "Lord Iffey and Lady Meriwell. Were they still in the drawing room when Stephen came in?"

"Oh yes," Persimone said. "Lord Iffey was concerned and tried to suggest several times that her ladyship should retire, but she wouldn't hear of it. She wasn't about to leave guests to fend for themselves—she was quite adamant about that."

Penelope stirred and, when Persimone looked her way, mildly said, "We gathered that your visit here was by way of getting to know Stephen Meriwell and his family. We've heard your parents' views on Stephen's suitability as a potential suitor for you." Her gaze on Persimone's face, Penelope tipped her head. "What are your thoughts on the matter?"

"On Stephen?" Persimone didn't seem perturbed, much less flustered by the question. She considered, then offered, "I appreciate that he presents as a respectable, reliable, steady gentleman of established means. Outwardly, he appears to be a highly suitable parti. But as to the man himself, I have reservations, which is why I agreed to us coming to Meri-well Hall. I hoped to learn more of Stephen's character, his nature and temperament. While I perceive no grounds on which to reject his suit, there is more I would seek to know before I would feel comfortable accepting it."

Persimone met Penelope's eyes and smiled somewhat wryly. "If that makes me sound like some vacillating ninny..." She shrugged. "I would simply rather be sure than sorry."

Penelope's smile was genuine and approving. "A laudably sensible approach." After a swift glance at Stokes and Barnaby, neither of whom had anything to add, Penelope nodded to Persimone. "Thank you, Miss Busselton. You've been a great help."

Persimone's gaze flitted over them again, and it was obvious her curiosity hadn't waned in the least. "Are you staying here, at Meriwell Hall? In case I remember something pertinent."

Penelope sternly suppressed a chuckle. "No. We find it helps our deliberations to abide elsewhere. But we are staying close by. If you recall anything you think might prove helpful, please alert Jensen. He will know where to find us."

She wasn't about to tell Persimone that they were staying at an inn a few minutes' walk away. The girl would appear there, supposedly getting a feel for the locality; had she been in Persimone's shoes, that was what Penelope would have done.

"Oh." Persimone managed not to look too disappointed. When Barnaby rose and came to escort her to the door, she stood and nodded a farewell to Stokes and Penelope. "Inspector. Mrs. Adair." She turned to Barnaby and inclined her head graciously. "Mr. Adair. Should I send my brother in?"

Barnaby smiled. "If you would, Miss Busselton, that would be helpful."

Persimone turned and walked to the door.

All three investigators smiled at the panel after it closed behind her.

Peregrine Busselton walked into the library even more openly agog to witness a police investigation in action than his sister had been.

He was tallish, still retaining the gangliness of youth; Penelope placed him at twenty years old at most. His pleasant, likeable features had yet to firm into their fully adult lines, and his expression was unguarded and devoid of all artifice.

Stokes waved Peregrine to the chair before the desk.

As he sat, he assured them, "I say, you can count on me to help in any way I can."

Stokes struggled to mute his grin. "Excellent." He glanced at Barnaby, delegating opening the questioning to him.

Barnaby smiled encouragingly at Peregrine and commenced with what were now their routine questions regarding the movement of the company into the dining room and the actions about the table thereafter.

Peregrine's answers—clear, concise, and surprisingly insightful for one of his years—quickly established him as their most useful witness to date. He confirmed his mother's and sister's accounts of the movements of people and the target of Lord Meriwell's glare. Peregrine, too, had registered the oddity of their host seizing his wine glass and quaffing wine before anyone else had been served. "Dashed strange, that was. It didn't seem like the sort of off-color behavior someone like Lord Meriwell would normally have indulged in."

Barnaby studied Peregrine's face. "I believe—we believe—that you're right in thinking the action was out of character for Lord Meriwell. If you had to hazard a guess, why do you think he might have done it?"

"Oh, he was angry," Peregrine said. "I spotted that the moment he walked into the drawing room. He was seething underneath, but it wasn't anything to do with the company—the gathering—so he was trying valiantly to squelch his temper." Peregrine paused, then offered, "If I had to guess, then I would say he quaffed the wine to help him swallow his rage. Only he choked." Peregrine's sharp hazel eyes studied Barnaby, then shifted to Penelope. "But that was the poison, wasn't it?"

"It seems so," Penelope admitted, then abruptly shut her lips.

Hiding a smile, Barnaby tapped the desk, drawing Peregrine's attention back to him. "Tell us how the company returned to the drawing room."

Peregrine recounted much the same tale as Persimone. "After a time, Peter left, saying he was going to see what he could find out, but he never came back. I wouldn't be surprised if, instead, he went off to find a stiff drink. A minute or so after that, Miss Meriwell claimed she was feeling quite ill and left, supposedly for her chamber. Sometime after that—perhaps ten minutes or more—Stephen returned to tell us the sad news. Arthur came through the door a little after Stephen. I'm fairly certain that Arthur had been drinking—he had that look about him."

Barnaby glanced to where Stokes was busily jotting notes, then returned his gaze to Peregrine. "What do you think about having Stephen Meriwell as a brother-in-law?"

Peregrine raised his eyebrows. "To be perfectly frank, I'm not sure Persimone will accept him. As for myself, when it comes to Stephen Meriwell, I'm very much on the fence. I haven't seen enough of him to make up my mind about what sort of man he is." He met Barnaby's gaze. "I mean, there's the outer man and the inner man, and you want some experience of the fellow to be reasonably confident that the inner man matches what you can see."

Barnaby inclined his head. "That's an excellent way to put it." It was also surprisingly astute and mature.

Peregrine looked from Barnaby to Stokes to Penelope. "I say, can I join in the hunt?"

Barnaby saw Stokes struggle to quash a smile. "No," Stokes said, "although we'd be glad if you kept your eyes and ears open and let us know of anything odd you might learn." When Peregrine shot faintly frowning glances at Barnaby and Penelope, Stokes deigned to explain, "Mr. and Mrs. Adair are long-standing official consultants to the Metropolitan Police. They assist at the commissioner's request, so you might say that they have legal standing. That's important in terms of giving evidence in court and is not a position that is readily available or that can be readily bestowed on anyone."

Peregrine sighed. "I see." Although he was plainly disgruntled, there was no sign that he didn't accept Stokes's verdict.

Stokes unbent enough to add, "We're staying nearby, and if you discover something you think we ought to know, Jensen will know where to find us. We'll be returning tomorrow and, most likely, be about the house during the day."

Peregrine nodded. "All right." He sat up and looked at the three of them. "Should I take myself off, then?"

The three of them couldn't help but smile.

Peregrine smiled back, rose, tipped them a salute, and ambled from the room.

When the door closed behind him, Penelope shook her head. "He's going to be one to watch in the future."

"After interviewing his sister," Stokes said, "I hadn't imagined the Busselton quiver would contain an even sharper mind."

Laughing, Barnaby agreed.

"What I found noteworthy," Penelope said, "was that while Mr.

Busselton was full of praise for Stephen Meriwell and ready to welcome him as a son-in-law with open arms, the rest of the family were a great deal more equivocal."

"Yes," Stokes said, "but that might be because George Busselton has spent more time with Stephen, and the other three all intimated that learning more about Stephen might yet win them over."

"True," Penelope conceded.

Barnaby rose and stretched. "Other than telling us that winning the support of Mrs. Busselton, Persimone, and Peregrine requires more than a winning smile and easy ways, I'm not sure the observation gets us much farther. It doesn't necessarily reflect in any substantial way on Stephen Meriwell."

Penelope sighed. "You are, sadly, correct." She smiled at Barnaby. "Now you're up, why not ring for a tea tray, and over tea and biscuits, we can review and decide what we need to ask Sophie Meriwell."

Peregrine returned to the drawing room to find that, while he'd been in the library, afternoon tea had been served.

He strolled into the room and made a beeline for where Lady Meriwell sat behind the trolley, dispensing cups of tea. To Peregrine's eyes, the old dear was holding up well; despite an aura of sorrow that draped about her like a shawl, she was determined to play her part as hostess in appropriate fashion. Peregrine could appreciate her devotion to society's conventions; such rules gave one something to hold on to in times of upheaval.

He smiled at her ladyship and accepted a cup and saucer from her.

"Have they finished with their questions for you?" she asked with a sad smile.

"Yes. I'm done." He glanced at the others gathered in several groups dotted about the room. "They didn't ask me to send in anyone else, so perhaps they, too, will be taking tea."

"I hope so." Her ladyship's blue eyes drifted to where Lord Iffey was speaking earnestly with Arthur and Peter. "I really don't know," her ladyship all but whispered, "what will come of this."

Peregrine didn't know how to reply to that, so he thanked her for his tea, picked up a bun off the plate beside the pot, and retreated to the side of the room.

After putting his back to the wall, he bit into the bun, finding it substantial and quite tasty. While he chewed, he surveyed the others in the room; no doubt the group included all the potential suspects. Along with the murderer.

Could he spot who that was?

The investigators might have declined his offer to join them, but that didn't mean he couldn't use his eyes and ears. Indeed, they'd encouraged him to do that, so what could he see?

His gaze returned to Arthur and Peter, currently standing in a tight knot to one side and discussing some subject with Lord Iffey. Judging by the glances they darted at Lady Meriwell and their serious expressions, the trio were evaluating the situation in a furtive manner they hoped would not be noticed by her ladyship.

Faint hope, that.

Regardless, Peregrine received the clear impression that both younger men were worried. What about was impossible to guess, but what did they have to fear, hmm?

Realistically, however, neither Arthur nor Peter struck Peregrine as having the stomach for murder, especially not the rather gruesome act of poisoning their uncle at his own dinner table. To Peregrine, that seemed a particularly dastardly act.

He shifted his attention to Lord Iffey. Given the man's solicitous behavior toward Lady Meriwell, it wasn't difficult to concoct a fantasy of Iffey carrying a torch for her ladyship for uncounted years.

Carrying a torch, yes. Fond and being close, yes. But to Peregrine's eyes, the elderly pair were the epitome of very old friends, deeply comfortable in each other's company. Even if their friendship had evolved into something deeper, could he imagine Iffey poisoning his old friend over the dinner table in order to claim that old friend's wife?

Peregrine considered the prospect. He knew such motives existed and that they could be extremely powerful, but he couldn't quite see why, if Iffey had been so murderously inclined, he would have waited so long and then acted now, when there was company at the Hall.

That made little sense, and Peregrine set Lord Iffey and her ladyship aside as unlikely suspects.

He shifted his gaze to those at the other end of the room. He skated over his parents, both of whom were doing their best to appear patient with the proceedings and altogether detached from them. In short, they were endeavoring to pretend that everything was more or less normal, which in situations like this was the way people like them behaved; it was, in effect, their way of supporting Lady Meriwell and Stephen by "doing the right thing."

Peregrine focused on his sister, who was standing and conversing in low tones with Stephen and Sophie.

Peregrine considered Sophie Meriwell to be a rather flaky sort, liable to act in some outrageous manner at any moment and for no apparent reason. From what little he'd seen of her, she appeared far too enamored of her own drama, a condition he read as her constantly wanting attention —constant attention—paid to her.

Nevertheless, at present, she seemed rather subdued, and from the way her gaze kept drifting to the door, she was concerned over what might walk through it...

Ah, right. Sophie hadn't been interviewed by the investigators yet.

Peregrine wondered if her being at the end of the list meant anything and decided he as yet knew too little of the investigators' ways to make anything of it.

Refocusing on the group including Sophie, he switched his attention to his sister and hid a smile behind his cup. To his educated eyes, Persimone was battling to rein in her curiosity and merely ask questions that were sufficiently innocuous to pass social muster.

Peregrine made a mental note to ask Persimone later what the investigators had asked her and tease out whether she'd learned or sensed anything he hadn't.

His mind drifted to the investigators. An odd and unexpected trio and definitely not what he had expected. That said, he'd got the definite impression that the three were accustomed to working together and had a very good grasp of what they were about. There'd been an almost seamless understanding of who would ask what, and they hadn't trod on each other's toes, not at any point.

All three were, Peregrine judged, highly intelligent, and while the inspector, Stokes, might be the legal anchor, Peregrine suspected that, in a situation such as this, the other two possessed certain society-based skills that Stokes could not possibly have. All in all, Peregrine could see that the trio made a formidable team.

He could certainly understand why Persimone was so intrigued, not to say fascinated and curious about them and how they operated.

He finished the bun and licked his fingers, then sipped the last of his tea. His gaze returned to Stephen and lingered. Peregrine could usually tell how he felt about a person, especially a gentleman, in short order, but he honestly could not make up his mind about Stephen Meriwell.

That, in itself, was strange. It was as if he couldn't quite get a handle on who Stephen Meriwell was.

Perhaps that was Peregrine's own lack of experience talking.

With an inward grunt, he acknowledged that was entirely possible.

But in terms of the investigation, Stephen seemed entirely calm, waiting and watching as all of them were and, in his case, showing no signs of perturbation or concern.

Stephen's self-assurance was easy to read, and within that, there was not a sliver of anything resembling guilt.

Accepting that, Peregrine swung his gaze back to where he'd started his survey of suspects—to the group including Arthur and Peter.

In terms of poisoning Lord Meriwell, they remained the standout candidates.

So, Peregrine asked himself, which one had found the gumption to actually do the deed?

∾

Sophie Meriwell sat in the chair before the desk in the library and stared at Penelope, Stokes, and Barnaby.

For this interview, Penelope sat in the center, in the admiral's chair, the better to be the principal questioner. Observing how Sophie was gripping the chair's arms with both hands, with her knees pressed together and her feet flat to the floor—as if she was poised to leap up and flee—Penelope considered their arrangement wise. She would need to keep Sophie's focus on her, to Sophie the least frightening person behind the desk.

Veronica had told them that Sophie was eighteen, and with her lustrous sable tresses, presently arranged in a fashionable and appealing style, her large brown eyes framed by lush lashes, and a fine-complexioned face of elfin cast, she would likely make her mark once she emerged into the ton.

To Penelope's mind, Sophie resembled a trapped butterfly, one newly hatched but, to this point, not allowed to fly free. The girl's fluttery, rather flighty movements and gestures added to the image. Her gray gown was à la mode, but youthful in style and, with its several ribbon-edged flounces, gave an impression that edged toward the frivolous.

One notable aspect of her appearance was the evidence of tears in her red-rimmed eyes; of all those they'd interviewed, other than her grandmother, she was the only one to bear physical signs of sorrow.

That, however, was to be expected; Sophie was undeniably young. From the tension that gripped her and the way she surreptitiously bit her lower lip, it was patently obvious that she was entirely unsure how she should behave. How she should react to the situation she found herself in. Confusion and uncertainty were readily discernible in her brown eyes.

Deeming it wise to reassure her, Penelope smiled understandingly. "We'd just like you to tell us what you remember of the evening in question, starting from the gathering in the drawing room." When Sophie didn't immediately respond, Penelope prompted, "Where was your grandfather when you entered the room. Was he already there?"

Sophie nodded. "Yes. I was the last down. Grandpapa was speaking with the Busseltons." She frowned and went on, "He seemed angry about something, but trying to hide it given we had guests."

"Do you have any idea what he was angry about?" Penelope asked.

Sophie shook her head. "He wasn't often angry—not like that, or at least not to that extent—and I was mystified as to what had caused it. He wasn't angry earlier in the day."

Penelope nodded and took Sophie through the movement of the company into the dining room. Her account was reasonably fulsome and matched the previous reports.

"Once your grandfather came in and sat at the head of the table, it seems he glared down the table, apparently toward you."

"Yes!" Sophie grew animated and sat straighter in the chair. "He did! It was quite distressing."

Penelope blinked, then asked, "Do you have any idea why he might have been glaring your way?"

"No!" Sophie all but wailed. "That was what made it so distressing!" She met Penelope's gaze directly. "He usually only glares like that at Arthur or Peter, and I was racking my brain as to why he could possibly be glaring at me in that way. He never normally did."

The genuineness of her confusion and puzzlement was written on her face.

Gently, Penelope suggested, "Might your grandfather's attitude have something to do with the argument between you about you going to London for the Season? We understand you and he disagreed strongly over that."

"Indeed, we did!" Sophie flared up like tinder to which a spark had been applied. Her features firmed into stubborn lines, her chin hardening with determination. "Can you imagine?" She appealed to Penelope. "He refused—categorically refused!—to allow me to go up for the Season this year. I'm already eighteen! Other girls make their come-outs when they're younger, but I agreed to wait until I was eighteen, and then he refused!"

Penelope shut her lips, not wanting to interrupt the pending tirade; tirades could be revealing.

Sophie duly rolled on, "I argued and argued, but he wouldn't be moved!" She fell silent, her expression close to a scowl as she dwelled on her grandsire's iniquities, then confusion once more overtook her features, and frowning in puzzlement, she looked at Penelope. "But surely, if that was the cause, then it should have been me glaring at him—not him glaring at me."

Penelope stared at Sophie's lost-and-confused expression and wondered why they hadn't realized that themselves. Holding Sophie's puzzled gaze, Penelope inclined her head. "You're correct. It can't have been that subject that your grandfather was reacting to."

"Well, then." Sophie continued to frown as she pondered the point. "As I said, Grandpapa only glares at Arthur and Peter like that—in that particular way—but they were on the other side of the table. It was me and Stephen on our side, and I can't imagine why he was glaring at me. I hadn't done anything…" She broke off, then in a choked voice rushed on, "And then he picked up his glass and drank, and… oh!"

Her hands flew to her face.

"Just so." Ruthlessly, Penelope cut off any impending hysterics. "Now, after your grandfather collapsed." She continued in a firm, clear voice, leading Sophie through the subsequent actions.

Forced to follow and respond to Penelope's simple questions, Sophie calmed.

When Penelope asked what Sophie had done after the company had returned to the drawing room, Sophie replied, "We all sat around for several minutes, no one knowing what else to do, then Peter said he was going to go and check to see if there was any news. He left, but didn't come back. I think he probably went for a drink. I kept thinking of Grandpapa—the look on his face as he choked—he was looking toward me, as you know, and it was simply dreadful, and I started to feel ill, so I excused myself and said I'd go up to my room, and I left. I knew by then that any news wouldn't be good—that Grandpapa was dead—and I was trying hard not to think about any of it. It was all too…well, *overwhelming*."

"Did you go straight to your room?" Stokes dared to ask.

Sophie glanced at him and nodded. "Yes. And I rang for Sally as soon as I got there. She came up straightaway and helped me undress and get into bed."

"You didn't see anyone else on the stairs or in the corridors?" Stokes asked.

Sophie shook her head. "No one. I think the others must still have been in Grandpapa's room."

Stokes nodded in acceptance and continued to keep his gaze on his notebook.

Barnaby caught Sophie's gaze and smiled gently, encouragingly. "Was there anything you noticed about anyone else that evening—family, staff, or guests—that seemed odd or strange to you?"

Her brow furrowed in thought, but after several moments, she shook her head. "No. Truth to tell, I can't remember much about what other people did. It was so deeply shocking that I wasn't really thinking about anything but Grandpapa dying." With that, her attitude—her posture in the chair, her spine, her shoulders, her entire being—seemed to wilt into despondency. "I really don't know what will happen now that Grandpapa is gone. I won't even be able to have a proper Season next year, because I'll still be in half mourning."

Penelope shared a brief glance with Barnaby, then she looked at Sophie and blandly said, "Thank you, Miss Meriwell. I believe that will be all. You're free to go."

Barnaby rose and walked around the desk.

After a brief frown at Penelope's crisp dismissal and her lack of appreciation for the invitation to further dramatize Sophie's future, Sophie decided it was better to leave. She rose and allowed Barnaby to usher her to the door.

After he closed the door and turned back to the room, Penelope blew out a breath. "That," she declared, "was a close call. Any encouragement, and we would have had a full-blown display of her histrionic abilities."

Barnaby smiled at his wife. "You handled her quite well, I thought."

"Rather you than me." Stokes dropped his notebook on the desk. "So who do we speak with next?"

They decided to speak with David and Veronica about how the poison got into the wine glass.

As the pair settled in the chairs before the desk, Stokes explained, "We thought that before we speak with the staff, we should ask if you have any ideas about how, exactly, the poison might have been put into the glass so we can adjust our questions accordingly."

Jensen had followed the pair in, carrying a fresh teapot and a plate of buns.

As the butler straightened from arranging the tray on the desk, Penelope said, "Jensen, I know time is getting on and soon the staff will need to prepare for dinner, and we're sorry to have to interrupt, but some questions need to be asked today and not later."

"We, the staff, quite understand, ma'am." Jensen met her gaze. "His lordship was a good master, always fair and generally even-tempered, and there's not one member of the staff who are happy that his time as master of Meriwell Hall was cut short in such a way. You will find all of us eager to assist in bringing his murderer to justice."

Penelope inclined her head. "We will call you as soon as we're ready."

Jensen bowed and withdrew, leaving Penelope filling and refilling cups while Barnaby passed around the buns.

Once everyone was supplied, Stokes sat back and looked at David. "Give us your thoughts on how the poison could have been placed in that wine glass."

David glanced at Veronica. "While you've been busy with your interviews, we've been investigating just that, and to begin with, it now seems certain that the poison was only in Lord Meriwell's glass."

"The other glasses were clean?" Penelope asked.

David nodded. "In order to cause such a rapid reaction in the victim, the poison had to have been in concentrated form, and so only a few drops would have been needed in the glass, and concentrated prussic acid is colorless."

Stokes nodded. "A few drops, and no one would notice."

"Exactly." Veronica lowered her teacup. "Jensen is quite meticulous, and if there'd been any liquid visible in the bottom of the glass, he would not have poured the wine."

"But a few drops in a crystal goblet wouldn't have been detectable," Barnaby said.

"That," David said, "is why we believe it must have been done that way—just a few drops of concentrated liquid dripped into the glass as the murderer passed by."

"Also, and you should check this with the staff," Veronica said, "it seems likely the poison could not have been placed in the glass ahead of the company entering the dining room. Usually, the glasses are set out by the footmen only minutes before Jensen leaves to summon the company, and the footmen generally remain in the dining room during the intervening minutes."

"And all our suspects were in the drawing room anyway," Stokes pointed out.

"Indeed," David nodded. "So the upshot is that we believe the poison was dripped into the glass—it would have taken less than a second, literally—by one of the company as they milled around the table prior to taking their seats."

"And by all accounts, mill they did." Penelope grimaced. "Given the room's dimensions, where they each sat, and the order they came into the dining room, they would have had to jostle past each other in order to get to their seats."

Barnaby arched his brows. "So essentially, we have murder by sleight of hand. The murderer knew enough to take the risk—"

"Not," Penelope interjected, "that it was that much of a risk given people would have been talking and therefore looking at each other's faces and others would have been pointing across the table at chairs—arms would have been extended over the table at various moments, all apparently innocently."

"Indeed." Barnaby inclined his head. "But my point was that our murderer knew—could guess and expect—that to be the case."

"Ah." Penelope adjusted her glasses. "You mean he was a local as it were."

Stokes humphed. "On the basis of our theory of how the poison got into the glass, we can cross George Busselton off the suspect list, but no one else."

"However," Barnaby said, "it's difficult to see how the other three Busseltons would have known about the cramped conditions of the Meriwell Hall dining room."

"It's also hard—or at least more convoluted—to devise a motive for Mrs. Busselton, Persimone, or Peregrine," Penelope added.

"Agreed." Stokes set down his empty cup and saucer and looked at Penelope and Barnaby. "Let's see if the staff can add any more details to our picture of how Lord Meriwell was poisoned."

CHAPTER 6

*T*he clock on the library mantelpiece had just finished chiming for five o'clock when Jensen responded to their summons.

David and Veronica had left to check on their patients, so once again, it was Barnaby, Penelope, and Stokes seated behind the desk when Jensen came to stand before it.

Barnaby didn't bother inviting the butler to sit. That would have only made Jensen uncomfortable. More uncomfortable.

Stokes said, "We'll keep this as brief as we can. How long before the guests entered the dining room was his lordship's wine glass placed on the table?"

Immediately, Jensen replied, "The wine glasses are the last items to be set out. Thomas fetched them from the sideboard and wiped each out with a linen cloth before setting them in place. I was watching and waiting until he set down the last glass, which was her ladyship's. I take that moment as my cue to go and inform the company that dinner is ready to be served."

Barnaby nodded. "Between you leaving for the drawing room and returning, was the dining room left unattended, even for just a moment?"

"No, sir," Jensen replied. "Jeremy had left to fetch the soup tureen, but Thomas remained. When I returned, he was waiting as usual at the far end of the room to assist with her ladyship's chair."

Penelope leaned forward. "You reentered the dining room ahead of...I believe it was her ladyship, Lord Iffey, and Mrs. Busselton."

"Indeed, ma'am. That's correct." Jensen paused a second, then added, "Her ladyship and Lord Iffey are generally the first in, as they have to go all the way down to the other end of the table. It's more difficult if they come in later and have to get past the other diners."

Stokes glanced up from his notebook. "What were you and the footmen doing during the time the guests were filing in and finding their seats?"

Jensen faintly grimaced. "With the space so tight, what with those four big sideboards, we've learned to stand back, more or less with our backs to the walls, to allow the diners to find their places. There were place cards put out."

"Where was the decanter of wine?" Barnaby asked.

"On the sideboard closest to me," Jensen replied. "It was stoppered at that point. I'd decanted it downstairs, in my pantry, and left it to air there, and I brought it up while Thomas and Jeremy were setting out the plates."

"When did you pick up the decanter and unstopper it?" Stokes asked.

"Jeremy came in with the soup tureen immediately behind his lordship and set it on the sideboard near the decanter. As usual, I waited until everyone sat before pouring the wine. Lord Meriwell was the last to take his place. He waited until Mr. Busselton sat"—Jensen paled a touch—"and as his lordship took his seat, I picked up the decanter and poured the wine into his glass."

Penelope quickly asked, "Was it normal for his lordship to immediately take a mouthful of wine, before you'd even filled another glass?"

Jensen blinked, then frowned. "No, ma'am. Now you mention it, I can't recall him ever doing so before. He was normally the most attentive and correct host."

Somewhat carefully, Stokes asked, "Why do you think he did so on this occasion?"

Jensen immediately pokered up. "I'm sure I can't say..." His voice trailed away, then he sighed, and his shoulders slumped. "As the master is dead, then...I believe he was furiously angry and trying to...well, almost drown his ire enough to get through dinner."

Penelope said, "We've heard from several people that his lordship was glaring down the table as he picked up his glass and swallowed."

Jensen nodded. "He was glaring in Miss Sophie's direction. Whether he was actually glaring at her, I couldn't say."

Barnaby said, "We've been trying to build a picture of what exactly happened in the last instants of Lord Meriwell's life. We've heard that once he'd swallowed the wine, the poison acted almost immediately, yet he tried to lift his left hand and point. Do you know at whom?"

Jensen grimaced and shook his head. "It was his left hand—the right was gripping the stem of the wine glass—and he seemed to be trying to point in the same direction in which he'd been glaring. But the poison overcame him before he could actually point at anyone, and his hand fell back to the tablecloth."

Stokes nodded. "Tell us about what happened immediately after his lordship collapsed."

Jensen looked over their heads, and his gaze grew distant. "At first, there was a stunned silence—you could have heard a pin drop—then Miss Sophie screamed, and several people stood up. It was obvious from the first that his lordship's condition was serious, and I sent Thomas running for Nurse Haskell. By then, Mr. Arthur and Mr. Peter had rushed to help his lordship. Mr. Peter reached him first, but Mr. Arthur pushed Mr. Peter aside and bent over his lordship, and Mr. Stephen came up on his lordship's other side."

Jensen paused to wet his lips, then continued, "Mr. Busselton had frozen—it was obvious he didn't know what to do for the best and was uncomfortable interfering. He sat back while the three nephews gathered around his lordship, trying to help him. No one really knew what was happening. Then Mr. Arthur, I think, suggested they take his lordship upstairs. Mr. Stephen agreed, and between them, they managed to lift his lordship up and turn toward the door.

"Nurse Haskell had arrived by then, but the nephews insisted they should first get his lordship upstairs and she could examine him there. I assisted, as did Jeremy. His lordship was quite a heavy weight to get up the stairs and to his room. Oh, and Gorton—his lordship's valet—was there, too. I think he arrived with Miss Haskell. She followed on our heels to his lordship's room."

Jensen paused, then added, "As we quit the dining room, Mr. Stephen told Mr. Peter to take the rest of the company to the drawing room, which I understand Mr. Peter did. I sent Thomas to assist."

Stokes took Jensen through the subsequent happenings. The butler's account matched Veronica's in every detail, all the way to when Jensen and Veronica returned downstairs in search of the wine glass, only to discover it had vanished.

"And you've been searching for it?" Stokes asked.

"Indeed, sir." Jensen looked troubled. "We've been quite thorough, but we've found no trace of it."

Barnaby clarified, "Only his lordship's glass went missing?"

"Yes, sir. All the other glasses, the cutlery and crockery—everything else that had been on the table—was still there, in its proper place. Only his lordship's glass had…vanished."

"When you returned to the dining room, did you see any of the family or guests in the corridors or on the stairs?" Penelope asked.

"No, ma'am." Jensen paused, then added, "I was later told that there were two glasses used in the library that evening. For brandy. I suspect one was used by Mr. Arthur and the other by Mr. Peter, although none of the staff saw either gentleman during that time."

"After you and Miss Haskell left the dining room, she was summoned upstairs to attend to Miss Sophie." When Jensen nodded, Penelope asked, "Where did you go?"

"Back to his lordship's room to warn Gorton and Jeremy that it would be better to keep our thoughts on his lordship's murder to ourselves until Dr. Sanderson could confirm our belief. After that, I went down to the drawing room, ma'am."

Barnaby inquired, "Who was there at that point?"

Jensen paused to consult his memory, then stated, "Lady Meriwell and Lord Iffey. Mr. Stephen and Mr. Arthur, and the Busseltons, all four of them."

Stokes looked at Barnaby and Penelope and arched his brows. Both shook their heads, and Stokes looked at Jensen and smiled kindly. "Thank you. You've been very clear."

"We appreciate that," Penelope said. "We understand this could not have been easy for you, watching your master die as he did."

"No, indeed, ma'am." Jensen offered them a bow. "I take it you would like to speak with the rest of the staff?"

Stokes glanced at Penelope. "Just the footmen—Thomas and Jeremy —to start with, I think."

"I'll send them in straightaway."

～

Jensen was as good as his word, and within minutes, the two footmen had presented themselves in the library.

Understandably, the pair were nervous, but between them, Barnaby and Penelope managed to lead them through the critical events, and they soon lost their hesitation and answered quickly and clearly, ultimately confirming all that Jensen had said.

After assisting Peter Meriwell to steer the remaining company to the drawing room, once dismissed, Thomas had retreated to the servants' hall to await further orders.

Jeremy, meanwhile, had remained with his lordship's body in his bedchamber. "Until Nurse Haskell looked in after seeing to Miss Sophie. She said we had to move the body to the laundry room in the basement, and Gorton sent me to get the stretcher for his lordship. I had to wake the gardeners to get it, so it was an hour or so before I got back, and by then, Gorton had the body ready, and Thomas, Jensen, and I helped him carry the stretcher down to the basement."

"Thank you," Stokes said. "That fills in several holes."

"One last question," Barnaby said. "Did either of you, at any time in the evening after his lordship's death, see any member of the family in the corridors or on the stairs?"

Both footmen shook their heads.

"Right, then." Penelope smiled on them both. "You may go, but if you would, please send Gorton in."

"Yes, ma'am," the pair chorused and left with alacrity.

Gorton arrived with commendable promptness. When Barnaby invited him to take the chair before the desk, he sat on the edge of the seat, his back ramrod straight, his hands on his knees as he looked at them expectantly.

He was relatively short and somewhat burly, yet his hands were small, the fingers neat. His pate was balding but partially concealed by well-combed brown hair, and his face was the sort usually described as comfortable, with uninspiring features that nevertheless appeared kindly.

At the moment, his expression radiated quiet sorrow lightened by expectation, possibly by the hope of helping to gain vengeance for his late master.

Stokes commenced by taking the valet through the events from the time he followed Veronica into the dining room to the moment when, with his lordship's body conveyed to the laundry, Gorton had closed the door on Lord Meriwell's earthly remains.

Gorton concluded, "I went up to my quarters in the attic after that, with the others—Thomas, Jeremy, and Jensen. We were all somewhat low and went straight to our rooms."

Penelope was frowning. "If you would, Gorton, think back to the moment when you first reached his lordship in the dining room. Can you say if, in your opinion, his lordship was still breathing?"

Gorton thought, then drew breath and admitted, "I don't think he was, ma'am. Looking back, I believe he was already dead by the time I reached him."

"I'm merely curious," Stokes said, "but what was the reason given for removing his lordship's body to his bedroom?"

Gorton's eyes widened. "I don't think anyone made the argument, Inspector. Someone, I think it was Mr. Arthur, suggested we should move his lordship to his bed, and everyone agreed, and we did. It seemed... well, more appropriate—more respectable—for him to be lying in his bed, dead or not."

Stokes nodded, as did Barnaby and Penelope.

"Now," Stokes went on, "several people have mentioned noticing that his lordship was angry from the moment he walked into the drawing room. Angry, but trying to hide it. You were with his lordship immediately prior to him coming downstairs. Did he seem particularly angry while he was dressing?"

Gorton nodded readily. "He was all but fuming, truth be told. But the anger didn't start until after the man who came to see him left."

Stokes stilled, as did Barnaby and Penelope, their gazes fixed on the valet. "The man who came to see him," Stokes parroted. "What man is that?"

"Earlier in the afternoon, about three o'clock, before the nephews and the Busseltons arrived at closer to five, a man called to see his lordship. I only glimpsed him in the corridor while Jensen was escorting him here, to the library." Gorton paused. "I wouldn't say the man was a gentleman but perhaps a businessman."

"And his lordship received this man." Stokes was scribbling in his notebook. "How long was their meeting?"

"About an hour, I would say. I don't know any more than that, but Jensen might."

Stokes nodded. "We'll definitely be asking Jensen later."

"Was Lord Meriwell angry before this visit?" Barnaby asked.

"No, sir. Not that I noticed." Gorton plainly thought back, then affirmed, "I spoke with him after lunch, and he was his usual genial self."

"What you're saying," Penelope summarized, "is that his lordship's anger was triggered by this man's visit—possibly by something the man told him."

Gorton lightly shrugged. "That's how it seemed. Before the meeting, he was relaxed, and after it, he was, at first, frowning, as if he was very unhappy—unsettled and disturbed. Then, as I dressed him for dinner, he got angrier and angrier. Not at me but over whatever it was that was bothering him. I could feel it. By the time he left his room to go downstairs, he was palpably furious, but over what, I have no idea."

Barnaby caught Gorton's eye. "Had you ever seen his lordship angry like that before?"

Gorton thought, then looked down and, in an almost puzzled tone, replied, "Not quite that way. Normally, I would have assumed he was irritated by Mr. Arthur or Mr. Peter—at their latest importunities. They are the two who most often put his lordship into a temper. But this time seemed...worse. More intense." Gorton raised his gaze to Barnaby's face. "In all honesty, I had never seen him in quite that sort of mood—so gripped by ferocious anger— before."

Both Stokes and Barnaby cast around, but there seemed nothing else Gorton could tell them, and they dismissed him with genuine thanks.

When the door closed behind him, Penelope let out a long breath. "At last, we have a real clue to follow."

They immediately recalled Jensen, but while the butler confirmed the unknown man's hour-long meeting with Lord Meriwell, he had little to offer by way of the man's identity or purpose.

"He was an entirely unremarkable man." Jensen frowned in concentration. "I would agree with Gorton's assessment that he wasn't a gentleman, but he was neatly dressed in good-quality clothes, and his manners were assured." Jensen looked at Stokes and Barnaby. "I would swear he was a man accustomed to dealing with those of higher standing. I did find it odd that he didn't give his name. He merely said that his lordship was expecting him, and as Lord Meriwell had warned me that he was expecting a man to call and I should bring him directly to the library, I did so. From what I glimpsed of his lordship greeting the fellow, he was, indeed, the man his lordship had been expecting."

Barnaby, Stokes, and Penelope frowned, puzzlement mixed with frustration.

After a moment, Barnaby looked at Jensen. "How did the man arrive? Horse? Carriage?"

Jensen looked relieved to be able to offer some actual information. "He drove up in a gig. A decent-enough carriage with a nice-looking bay. Not, I would venture, an equipage hired from hereabouts."

Increasingly frustrated, Penelope surveyed the desk and its many drawers. "Did Lord Meriwell keep a diary?"

"Not that I was ever aware of, ma'am. Her ladyship might know, but…" Jensen grimaced faintly. "Truly, I don't believe he did. His lordship was not one for writing things down."

Penelope sighed. Feelingly.

Stokes studied Jensen. "I don't suppose you had any indication of the tone of the meeting? No raised voices, for instance?"

When Jensen shook his head, Barnaby asked, "How did his lordship and the man interact when you came to see the man out?"

Jensen paused to think, then offered, "His lordship shook the man's hand. I would say that, toward the man, he was cordial and…grateful. But his lordship seemed unhappy and more tense than previously, presumably over what the man had told him." Frowning, Jensen paused, then added, "From all I saw, I took it that the man had reported something to the master, something that caused him serious concern."

Barnaby nodded.

Stokes glanced at Penelope, then thanked Jensen, adding, "We'll come down to the servants' hall in a moment. I don't expect we'll keep the staff for long."

"Very good, Inspector." Jensen bowed and took himself off.

The instant the door shut behind him, Penelope humphed. "This case gets stranger and stranger. Who was this mystery man with the upsetting news?" She eyed the desk severely. "While I'm reluctant to search his lordship's correspondence without knowing the man's name and therefore what we're searching for, if we don't get some clue as to what the man reported, which was presumably what sparked his lordship's temper, and some indication as to which of his family his ire was directed, I fear we'll have to do just that."

"Possibly," Stokes allowed. "But if his lordship was disinclined to write things down, searching his papers might not get us far."

"Indeed," Barnaby said. "But before we ponder that, we need to release the staff. They'll be waiting on us, and they do still have a dinner to serve." Barnaby uncrossed his long legs and rose. "Let's go and—faint hope—see if the staff can shed any light on our accumulating mysteries."

~

Sadly, as Barnaby had foreshadowed, the assembled staff could add nothing to the picture of events they'd already assembled.

Penelope thought to clarify, "The nephews don't bring staff with them —any gentleman's gentlemen or grooms?"

"No, ma'am," the housekeeper, Mrs. Hutchinson, said. "They use us."

Gorton added, "My understanding is that none of the three are sufficiently flush to have staff of the level to be brought into this household."

"So the footmen unpack their bags?" Penelope asked, but all the staff shook their heads.

Jensen explained, "The nephews have been visiting here since they were in short coats, and from the time each went to school, they've had a permanent room in the house. All three leave clothes and accoutrements here, so when they visit, they rarely bring much luggage. Just an overnight case at most."

"I see." Penelope glanced at the housekeeper and maids. "And the Busseltons?"

Mrs. Hutchinson replied, "They didn't bring any staff, either." She nodded at Gorton. "Gorton was deputed to assist Mr. Busselton."

Gorton nodded. "I offered my services, but other than pressing his shirt for the evening, he did not require my assistance."

Mrs. Hutchinson went on, "Pinchwell, her ladyship's dresser"—she waved at a tall, somewhat severe-looking gray-haired female—"and Sally, who tends Miss Sophie"—another wave indicated a cheery, younger maid with apple cheeks and blond hair—"assisted the Busselton ladies as well as their mistresses."

Penelope stifled a sigh. "I don't suppose anyone noticed anything odd —any unusual vials or bottles?"

The staff glanced at each other, but all shook their heads.

Faintly grimacing, Penelope looked at Stokes. She was out of questions.

Stokes duly thanked the staff. "And now, we'll get out of your way and let you get on with your duties."

That announcement was greeted with relief, and Penelope led the way up the stairs as the staff dispersed.

Barnaby, with Stokes beside him, followed at Penelope's heels as she led them back to the front hall.

They'd just emerged through the swinging baize-covered door at the rear of the hall when the front doorbell pealed.

All three of them halted, doubtless struck by the same thought.

Penelope looked down the hall toward the front door. As Jensen arrived and went past them to open it, she murmured, "It's nearly six o'clock. A curious time to call at any house."

As curious as Penelope regarding the caller, Barnaby waited with her and Stokes as Jensen swung open the door.

On taking in the personage waiting on the porch, Jensen exclaimed, "Mr. Wishpole, sir!" Surprise mixed with confusion in the butler's tone.

The man on the porch was garbed in a conservative suit in the dull black favored by those in the legal profession. He was at least sixty years old, with white, tufted hair and a face whose wrinkles bore testimony to his age. His broad brow, piercing gaze, and prominent nose gave him the appearance of a raptor, but he nodded amiably at Jensen and said, "Good evening, Jensen. I had hoped to be here earlier, but his lordship's summons rather took me by surprise, and there were matters I had to deal with before leaving chambers."

Jensen stuttered, "I didn't know…" Then he hauled in a breath, drew himself up, and bowed. "Do come in, sir."

The older man—Wishpole—obliged, and Jensen hurried to shut the door.

Even as Wishpole noticed the investigators, Jensen whirled and spoke to Barnaby, Penelope, and Stokes. "This is Lord Meriwell's solicitor, Mr. Wishpole of Lincoln's Inn."

Wishpole's sharp gray gaze had already fixed on them. Smoothly, he said, "Indeed, I have that honor. But I fear you have the advantage of me."

Before Jensen could fling himself into introductions, Barnaby went forward and offered his hand. "Barnaby Adair, sir." As Wishpole gripped his hand, Barnaby waved at Penelope. "And this is my wife."

Penelope came up beside Barnaby and returned Wishpole's greeting —a half bow and a murmured "A pleasure, ma'am"—with a polite if curious nod.

"And this"—Barnaby gestured at Stokes, who had followed at Penelope's heels—"is Inspector Stokes of Scotland Yard."

Wishpole's eyes widened even as he reached to shake the hand Stokes held out. "Bless me! What's this about?"

Stokes released Wishpole's hand. "I regret to inform you, sir, but your client, Lord Meriwell, is dead."

"Dead?" There was no doubting Wishpole's shock.

"Specifically," Stokes went on, "he was poisoned at his dining table yesterday evening."

Wishpole's bushy white eyebrows had climbed to his hairline. "Good Lord! But—"

Wishpole cut himself off, and his expression grew seriously perturbed.

Barnaby glanced at Penelope, then ventured, "Perhaps we might repair to the library, sir, and you can tell us what brings you here."

Wishpole came out of his sudden reverie to blink at Barnaby and Penelope. "My apologies, sir, but what connection do you have to this matter?"

"Mr. and Mrs. Adair are acting as official consultants to the Metropolitan Police," Stokes explained. "At the commissioners' behest."

"Ah." Wishpole's expression lit with understanding. "I have heard of your previous endeavors, I believe. With that case at Mandeville Hall?"

Penelope smiled. "Indeed. And several cases before that. But we are truly agog to learn what brought you to Meriwell Hall so opportunely, sir."

Wishpole's expression grew bleak, and he nodded. "And I fear I need to tell you forthwith." He glanced at Barnaby. "The library, I believe you said?"

After Wishpole confirmed to Jensen that he would be staying at least overnight—and possibly for longer—and Barnaby assured the butler that they needed nothing more from him at that moment, the four made their way to the library.

While Penelope settled Wishpole in one of the armchairs before the fireplace, Barnaby and Stokes fetched drinks from the tantalus.

Stokes handed Wishpole a healthy dose of brandy, then took the chair beside the solicitor, leaving Barnaby the chair opposite, beside the one Penelope had claimed. Barnaby handed her a small tot of brandy and sat.

Wishpole took a long sip of the fiery spirit, then cleared his throat. "Dear me. I must admit this is a shock." He raised his gaze and regarded the three of them with a shrewd eye. "But as to what brought me here, while I would not, normally, break the confidence of a client without their permission, in this instance, I feel you should be made aware that his lordship sent a message to my chambers yesterday. It arrived late in the afternoon, just before we closed. His lordship wrote that he wished to make a significant alteration to his will. He didn't include any further details and asked that I bring the current will and all else necessary here, as soon as possible, to legally make the change."

Stokes had extracted his notebook and was writing. "The message—who delivered it?" He glanced at Wishpole. "The household wasn't aware that his lordship had sent any communication."

Wishpole nodded. "It wasn't brought by one of his lordship's servants or agents but was delivered by a street lad. You know the sort, the young lads always ready to run a message for a few pennies."

"You didn't question the lad?" Stokes asked.

Wishpole replied, "It was my clerk who accepted the note, and he had no reason to. But in his lordship's message, which, I might add, was obviously written in haste, he mentioned that he was arranging delivery through the good offices of an acquaintance."

Leaning back in the chair, Barnaby steepled his fingers. "Did his lordship give you any idea of who that acquaintance was?"

Wishpole shook his head. "I have no idea, but plainly, his lordship was correct in thinking that speed was of the essence in this matter of changing his will." Wishpole's expression turned grave. "It seems that whoever would have been affected by the change his lordship intended to make must have learned of his lordship's intention and taken steps to ensure he didn't have the opportunity to effect the change."

Stokes nodded. "The timing is hard to discount."

Penelope asked, "Did his lordship give you any indication of what type of change he intended to make?"

Wishpole shook his head. "He wrote only that he wished to make 'a significant alteration,' which, given the nature of his will, I presumed meant a change to the bequests. Beyond that, I know nothing more."

Barnaby shared a grimace with Stokes. Once again, they appeared to be stymied.

Penelope ventured, "I take it you have his lordship's current—and therefore extant—will with you."

Wishpole regarded her warily. "I do."

Penelope smiled understandingly and asked, "Given the extraordinary circumstances, can you outline for us, in general terms, the major provisions as they currently stand?"

Barnaby hid an appreciative smile. His clever wife had phrased her request in such a way that Wishpole might see his way to oblige.

The solicitor frowned and clearly inwardly debated the request, then slowly, he nodded. "In the circumstances, I feel certain his lordship would wish me to share the general outline with you. So. Firstly, Clementina, his wife, retains the use of the house and grounds and the income of the associated unentailed estate for her lifetime. As for ownership of the unentailed estate, Miss Sophie Meriwell is the principal beneficiary. Ultimately, she will inherit all that is not entailed, except for the following specific bequests to his lordship's nephews, the sons of his late brother, Claude. Those bequests are, to Stephen Meriwell, a certain sum of money, to Arthur Meriwell, the ownership of a specific horse from his lordship's stable, and to Peter Meriwell, a sum of money specifically intended to settle his debts. As to the title and the entailed estate, they will, of course, go to his lordship's senior surviving male heir."

Wishpole looked at Penelope, then at Barnaby and Stokes. "That's more or less the sum of it. It's a fairly standard will for these times."

Barnaby nodded. Distantly, from deeper in the house, the sounds of activity reached them.

Penelope glanced at the clock on the mantelpiece. "Time is getting on, I fear."

"Thank you for your information, Mr. Wishpole." Stokes rose and nodded to the older man. "You've given us a great deal to think about. We may need to speak with you again."

Wishpole inclined his head. "Of course."

Barnaby, too, got to his feet. "Should you need us, we're staying at the Angel Inn, which is only a few minutes away."

"That's good to know." Wishpole pushed out of the chair as Penelope rose. "I imagine I'll remain here for at least several days. Quite aside from having a very real interest in how the investigation progresses, I should be here to support her ladyship and Miss Sophie as needed." His expression clouded, and he added, "I know that's what Angus—Lord Meriwell—would have wanted me to do. He was a valued client and a good man. He might have been elderly, but he didn't deserve to have his last years taken from him."

"Indeed." Penelope inclined her head to Wishpole. "We'll leave you to get settled. No doubt we'll meet tomorrow."

With that, Barnaby, Penelope, and Stokes left the room and made for the side door and the Angel Inn.

CHAPTER 7

*H*alfway along the corridor to the side door, Penelope slowed. "We've learned all sorts of bits and pieces. Now, we need to juggle them into a coherent picture." She halted and looked at Barnaby and Stokes. "Might I suggest we invite David and Veronica to join us over dinner? Both will have insights into Meriwell family members that could shed light on what happened."

Barnaby nodded. "Specifically, illuminating who poisoned his lordship."

"Wait here." Stokes turned back. "I'll fetch them."

He reappeared minutes later with a curious David and Veronica, both shrugging into their coats, in tow.

"We need your specialized knowledge," Penelope informed them as she linked her arm with Veronica's and turned to continue to the door.

"In more ways than one," Barnaby added as the three men set out in the ladies' wake.

They walked out of the door, onto the terrace, and started around the house.

"It might be best," Stokes said, "to leave all discussion until after dinner." He glanced at Barnaby. "I don't know about you, but my head's spinning with so many disjointed facts."

"A short mental break will do us all good," Penelope declared and strolled on into the wood, following the path to the Angel Inn.

It had been a gentle May day, with sunshine and light clouds scudding across a pale-blue sky, and the evening looked set to remain pleasant, with nothing more than an errant breeze cooling the shadows beneath the trees.

The walk to the inn was uneventful. Penelope led the way inside and waved at their host, at her station behind the counter in the main bar, then she steered Veronica in the opposite direction, to the private parlor they'd commandeered.

The men followed, and the attentive innkeeper appeared on their heels. She took their orders and, after promising to have everything delivered promptly, retreated.

Penelope and Veronica sat at the table and waited while Barnaby, Stokes, and David drew up extra chairs. The men had only just settled when the door opened, and the innkeeper and two maids ferried in dishes, plates, cutlery, napkins, glasses, and mugs.

In short order, their meal was laid before them, and they gladly addressed themselves to the fare.

While she ate, Penelope mulled over all they'd learned since they'd arrived at Meriwell Hall and was sure Barnaby and Stokes were doing the same. David and Veronica were content to allow them time to cogitate, but once the dishes were emptied and the plates had been cleared and slices of fresh apple pie and a jug of cream were placed before them, along with a bottle of good brandy and—at Penelope's insistence—five glasses, and the servers withdrew, she reached for the brandy bottle, pulled out the stopper, and poured herself a small amount, then did the same with another glass and pushed it toward Veronica. "Trust me, it will help."

With that, Penelope handed the bottle to Barnaby, picked up her glass, and took an appreciative sip.

The warming burn of the liquid as it slid down her throat helped her focus on the investigation. "I can barely believe that we arrived at Meriwell Hall only"—she consulted the clock above the fireplace—"less than eight hours ago."

Cradling a glass of amber liquid in his hands, Stokes nodded. "And from the moment we stepped through the front door, we've been learning facts, bits and pieces, here and there, at a rapid rate. But how many are relevant and—or even whether—they fit together is not at all clear."

Barnaby sipped, then lowered his glass. "That's the challenge before us now—to make sense of things and discover what else we need to learn."

"So where do we start?" Stokes asked.

After a moment of silence, Penelope suggested, "Let's begin by assembling a timeline of Lord Meriwell's movements on the day he died, then, working from that, create a list of potential suspects—those who could have done the deed."

"And who had cause to do the deed," Barnaby added. "Motive and opportunity, and let's start with his lordship's meeting with our unknown man."

David blinked. "Unknown man?"

Veronica, too, looked surprised. She glanced at David. "We haven't heard anything about any meeting."

"Likely it wasn't known to anyone other than Jensen and Gorton. And his lordship, of course." Penelope outlined what they'd learned of the unidentified stranger and how, after having Wishpole turn up at the door, they'd learned that he'd been summoned by his lordship via the unknown man.

"Would that we could identify the man," Stokes said, "but as of yet, we have no notion of his identity."

"It seems odd to have his lordship's solicitor turn up at this point," David said. "Did he say why?"

"Indeed." Barnaby outlined what Wishpole had told them of his lordship's intentions.

Veronica's eyes had widened. "But surely that gives someone—one of the family—a very good reason to murder his lordship. It can't be a coincidence that Lord Meriwell decides to change his will, and within hours, he dies of poison."

"Not only that," Penelope darkly said, "but that might also explain why now." She met Barnaby's eyes. "I've been puzzling about why the murderer turned up with poison, all ready to do the deed. Perhaps he or she suspected his lordship was about to learn whatever secret the unknown man delivered, and so our murderer came prepared, then realized that, indeed, his lordship knew—his lordship's seething anger would have given that away—and so the murderer acted, then and there."

Slowly, Barnaby nodded. "The murderer couldn't have known that his lordship had summoned Wishpole, but he could have known, in light of whatever the secret is, that his lordship might react in just that way."

"Given what we've learned from several sources about Lord Meriwell's abiding obsession," Stokes said, "namely the family's reputation, then any scandalous secret that threatened that would have made him see red."

Penelope nodded. "It does seem certain that the news the unknown man brought his lordship was what tipped him into his subsequent rage."

David was frowning. He glanced at Veronica. "This is the first I've heard about his lordship being in a rage."

But Veronica was looking at Barnaby, Penelope, and Stokes, with an expression of dawning recollection on her face. "I might know something to the point. I was in the gallery when the Busseltons and Stephen arrived. I was on my way to see Sophie, to remind her to go down and be agreeable, and I stayed out of sight while the usual greetings were exchanged, and I thought even then, purely judging by his lordship's tone, that he was very angry, but doing his best to hide it. Then once the Busseltons moved on into the drawing room, where her ladyship and Lord Iffey were waiting, Lord Meriwell hung back and, in a furious whisper, said to Stephen"—Veronica closed her eyes, presumably the better to recall—"that he—his lordship—needed to speak with Stephen later, after dinner, in the library. And his lordship added that it was about the business in Seven Dials."

Penelope's eyes flared wide. "Seven Dials?"

Veronica opened her eyes and nodded. "That was my reaction, too."

Stokes was busy scribbling. "How did Stephen react?"

"He readily agreed," Veronica reported, "but it sounded as if he didn't have any idea what Lord Meriwell was referring to." She paused, then added, "That was the extent of the exchange. They went into the drawing room, and I went on to see Sophie. I assumed that the business in question was either Arthur's or Peter's latest scandalous exploit."

"Very likely," Stokes somewhat grimly agreed.

For several moments, silence reigned as they puzzled over the various facts.

Eventually, Penelope blew out a breath. "Now we've got a new fact, we should go back and follow the trail—the sequence of events—from the beginning and slot it in and see how it fits and what more it might suggest."

"Right." Stokes nodded. "So, yesterday afternoon, Lord Meriwell met with some man whom he was expecting. We don't know who that man is, but whatever he imparted to his lordship—possibly a report about a business in Seven Dials—had two verifiable results. One, his lordship sent for Wishpole, telling him he wanted to make a significant alteration to his will. He didn't tell Wishpole more than that, so although Wishpole has confirmed that the beneficiaries of the will are her ladyship, Sophie, Stephen, Arthur, and Peter, we don't know which of them might be the one who'd been about to be struck from the will."

"While it might be tempting to discount the ladies," Barnaby said, "especially with respect to anything in Seven Dials, I suggest we consider them potential suspects until we learn more."

Stokes nodded. "The other thing that arose from that meeting— presumably due to what his lordship learned from the unknown man— was that his lordship's temper flared. His valet, Gorton, said his lordship was unruffled prior to the meeting, but in its aftermath, his lordship's fury built and built, and Veronica heard his suppressed anger in his exchange with Stephen. Subsequently, when his lordship was in the drawing room before dinner, several people, including her ladyship and Mrs. Busselton, noticed his seething anger."

"All the ladies, and even Jensen, commented on that," Penelope said. "And it seems his lordship's anger had him glaring down the dining table, then uncharacteristically quaffing a mouthful of wine the instant the wine was in his glass, before anyone else had even been served."

Frowning, David observed, "Lord Meriwell was a stickler for correct behavior."

"So we've gathered," Barnaby said, "which further suggests that whatever he learned was shocking enough to have driven him into a rage far beyond his usual limits."

"None of our witnesses," Stokes said, consulting his notes, "were certain about whom his lordship was glaring at, just that he was glaring toward his granddaughter. Sophie, however, believes it was, indeed, her his lordship was glaring at, but she has no idea why, and in that, I believe her." Stokes looked at Penelope. "She seemed genuinely confused."

Penelope agreed. "She was at a complete loss to explain it."

Barnaby went on, "All agree that his lordship swallowed the wine, choked, gasped twice, tried to lift his left hand, presumably to point in the direction in which he'd been glaring, but collapsed before he actually pointed at anyone."

From his notes, Stokes read, "It seems likely his lordship died at the table, but the nephews and his staff sought to move him to his bedroom anyway, deeming it more appropriate and respectful. Once there, you"— Stokes nodded at Veronica—"examined him and pronounced him dead."

Penelope frowned. "The movement of people through the next

minutes is somewhat unclear, at least to me. While you were upstairs, Peter was delegated to usher the remaining members of the company to the drawing room, which he duly did. However, some untold minutes later, Peter left, supposedly to learn what was happening, but he never returned to the drawing room."

"Most likely, he went to the library," Stokes said, "where, according to Jensen, at least two people helped themselves to brandy."

"Also, Peter's departure from the drawing room gave Sophie an excuse to plead illness and leave as well. She says she went upstairs and called for her maid, Sally, immediately." Penelope looked at Stokes. "We should check with Sally."

Stokes nodded. "And sometime after that, Stephen and Arthur left his lordship's bedroom and went downstairs, supposedly to report to those gathered in the drawing room—which is what each told us they did—but it seems they separated, because when Stephen entered the drawing room, Arthur followed, but not closely enough to be seen by those in the drawing room as having been *with* Stephen, and we think it must have been Arthur who used the second glass in the library. However, when he did that is yet to be determined." Stokes frowned. "Did Arthur merely lag farther behind Stephen in going to the drawing room? Or did he—or both of them—detour to the library first?"

Barnaby shifted. "Those movements are pertinent because, between the time the company vacated the dining room and you"—he glanced at Veronica—"returned with Jensen, his lordship's wine glass went missing."

"Correct me if I'm wrong," Stokes said, "but during that period, we've at some point lost sight of Peter and Sophie and, potentially, Arthur and Stephen. All were or could have been out of sight of others long enough to have taken and hidden the glass, and all know the house extremely well."

Penelope wrinkled her nose. "I've just had an unhelpful thought."

Stokes sighed. "I'm not sure I want to hear it."

Penelope pushed up her glasses. "Depending on how the company filed out of the dining room, it's possible one of the others was able to remove the glass and hide it nearby, to be collected later, during the night."

David grimaced. "Given how distracted they all must have been, I would consider it possible that one might have done that with no one else noticing."

"We already know that whoever put the poison in the glass was a past master at doing something in full view of others without attracting attention," Barnaby pointed out. "We know that the poison was introduced into his lordship's glass at some time between Jensen leading the company into the dining room and Jensen filling his lordship's glass. Everyone was about the table, talking and settling, and not one person saw anything to the point." Barnaby met Penelope's eyes, then looked at the others. "Our murderer doesn't lack for confidence in his ability to act and get away with it."

They all pondered that, then Penelope suggested, "Let's return to basics—to motive and opportunity."

"Opportunity first," Stokes said. "Who couldn't have done it?"

"George Busselton," Barnaby replied. "He walked in with Lord Meriwell, and everyone else was seated by that time. No cover, plus his lordship was there and Jensen was watching."

Penelope nodded. "I agree. Is there anyone else we can definitely rule out purely on the basis of the chance to put the poison in the glass?"

"Well, the staff," Veronica said. "But that was obvious from the first."

"In general, yes," Penelope acknowledged. "But Thomas placed the glass on the table. Although he was supposed to be wiping each glass with a cloth as he put them out, he could have dripped poison into his lordship's glass without Jeremy or Jensen noticing." She tipped her head, considering. "Or he might have put the poison in when he was alone in the room while Jensen summoned the diners and Jeremy fetched the soup course."

The others all looked at her. Eventually, Barnaby asked, "Are we really considering Thomas the footman as a viable suspect?"

Stokes grunted. "To my mind, we have enough suspects with the family and even the guests. I can imagine a scenario where, for some reason we've yet to divine, Persimone Busselton or even her brother poisoned his lordship." He looked at Barnaby. "The Busseltons were looking to ally themselves with the Meriwells, so his lordship's obsession might already have focused on them."

Barnaby pulled a face. "Sadly, that's true. He might have had someone look into the lives of the Busseltons—perhaps that was what the unknown man reported on."

They pondered that, then Stokes stirred. "Let's move on to motive. Actual motive that we have evidence of, not motive arising from our imaginations."

Barnaby grinned and supplied, "Via the will his lordship sought to alter, his three nephews, Sophie, and her ladyship all stood to gain in some way."

"And," Penelope said, "by association, given his long-standing affair with her ladyship, Lord Iffey should also be on our list."

"Right," Stokes said. "And apropos of motive, I've just realized that none of the Busseltons have one, not if we believe that whatever the unknown man reported to Lord Meriwell was what drove his lordship to decide to change his will. The Busseltons aren't affected by the will, and even if Persimone marries Stephen and we consider that connection, it doesn't sound as if Stephen needs the inheritance to any real degree. I can't see a believable, much less compelling motive to poison Lord Meriwell for Persimone, her brother, or her mother."

Penelope added, "Especially as those three aren't exactly tripping over their feet to encourage Stephen Meriwell's suit." She looked at David and Veronica. "All three, independently, gave us to understand that they were definitely on the fence. Persimone is *considering* Stephen Meriwell as a potential husband. There's been no decision made, not on the Busselton side."

Veronica frowned. "From what I gathered, including from comments Lord Meriwell made, he seemed very keen to further the match."

Stokes nodded. "Duly noted, but it seems the enthusiasm was, at least at this point, shared only by Mr. Busselton."

"All right." Penelope folded her arms on the table and leaned on them. "Let's take our suspects one by one. Sophie had a falling out—a major and active one—with her grandfather over him vetoing her London Season this year. That said, I can't see how killing her grandfather advances her cause. Indeed, as she herself remarked, she now won't have a proper Season next year, either, as she'll still be in half mourning."

Veronica gave a disgusted huff. "That sounds exactly like Sophie's way of thinking."

Penelope nodded. "Which is why I can't see her as his lordship's murderer. She might stand to gain financially under his will, but she doesn't strike me as sparing much thought for her financial future."

"No, indeed," Veronica agreed. "She's quite naive and unworldly and expects others to take care of her." She paused, then added, "Given her upbringing, that's hardly surprising. She's lived a very secluded, protected life."

"I would also suggest," David added, "that obtaining concentrated prussic acid was beyond Sophie's capability. Thanks to her grandfather, she's been more or less fixed here, and she would have no chance of buying such a thing in the local area. Not without someone commenting."

Stokes was making notes and nodded without looking up. "Good points all."

"So," Barnaby said, "that brings us to her ladyship and Lord Iffey."

Penelope frowned. "Given how long-standing their affair is and that we've found no evidence at all that his lordship knew—" She broke off and sat up. "Wait! Could his lordship have finally grown suspicious and had them investigated? Was that what the unknown man reported—that Iffey and Clementina were having an affair?"

Stokes frowned. "Could Meriwell change his will to deny his wife use of the house and estate after his death?"

Barnaby tipped his head. "I suppose that might be possible, but it seems..."

David offered, "Out of character for a man who was so powerfully driven by virtuous consideration, meaning trying to do the right thing in the manner society expected."

"Yes." Barnaby nodded. "That."

Stokes looked at the faces around the table, then said, "Let's move on to potentially greener pastures—the nephews. According to what we've learned, via his lordship's death, Arthur and Peter each gain something they want. On current information, how desperate either of their wants might be is difficult to judge, but it's possible that one or both might have a sufficiently urgent reason to lay their hands on their inheritance, a reason compelling enough to prompt murder."

Penelope inclined her head. "That's an accurate summation." For David and Veronica, she added, "Arthur needs a particular stallion his lordship owns in order to placate a long-standing creditor, and Peter has debts of mounting significance."

Barnaby tapped a finger on the table. "We shouldn't forget that this murder was premeditated. Our murderer came prepared with concentrated prussic acid. Did Arthur or Peter—or indeed, any of our other potential suspects—have something change that made gaining what they stand to inherit suddenly imperative?" He looked at Stokes. "Did any of our suspects experience some goad that spurred them to murder his lordship?"

Stokes returned Barnaby's regard, then said, "The only goad I can think of is the unknown man who reported to Lord Meriwell. It's possible that, before our murderer set out for Meriwell Hall, he discovered that the unknown man had learned his secret and it was about to be revealed to his lordship. So our murderer came prepared."

Barnaby and Penelope nodded. Penelope remarked, "That fits."

After a pause while they all thought of what they knew and what they didn't, David looked at Barnaby, Penelope, and Stokes. "What about Stephen Meriwell?"

Barnaby said, "No matter our preconceptions, we need to keep him on our list. Both in terms of motive and opportunity, he qualifies. He could have placed the poison in his lordship's wine glass, he could have removed the wine glass later, and he is a major beneficiary under his lordship's will."

"That said," Stokes observed, "Stephen's motive appears the weakest. By all accounts, he's well-to-do and financially sound—"

"And that must be so," Penelope pointed out, "or the Busseltons would never allow him near their daughter, much less be even vaguely entertaining his suit."

"Indeed." Barnaby inclined his head. "Stephen doesn't appear to have a financial need, and although it seems he will inherit the title and the entailed estate, I can't see how that gives him any great motive to kill his lordship *now*."

Penelope commented, "In terms of gaining the Busseltons' acceptance of his suit, the prospect of the title is just as good as having the title, at least in this instance."

Frowning, Veronica glanced at the others. "We seem to have forgotten the 'business in Seven Dials.'"

The others stared at her.

Stokes sighed. "That's precisely what I mean about having so many disconnected bits and pieces whizzing about in our minds."

"We can't see the needle because of the hay," Barnaby wryly said.

Stokes frowned. "What's interesting is that no one else has mentioned any business in Seven Dials."

Clasping her hands on the table, Penelope sat straighter. "Can we assume that the business in Seven Dials was the matter on which the unknown man reported to his lordship?"

"Timing-wise," Barnaby said, "that would fit."

"Which suggests," Veronica said, "that the information about the business in Seven Dials was what sparked his lordship's anger. That was certainly the impression I received from what I overheard."

Barnaby looked at Stokes. "We should ask Wishpole if he knows anything about such a business."

Stokes jotted a note. "Our other outstanding item is that missing glass." He looked at Veronica and David. "With woods all around the house, it could be anywhere, yet at the same time, the murderer wouldn't have had unlimited time to wander off and hide it."

"What if," Penelope suggested, "the murderer took the glass from the table and simply hid it somewhere it wouldn't have been immediately noticed? Those monstrous sideboards in the dining room spring to mind. He could well have counted on no one registering that the glass was missing—if Veronica hadn't detected poison and come looking for the glass..."

David shifted and said, "Very likely, this murder was intended to pass as death by natural causes." He met Barnaby's, Penelope's, and Stokes's gazes. "The reality is, in most cases with a man of his lordship's years, the death would, indeed, have been put down to a heart attack or seizure of some sort. The local doctor would have been summoned and would very likely have issued the death certificate saying just that." David glanced at Veronica. "If Veronica hadn't been there and been so observant, the murderer would have gained his objective without anyone being the wiser."

Stokes nodded. "And we wouldn't be here, poking around and searching for that glass."

"Exactly," Penelope said. "So the murderer—assuming the death would be explained by a heart attack or seizure—hid the glass...why?"

She looked at David, who obliged, "Presumably because the glass, having contained concentrated prussic acid, would likely still carry enough poison to be detected, even by someone not trained to be suspicious."

"Or," Veronica said, "the murderer might have been worried that whichever member of staff collected the glass—remember, it still had wine in it—might be tempted to take a sip—"

"And if they died, too," Penelope concluded, "it would have been obvious that his lordship was poisoned." She nodded. "Right. So the murderer hid the glass and wine, and I have to say my bet is on him using one of those sideboards."

Stokes continued to scribble. "And then, later in the night when there was no one else about, he came down, took the glass and wine, and disposed of both in some way."

Barnaby narrowed his eyes, imagining that. "I doubt he could have gone far, even then. He would have to be in his nightclothes in case he ran into any staff or other guests, so I doubt he went far from the house. If he left the house at all."

Penelope sighed. "It's a large house, with attics and basements, and all our suspects know it well. The glass is likely hidden somewhere, but finding it might not be easy."

"Regardless," Stokes said, "we should ask Jensen to search again and this time go through the bedrooms as well. I seriously doubt they did that the first time."

Veronica asked, "Could all of our suspects have taken the glass?"

Everyone paused to think, then Penelope stated, "Possibly not. None of the Busseltons are likely to have done so—we agree on them not being suspects—and we were told that they preceded her ladyship, Lord Iffey, and Peter from the room and took Sophie with them. But the Busseltons and Sophie waited outside until the other three joined them, and then the Busseltons, with Sophie, followed her ladyship, Iffey, and Peter to the drawing room." Penelope frowned. "I really can't see how any of that group could have secreted the glass without one of the others seeing, noting it, and subsequently telling us."

Stokes nodded. "But Peter and Sophie had an opportunity to collect and hide the glass later, after they'd left the drawing room."

"And," Barnaby added, "Arthur and Stephen both had time to do so—they were downstairs and, it seems, each was out of sight of others for a short time during the critical period."

"So." Stokes looked down at his jottings. "On the basis of having an opportunity to remove the glass, the three nephews and Sophie remain on our suspect list. That said, given we really don't know exactly how Peter, her ladyship, and Iffey exited the dining room, there's an outside chance that Iffey might have slipped back for just long enough to move the glass"—Stokes tipped his head at Penelope—"into one of those sideboards. The long and short of that is that I don't think we should rule him out yet."

Penelope nodded. "Let's leave him on our list for the moment. By my reckoning, that leaves all three nephews, Sophie, and Iffey."

"And we have two avenues to further investigate." Barnaby met Stokes's eyes. "We need to learn about the business in Seven Dials, and if at all possible, we want to find the missing glass."

Stokes nodded. "Even at this point, finding where the glass is might give us a clue as to who put it there. Or who could have. Any information that reduces our suspect list is welcome."

The others agreed, and on that note, they pushed back from the table and stretched, and after noting the hour, Barnaby offered to drive David and Veronica back to the Hall.

David cast a questioning glance at Veronica, but she smiled and told Barnaby, "The weather's May-mild, and the night's clear. The moon's out, too, so it'll be easy enough to find our way through the wood, and it's hardly far. No need to disturb your horses. Indeed, it's probably quicker for us to walk."

David supported the notion, and the others saw them off before retiring to their beds.

Veronica had spoken truly. The air was mild, and the path through the wood was bathed in soft shadow, with moonbeams dancing through the rippling canopy and dispensing a silvery, diffuse illumination that was more than enough for them to find their way.

Despite the specter of a murderer lurking at Meriwell Hall, in the wood, tranquility and peace held sway.

The path was relatively even and clear. There was no reason David needed to offer Veronica his arm, and no reason for her to take it; nevertheless, she did.

Walking closer, arm in arm with him, aware of the warmth of his body beside hers, as the night's quiet embraced them, she glanced at his face, studying the strong lines etched by the silvery light. Facing forward, she said, "Thank you for responding to my note so promptly."

He glanced at her; she felt his gaze trace her cheek. "Believe me when I say that I will always come to your aid as quickly as I'm able."

"Be that as it may, I couldn't be sure that you would be free." After a second, she added, "Or that you would credit my observations and deductions that his lordship had been poisoned and act so decisively, even to the point of notifying Scotland Yard."

She sensed him hesitate as if searching for words.

"Veronica..." He halted and swung to face her, and as her arm slid from his, he reached for her hands, capturing one in each of his. "My dear, you must know that I have complete faith in your professional abilities."

Her heart beat faster.

Through the dimness, his gaze locked with hers. Then, somewhat wryly, he grimaced and said, "If you want the truth, my major motive in recommending you for this position, here at Meriwell Hall, was that I wanted a way to maintain contact—professional contact—until…" He paused to draw in a deeper breath. "Until I could work out how to forge a more permanent—different—partnership with you. So I sent you here for my own reasons, and on reading your letter and learning that in following my own agenda, I had placed you under the same roof as a murderer… well, of course I acted. I called in Stokes and Barnaby and Penelope because I wanted their help to keep you safe." Impatiently, he dipped his head. "Yes, to find the murderer as well, for all the obvious reasons"—his eyes again found hers, and he held her gaze—"but my principal and over-riding motive is and will continue to be to keep you safe."

David paused, and somehow, at last, the words flowed more easily. "You are very precious to me, my dear."

Her eyes had widened, and she searched his expression. He had no idea what she might see; courtesy of the demands of his profession, his face rarely reflected his emotions.

Then he saw her swallow, and quietly, she asked, "You mentioned a permanent—different—partnership. Once this is over and the murderer caught—and surely, given Barnaby, Penelope, Stokes, and his men, that will happen soon—then in reality, looking ahead, there is no need for me here. Her ladyship needs a companion more than a nurse, and Lord Iffey is just waiting to fill that role. And Sophie…if she's made to stand on her own two feet, she'll discover she can and will go forward from there. She truly does not need a nurse, not of any kind." Her gaze steady on his face, she tipped her head. "So once this is over, I will not be needed here. I'll be free to find other employment."

David had wondered—had even hoped—that through the pressures of the investigation, his time to speak might come. And now it had. He'd toyed with the notion, imagining what might be for months—ever since he'd first made Veronica's acquaintance—but he'd shied from chancing his hand, citing one excuse after another, but he didn't dare put off speaking any longer. Life was too short; who knew what might come? "I suspected the assignment here wouldn't last long. I felt sure you would come to the same conclusion regarding Sophie as I had, even from my limited time with her, and I had already planned, once you were free, to ask if you would consider joining me in my practice."

A faint frown formed in her eyes, made lustrous by the moonlight. "You mean, as your nurse?"

He couldn't stop his lips from gently curving. "As my principal nurse, but not just as that. My dear, I'm asking if you would consider becoming my partner on a wider stage." Holding those glorious eyes with his, he raised her hand and kissed the backs of her fingers. "I'm standing here in this moonlit wood and asking you to be my partner in all things. In short, dearest Veronica, I'm asking if you will do me the honor of becoming my wife."

Her eyes flared. Although he searched them, he couldn't see beyond her stunned surprise.

Sudden uncertainty had him rushing to explain, "I've been rehearsing words like those for months, ever since we met at old Lady Ardlington's house, but it took the shock of knowing you were under the same roof as a murderer and that I had put you there—"

"Stop." She freed a hand and placed her fingertips over his lips. But she was smiling as she said, "You're babbling. I've never heard you babble before."

He blew out a breath. "Yes, well, if you must know, that's what you do to me. I lose a great deal of my self-assurance…" He tightened his grip on the hand he still held and locked his gaze with hers. "Please say yes, Veronica. I feel as if, quite literally, my life and yours, too, depend on it."

Veronica stared into the face that had inhabited her dreams for the past months. Her heart felt as if it were bursting from her chest; she might have dreamed, but she'd never expected… "Yes." She stared into his rich brown eyes. "Yes," she repeatedly more firmly.

Then, on a surge of joy, she shook her hand free and raised both palms and cupped his lean cheeks, and she stretched up and kissed him and gave him her answer in a language impossible to misconstrue.

And he kissed her back, gently at first, but they were both too eager, too impatient, and soon, she was wrapped in his strong arms, and the communion of their lips had plunged into heated waters.

In the night's quiet, they kissed and hoped and let the dreams each had dared to dream crystallize.

When, much later, they continued on their way, his arm around her and her head resting against his shoulder, despite having a murderer yet to catch, they were both smiling.

CHAPTER 8

$\mathcal{T}$he following morning, Veronica was still smiling in besotted fashion as she started down the service stair, heading for breakfast in the servants' hall.

She was two steps above the first-floor landing when an earsplitting scream rent the morning's peace.

Veronica froze. Her smile vanished, and her heart thudded twice, then she hauled in a breath, rushed down to the landing, and pushed through the service door, emerging at the end of the first-floor corridor.

The scream had come from somewhere along there, and although subsiding in volume, continuing sounds led her to Sophie's room.

The door was not quite shut.

Veronica pushed it wide, stepped inside, and halted.

Sally, with both hands clapped over her lips in an ineffectual attempt to mute the half shrieks, half whimpers that spilled from her, was backing, step by slow step, away from the four-poster bed.

Veronica's gaze shot to the bed.

To the figure beneath the covers.

Sophie lay on her back with her eyes closed and her arms stretched to either side. She appeared to be serenely sleeping, but her color...

Veronica pushed past Sally and rushed to the bed. She reached for Sophie's wrist, but even before her fingers touched the too-cool skin, she knew it was too late.

"Oh no." She stared at the still features, then releasing Sophie's wrist, stepped back.

On the bedside table sat a tray with a cup of hot chocolate and a plate of buttered toast upon it. Sally had brought up the tray, then tried to wake Sophie and discovered...

Veronica turned and went to Sally. "Here." Gently, Veronica closed her hands around Sally's shoulders and steered the maid to a straight-backed chair set against the wall. "Sit."

Gulping, Sally sat. Tears swamped her eyes, and her cries had muted to shaky whimpers.

Hearing the thunder of approaching footsteps—most of the staff would have been downstairs, and the family and guests in nearby rooms would have been asleep—and judging that Sally wasn't about to descend into hysterics, Veronica returned to the doorway.

The first to arrive—*thank God*—was David.

He'd been given a room in the opposite wing and had plainly dallied only to throw on his clothes before racing there. He took one look at Veronica's expression, and his features set. Without a word, she stepped back and let him into the room.

David glanced at the bed, then said to Veronica, "Keep the others out. We need to send for Stokes and the Adairs."

She nodded and moved to bar the doorway.

As David made for the bed, he heard her relay the order to summon Stokes and the Adairs from the Angel Inn with all speed. From the sound of the reply, it was the younger footman, Thomas, who dashed off to carry the message.

The chintz curtains hadn't been drawn around the bed but left looped and tied to the four posts, leaving the occupant readily visible. To David's educated eyes, Sophie was dead and had been for some hours. Her features were inert, and her skin had taken on a grayish hue. For the record, he checked for a pulse in her wrist, then in her throat, but her skin was so cold it was obvious death had claimed her in the small hours of the night.

A brown bottle with an apothecary's label stood on the bedside table on the other side of the bed. A folded sheet of paper lay beside the bottle. David couldn't read the label across the width of the bed, but he didn't recognize the bottle.

The burgeoning cacophony at the door intruded, and he heard

Veronica explaining to Jensen and others that it seemed Sophie had died and that Stokes had been sent for. Then more-commanding voices joined the chorus of questions, and his lips tightening, David turned and crossed the room to Veronica's side.

Instantly, all attention—expectant, apprehensive, and in some cases, almost ghoulish—swung his way.

Stephen Meriwell asked, "What's happened? Has Sophie been taken ill?"

Without inflection, David stated, "It appears that Sophie passed away during the night."

Veronica had said the same, but him saying it made it real and uncontestable.

The crowd fell silent, some sucking in shocked breaths.

From the rear, Peregrine Busselton asked, "How did she die? Was it poison again?"

Calmly, David responded, "At this time, I can't say, but I do know that Inspector Stokes, who is on his way to the house, would not want anyone else coming into the room prior to him and the Adairs examining the scene."

Veronica looked at Stephen. "Perhaps, Mr. Meriwell, you might escort Miss Busselton and Mr. Busselton downstairs to await developments."

David backed the suggestion with a decided nod. "Please do not spread the news at this point. Once I've spoken to the inspector, I will break the news to her ladyship myself."

Stephen and Arthur, who had joined the group in time to hear Peregrine's question, looked relieved that they would not have to perform that duty.

Jensen said, "Perhaps I should leave Jeremy here, sir—outside the door—to make sure no one thinks to venture inside."

David nodded. "An excellent idea. I'm sure Stokes will take charge once he gets here."

"Indeed, sir. We'll direct the inspector and the Adairs up as soon as they arrive." Jensen bent a severe eye on the maids, grooms, and other staff who had gathered, and reluctantly, they dispersed. Under David's gaze, Stephen and Arthur gathered the Busseltons—both still trying to sneak looks past Veronica and David at the bed—and herded the pair toward the main stairs.

David reached for the door and, when Veronica stepped back, firmly shut it. He glanced at the maid, who was sniffling but looked to have calmed, then caught Veronica's eye and tipped his head toward the far side of the bed. Quietly, he said, "Come and tell me what you know about this."

Puzzled, she followed him around the bed.

He stood back so she could see what was on the bedside table.

Her gaze fell on the brown bottle and the folded note, and her puzzlement turned into a frown. "What on earth's that?"

She walked forward and picked up the brown bottle, angling it so the light from the window fell on the label.

David drew closer so that he could read the small, typed letters, too.

"Good Lord." Veronica met his eyes. "It's high-strength laudanum."

He frowned. "I thought I gave orders that none of that was to be kept in the house."

"You did, and there's none of this concentration in the drugs cabinet in the still room." Veronica tipped the label more to the light and squinted to read the tiny print along the bottom. "This is from Melchoir's Apothecary in the Strand."

They both stared at the bottle. Melchoir's was one of the larger apothecary emporiums in the capital.

David shook his head. "How did she...?"

"I can't imagine." Veronica set down the bottle and picked up the note.

It was a sheet of letter paper of the rag-pressed sort that young ladies favored and had been folded in half.

She unfolded it, scanned it, and frowning anew, reported, "There's really only one line. It says, 'I'm so very sorry.' And then comes her signature. 'Sophie.'"

Frowning in even greater puzzlement, Veronica lowered the sheet. She looked at the bottle, then met David's eyes. "This makes no sense."

His lips compressed, David nodded. "But now that I know what I'm looking at..." He turned to the bed. "I'll do a more detailed examination while we're waiting for our investigators."

Penelope was grimly shaking her head when she walked into Sophie's room. "I can't believe it! Why kill Sophie?"

Immediately, Sally, until then sitting morose and silent on the chair against the wall, let out a wail, then mortified, gulped and blurted, "She did it! She took her own life!"

Barnaby and Stokes had followed Penelope into the room, and Stokes promptly shut the door on the no-doubt-interested footman standing in the corridor.

Along with Barnaby and Stokes, Penelope walked closer to the bed. They spent several moments silently studying the still figure, then all three turned inquiring gazes on David and Veronica, who were standing before the window and had clearly been waiting for them.

With her hands clasped at her waist, Veronica began, "Sally"—she nodded at the maid, busily dabbing at her eyes—"brought up Sophie's breakfast tray as usual, set down the tray, tried to wake Sophie, and found her unresponsive. Sally screamed. I was on my way down the servants' stair, so I was close and came running. I checked Sophie in case there was any hope, but she was already gone."

"I arrived about that time." David took up the tale. "I, too, checked for a pulse, but there was none. In my opinion, Sophie has been dead for at least six hours, possibly more."

Stokes was jotting in his notebook. "Cause of death?"

"As to that…" David glanced at the side of the bed closer to him and Veronica. "You'd better examine what we found left on the bedside table."

When he waved in that direction, Penelope bustled around the bed, with Barnaby and Stokes on her heels. She spied the bottle and note on the table and eagerly went forward.

She picked up the bottle and held it up to the light. Her excellent spectacles made reading even the tiniest print easy. "Maximum-strength laudanum from Melchoir's in the Strand." She handed the bottle to Barnaby and picked up the note.

She read the single sentence and frowned. She turned the letter and inspected the back, but it was free of marks. She flipped it over and studied the writing through narrowing eyes. "Hmm." She handed the note to Barnaby, adjusted her spectacles, and looked at Veronica and David, who were waiting for their reactions. "The letter is odd," Penelope declared. "As a suicide note—if that's what we're supposed to believe it to be—it lacks several indicators."

Stokes had been studying the bottle. He cocked a brow at David. "In your opinion, is this what killed her?"

David replied, "While waiting for you, I conducted a thorough examination. For the record, it's my opinion that Sophie died of an overdose of laudanum." With his head, he indicated the bottle. "Exactly what would have happened had she been dosed with what should have been in that bottle. That said, obviously, I cannot swear that it was the contents of that particular bottle that she ingested and that killed her."

Stokes grimaced. He pocketed the bottle and accepted the note from Barnaby. He glanced at it, then looked at Penelope. "You're our writing expert. What's your verdict on this?"

She wrinkled her nose. "I can't claim to be an expert on suicide notes. However, several things strike me as unusual. First, the layout of the note is not conventional. If you were to sit down and write that sentence as your suicide note, you would almost certainly start with some form of salutation, and even if you didn't, you would almost certainly start the sentence farther down the page. Instead, this sentence is written at the top of the page. She also doesn't state what she is sorry about. I assume we're meant to leap to the conclusion that she's apologizing for poisoning her grandfather, but this letter doesn't say so. If you were going to confess to poisoning your grandfather, wouldn't you write more than that? And last, she signs it simply 'Sophie.'" Penelope stared at the note in Stokes's hand. "Most people would consider their final letter to the world to be worthy of their full name. If that truly was her suicide note, then I would have expected her to sign it as Sophie Meriwell, at the very least."

Struck by a thought, Penelope frowned and looked at Veronica. "Are we sure this is Sophie's handwriting?"

Veronica came forward, took the note and studied it, then said, "I think it is, but I've not been here long enough to have seen her writing sufficiently to be sure."

She raised her head and looked at Sally, then crossed to stand before the maid. "Sally, pull yourself together. This is important." She waited until Sally sat up and, somewhat trepidatiously, looked at her.

Penelope had followed Veronica. "Sally, we need you to look at this letter, but you absolutely must keep what you see as well as all that you hear us say to yourself. All right?"

Eyes widening, Sally nodded. "Yes, ma'am." She glanced at Veronica. "I'm ready to help if I can."

Veronica found an encouraging smile. "You've seen Miss Sophie's writing before, haven't you?"

Sally nodded. "Often enough. She's often writing away when I'm around."

"I thought so." Veronica held out the letter. "Is this Miss Sophie's writing?"

Sally took the sheet and studied the words. "I think it is, but I couldn't swear to it. But the thing I can swear to is that this is Miss Sophie's letter paper." Sally held up the sheet. "See how it's faintly pink?" She held the letter to her nose. "And there's a faint rose scent to it, too." Sally handed the paper back to Veronica. "There's more of that particular paper in the top drawer of her desk."

Barnaby was already on his way to the lady's desk set before the second window. He drew out the top drawer, looked inside, then turned to the others. "Sally's correct. There's a small stack of that paper here."

Penelope glanced at Stokes. "That's good enough, I think, to say that Sophie wrote the letter. The point I would, at this stage, take issue with is the notion that she wrote it as a suicide note."

"So you're saying," Stokes clarified, "that this is not a suicide but… what? An accident? Or another murder?"

"The latter," David said. When the others, including Sally, looked his way, he went on, "That bottle of laudanum is not one I've ever prescribed for anyone in this house. Indeed, when I first took over his lordship's care about five years ago, I visited and checked the drug cabinet, and I got rid of all the old drugs, and that included the high-strength laudanum that the local doctor had previously prescribed for Sophie. And those bottles came from a local dispensary in Kingston, so this bottle isn't one that Sophie had somehow secreted away."

Veronica added, "And I can verify that it's not from any current household stock. I hold the keys to the drug cabinet, and as of yesterday evening, when I last looked, everything there was as usual and nothing had been added or was missing."

"So," Stokes asked, "how did this bottle turn up here, in Sophie's room?"

David said, "I can't imagine how she could have laid hands on it."

"Especially not coming from Melchoir's." Penelope looked at Stokes. "That's such a busy shop with such a large clientele, I don't like your chances of tracing who bought such a bottle recently, much less not so recently."

Stokes sighed. "So we have a note that might not be a suicide note and a bottle of the drug that most likely brought about Sophie's death, but we can't see how she might have got hold of it."

His expression bleak yet intent, Barnaby had been gazing at the body.

Now he looked at David and arched a brow. "There were no signs of violence on the body?"

David blinked, then shook his head. "No. None. But there wouldn't have been if she'd taken the drug herself."

Barnaby nodded. "That's my point. The note is ambiguous—it could indicate suicide, or it could indicate murder. The bottle, however, suggests murder, not suicide. However, it seems she took the drug willingly, which bolsters the case for suicide."

"Ah." David's expression blanked.

"Oh." Veronica looked as if she saw some light.

But it was Sally who, in a small voice, said, "It must've been in her cocoa."

Veronica nodded. "Sorry. We didn't mention that Sophie was in the habit of taking a small dose of laudanum—*very* small—in her cocoa every night. She insisted she needed it to help her sleep." Veronica exchanged a resigned look with David. "Whether she truly did or not is open to debate, but Sophie liked to think of herself as fragile, so she was adamant that she needed it every night."

Stokes was scribbling again. "How was the drug—her usual dose— put into the cocoa?"

"It was added directly to the mug of cocoa, by me, every night." Veronica went on, "For instance, last night, Sally brought the mug of cocoa to the still room, where I keep the household's stock of laudanum under lock and key. Her ladyship occasionally has need of it, too, but the stock we hold is very much more dilute than the solution that would have been in the bottle we found here."

David sighed. "Her grandparents were always concerned that in one of her dramatic flights, Sophie might take it into her head to stage"—he waved at the bed—"well, a scene much like this one. So his lordship had a new cabinet installed to keep any potentially dangerous drugs under lock and key."

Barnaby asked, "So what happened next, after you added the correct dose to the cocoa?"

Veronica looked across the room at Sally. "Sally left, taking the cocoa, and I locked up the cabinet and the still room."

Barnaby smiled encouragingly at Sally, who was looking exceedingly uncertain.

Penelope had been watching the maid. "Don't be frightened. No one is blaming or is likely to blame you. Just tell us what happened from the time you went to make up the cocoa."

Finding herself the focus of everyone's attention, Sally sat straighter in the chair, then said, "I went down to the kitchen and put the milk to warm on the stove, then fetched a mug from the sideboard in the servants' hall."

"Was it a particular mug?" Penelope asked. "One only Miss Sophie used?"

"No, ma'am. It was just one of the mugs the family uses for such drinks." When Penelope nodded, Sally went on, "I took the mug to the kitchen and got the cocoa powder from the pantry and added that to the mug, then when the milk was ready, I poured that in and stirred and stirred, like you have to."

Being fond of hot cocoa herself, Penelope nodded in understanding. "And once the cocoa was ready?"

"I took the mug to the still room for Nurse Haskell to add the laudanum." Sally looked at Veronica. "The still room's in the basement, and she was there, as usual, and put the stuff in, just as usual."

Penelope glanced at Veronica. "How did you know to be at the still room?"

"It's always the same time," Veronica replied. "Sally arrives at the still room just after ten o'clock. Making up Sophie's cocoa and delivering it to her room is the last duty each of us performs every night."

Sally nodded in agreement.

"So," Barnaby said, "you now have the cup of correctly dosed cocoa on your tray, and you leave the still room in the basement. What did you do next?"

"I came up here by the servants' stair." Sally tipped her head to the left. "It comes up at the end of the corridor. I carried the tray with the mug to Miss Sophie's door, knocked, and when Miss Sophie said to come in, I opened the door and walked in."

"Where was Miss Sophie?" Barnaby asked.

Sally looked toward the writing desk. "She was where she usually was at that time of an evening, sitting at the desk, writing. I put the tray— it's a small one—on the corner of the desk, just like I always do. I asked her if there was anything else she needed—she was already changed and ready for bed—and she said no, I could go. So I did."

"Did Miss Sophie appear overly sleepy or drugged to you at that time?" Penelope asked.

Sally shook her head. "No. She looked like she always did at that time. Still wide-awake."

"Was anyone else in the room?" Stokes asked.

"No," Sally replied. "Just Miss Sophie."

"Did you see anyone in the corridor when you left?" Barnaby asked.

Again, Sally shook her head. "There didn't seem to be anyone about."

Stokes glanced at Veronica. "We'll need to check the household cabinet and the stock it contains." He glanced at the others. "But assuming the drug that killed Sophie didn't come from the household stock, and she didn't knowingly add it herself, then it must have been—somehow—slipped into her cocoa by someone she allowed into her room after Sally left." He looked at David. "There's no sign that she was forced to drink the doctored cocoa, but wouldn't she have noticed a difference in taste?"

David grimaced. "Yes, the cocoa with a greater amount of laudanum would have tasted more bitter, but taste is a funny thing. Sophie had been accustomed to drinking laudanum in her cocoa for many years—long before I took over her care and reduced the dosage. The local man started her on it when she was barely thirteen and at a much higher dose, albeit still less than that used to kill her. To Sophie, the increased bitterness, assuming she registered it, might even have tasted better."

Stokes nodded and made several notes.

Barnaby shifted. "All the aspects of Sophie's death, which is looking increasingly like murder, once again underscore that our murderer—and I believe we're on solid ground in assuming we have one murderer who has now killed twice—is a member of the family." He pulled a face. "Or Lord Iffey. It has to be someone familiar with Sophie's nighttime routine."

Penelope was looking around. "Where's the mug?"

Sally leaned forward, peering at the desk. "I don't see it. Or the small tray. They should be waiting on the desk for me to collect."

They all looked at each other, then started searching.

It didn't take them long to confirm that neither the mug of cocoa—most likely the vessel carrying what amounted to poison for Sophie—or the small tray were there.

Penelope huffed. "Could our murderer be any more obvious in declaring he's the one behind this? We now have two vanishing vessels-used-to-poison."

Muted voices reached them through the door.

Stokes sighed. "I suspect we've run out of time to stand here and speculate."

"I think that's Iffey outside." David glanced at Veronica. "I'd better go and break the news to Lady Meriwell."

"If you would," Stokes said, "that would likely be best." He glanced at the bed, and his features firmed into stoic lines. "What about the body?"

David confirmed that he'd completed his examination, and they agreed that the body should be removed to the laundry room and laid out with Lord Meriwell.

"Mrs. Hutchinson will see to it." Veronica looked at Sally. "Sally, if you would remain here until Mrs. Hutchinson arrives?"

Dully, Sally nodded. "I'll keep watch, miss."

Stokes tapped his pencil on his notebook, then glanced at Veronica. "Unless you feel you need to go with David, I should look at the still room as soon as possible."

Veronica exchanged a fleeting look with David, then nodded. "I'll take you there now."

They left Sally staring morosely at the bed. On emerging from the room, they saw Lord Iffey retreating down the corridor, and David strode off to join him and go on to her ladyship's room.

Stokes paused to give the footman, Thomas, orders to convey to Mrs. Hutchinson, and once Thomas had hurried off, Veronica led Stokes, Barnaby, and Penelope in the footman's wake.

They descended the servants' stair past the ground floor and on to the basement.

Although the air down there was cool, it was also dry. Veronica led them along a corridor to a sturdy door, which was locked. As she searched for the right key on the ring she pulled from her pocket, she said, "Only Mrs. Hutchinson, Jensen, and I have keys to this room. It's always kept locked unless one of us is in here."

Stokes made an approving noise.

Once the door was unlocked, Veronica opened it, and she, Penelope, and Barnaby went inside.

Stokes paused at the door to check the lock. When he straightened and saw the others looking his way, he stated, "No one's tried to pick or force the lock."

Veronica showed them the metal drug cabinet, then unlocked it and drew out the bottle of laudanum stored there and held it up to check the level. She nodded and handed Penelope the bottle. "This is the laudanum I use for Sophie or her ladyship. I keep a ledger of the doses dispensed"— she pointed to a small book tucked inside the cabinet—"and that's the correct amount still left in the bottle. I check the level every night, and it hasn't changed since last night."

Penelope turned the bottle over and around. It was another brown bottle, but of a different style to the one in Sophie's room, and was about half full.

Penelope handed the bottle to Stokes, and after he and Barnaby had examined it, they returned the bottle to Veronica, and she put it back in the cabinet. As she closed and locked the door, she added, "As far as I know, that's the only laudanum the household has. As David mentioned, there was a reason we all felt it best to keep the stuff under lock and key."

Stokes subjected the cabinet to a cursory inspection, but it, too, was entirely undamaged. "Right." He looked at the others. "I think we can deem the laudanum used to drug and effectively murder Sophie to have come from somewhere other than the household stock."

They nodded in agreement.

"Let's head back to the library," Barnaby suggested. "We need some time and space to think."

No one disagreed. After Veronica had relocked the still room door, they trooped up the stairs to the front hall and continued to the library.

They'd barely fallen into the armchairs near the fireplace when David opened the door, saw them, and came in. He drew up another chair and joined the circle. He sighed as he sank into it. "Her ladyship is understandably overset. The good news is that she doesn't wish to be sedated, and I see no reason to insist. She's in reasonably sound health, and Iffey is with her. For what it's worth, both seemed sincerely shocked and stunned at the news of Sophie's death."

Stokes studied David. "Did they ask how she died?"

David nodded. "I told them she'd died of an overdose, and I also felt I had to say that at this juncture, there was no reason to believe she'd committed suicide." His lips twisted in a grimace. "Luckily, neither were in any state to question me further as to whether that meant it was murder or not."

Grimly, Stokes said, "Sophie being murdered is bad enough. It wouldn't be kind to allow them to imagine it was suicide if it wasn't."

David let out a breath. "Exactly." He paused, then added, "Jensen mentioned that Stephen, Arthur, Peter, and the Busseltons have sensibly broken their fast and are now waiting, not entirely patiently, in the drawing room. As for Wishpole, apparently, he was more affected by the news—more deeply shocked. Jensen has settled him in a parlor, out of the way, and is keeping an eye on him."

"Right," Stokes said. "We'll go and speak with everyone shortly, but first, I'd like to get some idea of how we all see this."

"Meaning," Penelope asked in a faintly disgusted tone, "do we believe Sophie's death was suicide? Or was it murder made to look like suicide?"

Barnaby raised a hand. "My vote is for the latter."

David nodded. "As is mine."

"And mine," Veronica firmly said.

Regarding them, Penelope tipped her head. "Just to play devil's advocate—which I hope will shore up our reasons for believing as we do—if Sophie had, indeed, poisoned her grandfather, then fallen into a funk and committed suicide by way of atonement, how did she get either poison? The cyanide for his lordship and the high-strength laudanum for herself?"

"Her having such poisons screams premeditation," Barnaby pointed out, "which does not fit with anything we've learned of Sophie."

Penelope nodded. "Indeed. But did she, for instance, go up to London recently?"

"No," David answered. "She's been stuck here, quite literally, for a year and more. That was a large part of her gripe against his lordship."

"Very well," Penelope said. "But did she have a bosom-bow in London, a close friend she wrote to constantly, whom she might have prevailed upon to obtain and send or bring her such poisons?"

"I remember her complaining that she hadn't had anyone her age visit here since last autumn," Veronica said. "I can't see Sophie planning anything that far from execution."

"No." Penelope thought, then stated, "I believe we can answer our Lucifer's advocate's questions." She focused on Stokes. "Sophie was murdered. She was our murderer's second victim, and presumably, she was killed to provide our murderer with a scapegoat."

Barnaby nodded. "If Veronica and David hadn't been here—on site to examine the body and understand the dosages of laudanum—then the chances are the murderer might well have got his wish."

"Hmm. I believe," Penelope said, "that the murderer hoped his lordship's murder would be put down to old age, but if it wasn't—as it wasn't—then he came prepared to offer Sophie up as the sacrificial scapegoat to appease the gods of justice."

Stokes grunted. "Very poetic, but essentially on point."

"And," Barnaby said, "we still have two missing vessels—his lordship's wine glass and Sophie's mug."

David stirred. "Wishpole turned up yesterday, by which time our murderer knew his lordship's murder wasn't going to be dismissed as natural causes. It's possible our murderer thought that Wishpole could have information that might have inclined us to look more closely at him —the murderer—so he enacted his back-up plan and threw the authorities a ready-made, self-confessed murderess in Sophie." David glanced around their circle. "He hopes we'll all swallow the story and go away."

Everyone agreed.

"Yet it's interesting," Barnaby said, "that he came prepared with both cyanide and high-strength laudanum."

Stokes nodded. "That suggests that Sophie's death was always a part of the murderer's plan regardless of Wishpole turning up. He—the murderer—always intended to kill Lord Meriwell and follow up by casting Sophie as the murderer. To our villain's mind, that would end the investigation and leave him free and unencumbered to enjoy his ill-gotten gains, whatever those might be."

"All of that," Penelope said, "confirms that the murderer, whichever of our suspects he is, is still here, in the house."

"And most likely," Stokes said with a small, feral smile, "he's waiting for us in the drawing room." He glanced at the others. "I suggest it's time we speak with the assembled company." He looked at David. "Is her ladyship well enough to join the gathering?"

"I can't say as to well enough, but I believe she will want to be present." David rose and glanced at Veronica. "We should at least give her the choice."

Veronica got to her feet. "I'll go with you."

"And," Stokes said, "please send Iffey down, regardless."

Veronica nodded, and she and David left to fetch Lady Meriwell and Lord Iffey.

Barnaby rose and tugged the bellpull. When Jensen arrived, Barnaby asked him to invite Wishpole to join the group in the drawing room. "Her ladyship and Lord Iffey are expected down soon with Dr. Sanderson and Nurse Haskell. Once everyone's gathered, Inspector Stokes, Mrs. Adair, and I will address the company."

"Very good, sir." Jensen bowed and departed.

Barnaby looked at Penelope and Stokes. "It occurs to me that in this scenario, Wishpole will, very likely, be an excellent additional pair of eyes and ears."

～

With Penelope and Stokes, Barnaby paused in the shadows of the library corridor and watched as David and Veronica, walking a little behind Lady Meriwell and Lord Iffey, met Wishpole in the front hall and drew the solicitor with them into the drawing room.

As Jensen shut the drawing room door, Barnaby exchanged a questioning look with Penelope, then Stokes, and by unvoiced agreement, they remained where they were, allowing those who had just entered a few minutes to receive and offer condolences and get settled.

Eventually, Penelope sighed. She glanced briefly at Barnaby, then she walked forward and nodded to Jensen, and when he opened the door, she led the way inside.

Barnaby followed, and Stokes came in behind him.

A quick survey of the room, left to right, showed Wishpole ensconced in a deep armchair set unobtrusively by the wall, with Veronica and David in straight-backed chairs nearby.

Lady Meriwell sat in an armchair to the left of the hearth, with Iffey in its mate beside her and Arthur and Peter Meriwell in straight-backed chairs set a little apart from his lordship.

Opposite, to the right of the hearth, the Busselton ladies sat on a sofa, with Miss Busselton nearer the fireplace and Mr. Busselton occupying an armchair alongside his wife. Stephen Meriwell stood protectively behind Miss Busselton, while Peregrine, apparently nonchalant, lounged against the back of his father's chair.

Somewhat grimly, Barnaby noted that the expressions on the faces turned their way ranged from concerned, anxious, and wary to, in the younger Busseltons' cases, intrigued. With apprehensive expectation, the company watched as Stokes walked forward to stand centrally before the gathering, his back to the door. Barnaby and Penelope flanked him, all three of them looking grave.

Stokes commenced, "I regret to have to inform you of the death of Miss Sophie Meriwell. She passed away in her sleep early this morning."

Barnaby and Penelope's joint task was to monitor the reactions of their suspects to the news as Stokes lugubriously doled it out.

Stokes used the ploy of consulting his notebook to punctuate his revelations. "It appears Miss Meriwell died of a large overdose of laudanum."

There was a swift intake of breath from the Busselton ladies, but none of the Meriwells seemed all that surprised. Most likely, Sophie's addiction to laudanum was well known within the family.

"A note was found beside the body," Stokes continued, "on the bedside table, and we believe it to be in Miss Meriwell's hand."

In a brief discussion before they'd quit the library, they'd agreed that no purpose would be served by holding back the facts as they knew them.

"The note," Stokes stated, "simply says, 'I'm so very sorry' and is signed 'Sophie.'"

The older Busseltons exchanged a telling look, but then glanced at Lady Meriwell and composed their features and said nothing. The younger Busseltons likewise shared a glance, but their expressions had more in common with hounds on the scent, expectant and waiting to see what would come next.

Of the Meriwell nephews, Stephen frowned, then looked at his aunt, and his lips tightened.

Both Arthur and Peter seemed to be restraining themselves from speaking, from giving voice to the conclusion the murderer had hoped they would all leap to, namely that Sophie had murdered her grandfather, then in a fit of remorse, killed herself.

Only her ladyship and Lord Iffey—both of whom had been informed that the investigators did not believe Sophie had committed the sin of suicide—remained focused and watchful, waiting to hear what Stokes would say next.

Finally, Stokes obliged, stating, "Despite what those facts might suggest, there are several observations that argue against us labeling Miss Meriwell's death a suicide rather than a murder." Stokes paused, then amended, "A second murder, one designed to deflect attention from the true murderer."

This time, the intake of breath was more pronounced. The Busseltons looked faintly alarmed, no doubt having just realized that Sophie's death did not mean that all danger within the household had been eliminated. That, on the contrary, the murderer stalking Meriwell Hall had struck a second time. Mrs. Busselton looked in consternation at her daughter, then glanced at her son. Her thoughts were easy to read in her face.

Mr. Busselton, too, was increasingly worried about the turn the investigation had taken, not just on the personal front but on the professional front, too. His mounting anxiety was even easier to read than his wife's.

As for Persimone and Peregrine, shielded by the invincibility of youth, especially that of those well-sheltered, the gleam in their eyes testified that they viewed hunting for a murderer as not far removed from a particularly exciting parlor game.

Her ladyship and Lord Iffey remained steadfast and largely unmoved. Their expressions bleak and rather stoic, they steadily regarded Stokes, patently waiting to see what else he would tell them. Having known the investigators were not entertaining death by suicide, the pair had already come to the obvious conclusion, namely that Sophie's death was, in fact, another murder. If anything, neither were capable of being further shocked.

As for the three nephews…

Looking from one to the other, Barnaby inwardly cursed. All three had reacted, but in exactly the same way. Or as near to the same as made no difference.

All three looked puzzled, even confused. Uncertain, unsure.

Definitely unable to decide what they should do—what they should say or how they should behave.

Transparently, all three vacillated as to what their response should be.

Eventually, in a hesitant tone that made it clear he was not challenging the investigators' conclusion, Arthur ventured, "Perhaps, Inspector, if you could tell us what makes you think Sophie's death was not some ghastly accident but another deliberate act?"

Stokes had been waiting for the question, but still took his time replying. "One anomaly is that we know of no way that your cousin could have gained access to the bottle of concentrated laudanum that was found beside her bed. It was purchased from an apothecary in the Strand and is of a very different strength to that stocked in the household. There is also the matter of the mug from which she presumably unknowingly imbibed the drug. It's missing from her room." He paused, then added, "Just as the wine glass used to poison his lordship is also missing."

They'd agreed that their best way forward was to lay those issues before their suspects and see who came forward to offer solutions consistent with Sophie committing suicide.

To prod the murderer onto that track, Stokes added, "Unless and until we can find rational and viable explanations to account for those two logical stumbling blocks, we cannot deem Miss Meriwell's death a suicide. At this point, based on the evidence, it appears more likely that her death was a second murder."

Stokes waited, but when no one rushed into speech, he glanced around the gathering. "Given the current situation, I have to inform you that you will need to remain at Meriwell Hall until we get to the bottom of what has occurred here. I'm sure that none of you would wish to see a murderer, likely now a double-murderer, walk free."

No one was about to argue that point.

Stokes paused, once again raking the company with his gaze. "Is there anything anyone here knows that might be pertinent to Miss Meriwell's death?"

Arthur shot a glance at his aunt, then flung a brief look at Veronica, sitting beside David. Distinctly uncertain, Arthur cleared his throat and ventured, "Most of us—the family—know that there's always been laudanum in this house. Are you"—Arthur fixed his gaze on Stokes—"sure this other bottle isn't a red herring, as it were, placed there to, perhaps, cover up some accident?"

Veronica stiffened, her eyes flaring in outrage.

Beside her, David bristled, appearing quite furious, but at a look from Barnaby, David clamped his lips shut and closed his hand about Veronica's in warning.

Veronica glared daggers at Arthur, but it was Stokes who replied with cutting iciness, "Quite sure, Mr. Meriwell. For your—and everyone else's—information"—Stokes swept the company with a steely gaze—"we have checked the household stocks, which are kept under lock and key— two locks, two keys—and determined that all is as it should be. Furthermore, Dr. Sanderson has confirmed that the household stocks could not have been used for this purpose."

That was a trifle more than David had actually said, but Barnaby judged it to be an accurate statement nonetheless.

An awkward silence ensued.

Finally, Stokes repeated, "Does anyone have any pertinent information?" When no one answered, he nodded curtly. "In that case—"

Mr. Busselton cut Stokes off. He didn't have any information, but he did have questions.

As did his wife and children, and then Peter Meriwell joined the circus.

Along with Penelope, who was standing back on Stokes's other side, Barnaby dutifully observed as, with a stoic patience that had matured with the years, Stokes dealt with every last question.

CHAPTER 9

 hen the questions eventually ran out, Stokes excused
himself, Barnaby, and Penelope, and at a whispered
suggestion from Penelope, he and Barnaby left for the library while she
crossed to where David and Veronica were quietly speaking with Mr.
Wishpole.

With an inviting smile for all three, Penelope said, "We're adjourning
to the library to compare notes and decide what's next on our agenda and
would appreciate your input."

David and Veronica readily rose, but Wishpole gently smiled and
shook his head. "I believe, dear lady, that at this juncture, you and your
colleagues will do better without me." His shrewd gaze slid past Penelope
to the rest of the company, all of whom were already absorbed in
discussing what Stokes had deigned to tell them. "I'll wait quietly here.
Once you leave, I daresay the rest will forget I'm in the room. Who
knows what I might see and hear?"

Having a healthy regard for an experienced solicitor's acumen, Penelope inclined her head, then she, David, and Veronica made for the door.

They reached the library to find Barnaby and Stokes already settled in
the chairs before the fireplace.

Stokes waited until Penelope, Veronica, and David claimed seats, then
said, "So, did any of our potential suspects react in a telling way?"

Penelope sighed. "Not that I saw." Brows rising, she looked at
Barnaby.

"They reacted to your revelations, certainly," Barnaby said, "but not in any way that stood out as strange or noteworthy or that would distinguish the murderer. In fact, the three showed much the same response. At first, they patently leapt to the conclusion that Sophie had taken her own life. It was plain they were ready to embrace that explanation. As your exposition continued and it grew clear we weren't accepting Sophie's death as a suicide, all three looked puzzled, then increasingly anxious, a touch wary, and possibly even apprehensive. Unfortunately, all three have reason to feel so. Regardless of whether they are the murderer, each is sufficiently intelligent to see that they will be a suspect. A suspect in both murders."

"And in Arthur's and Peter's cases, we have already identified definite motives." Penelope grimaced. "And Stephen will be anxious as to how the case will impact his courtship of Persimone Busselton."

"What about Iffey?" Stokes looked at David. "How did his lordship react when he heard the news of Sophie's death? He was with her ladyship when you broke the news, wasn't he?"

David nodded. "He was, and I would say that he was as genuinely shocked and stunned as her ladyship."

Veronica added, "In the drawing room, when you made it clear that Sophie's death was being viewed as a murder rather than a suicide, if anything, Iffey looked pleased. Meaning he was pleased that you'd made that point public knowledge, and therefore, her ladyship wasn't going to have to deal with a scandalous suicide on top of his lordship's murder."

Stokes grimaced. "In other words, Iffey behaved exactly as one might expect in the circumstances."

"One point that Wishpole raised." David glanced around their circle. "Could we have foreseen Sophie's murder and prevented it?"

They all pondered that uncomfortable question, then slowly, Barnaby shook his head. "I can't see how we might have predicted it."

Penelope nodded decisively. "And if we couldn't have predicted it, we couldn't have prevented it." No one argued, and she added, "Not that any of us or, indeed, anyone other than the murderer is happy about that. Sophie might have been immature and trying, but she had her whole life before her, and she certainly didn't deserve to have her future ripped away."

"I presume," Barnaby said, "that Wishpole's question was prompted by the thought that Sophie was killed to throw us—the investigators—off the scent. In essence, that she was a sacrificial scapegoat, and her death became necessary only because we were actively pursuing the murderer. However, we shouldn't forget, first, that it was the murderer who killed her, not us or Wishpole or the investigation, and even more to the point, the murderer arrived here with the wherewithal to kill Sophie and make it seem like suicide."

Nodding, Stokes shifted in his chair. "Sophie's murder was planned, every bit as much as Lord Meriwell's."

Frowning, Penelope tipped her head. "The question is, was Sophie's death always a part of the murderer's plan, or was it a fallback safety measure, to be enacted only if Lord Meriwell's death wasn't accepted as due to natural causes?"

They all thought, but no one had anything further to offer in that regard.

After several moments, Penelope shook herself, then looked around the circle of faces. "I can't help thinking that this abstraction of ours is precisely what the murderer hoped to achieve with Sophie's death. He wants to distract us from our investigation of Lord Meriwell's murder."

Barnaby stirred. "Presumably because if we continue poking into his lordship's murder, we might stumble on something that will point to our villain."

Stokes nodded. "The situation does suggest there's some vulnerability there, if only we can find it."

Veronica had been looking from face to face. Now, she drew in a breath and firmly stated, "In that case, let's get back to the questions we decided yesterday needed to be followed up, namely, identifying the business in Seven Dials and finding the missing wine glass—and I suppose we should now add the missing mug as well."

Her brisk tone had the others sitting straighter and turning their minds to those subjects.

"The missing glass and mug are the easiest to deal with." Stokes rose and crossed to tug the bellpull. "The staff are best placed to handle any search, especially with Sergeant O'Donnell and Constable Morgan assisting."

Jensen arrived so quickly, he had to have been waiting for their summons.

Stokes gave orders for a second and even more thorough search of the house and grounds. "Literally, look everywhere. Our murderer almost certainly knows the house and grounds intimately, and he'll have chosen some place no one else is likely to think of."

"And," Barnaby said, "search every room, including the bedchambers, with only those used by the Busseltons to be excluded."

"You will need to quarter the grounds," Penelope said. "The missing wine glass and missing mug have to be somewhere."

Jensen looked pained. "As to the latter, ma'am"—he tipped his head toward Stokes—"Inspector, I have just been informed that a mug we believe to be the one Sally used to make Miss Sophie's cocoa last evening was found in the sink this morning by the scullery maid. She was surprised to find it there, but otherwise, thought nothing of it. She washed and dried it and put it away."

Penelope sighed.

Barnaby thanked Jensen for the news. "At least that's one mystery solved."

Jensen vowed, "We'll reinstitute the search for the wine glass immediately, Inspector." With that, he bowed and left.

Penelope hummed, then said, "Everything we know points to the murderer being one of the family. So who are we putting at the top of our suspects list?"

"Arthur and Peter," Stokes promptly replied. "I can't see anything to distinguish between them at this point. They might even be working together."

"I think," Barnaby added, "that for now, we have to leave Iffey on the list, albeit acting without her ladyship's knowledge. No matter her fondness or otherwise for her late husband, I cannot see Clementina Meriwell agreeing to allow her granddaughter—her only living descendant—to be sacrificed."

"No, indeed," Penelope agreed.

David nodded. "So we have those three—Arthur, Peter, and Iffey."

"Well," Penelope said, "if we're to be logical and consistent, then at least from a motive and opportunity perspective, we have to leave Stephen on the list, too, even though he doesn't appear to be a strong contender."

Stokes nodded. "Right. So at this moment, we have four suspects, and despite all we've learned, we cannot distinguish which of those four Lord Meriwell was referring to regarding 'the business in Seven Dials.'"

Veronica frowned. "I suppose that's true."

Penelope observed, "If any of them are hiding an unsavory secret, one of the magnitude that the phrase 'business in Seven Dials' conjures, then for any of those four, that would provide sufficient reason for Lord Meriwell to feel enraged to the point of altering his will and for our murderer to act decisively to keep his secret concealed."

"Yet to date," Stokes said, "we've uncovered nothing that ties that business, whatever it is, to any of our suspects."

"We need to ask Wishpole." Barnaby rose, walked to the bellpull, and tugged it. "He might well know if any of our four have a connection with such an enterprise."

When Jensen answered the summons, Barnaby asked him to request that Wishpole join them.

∼

By the time Wishpole arrived, they'd added another armchair to their circle, and once the aging solicitor was installed in its depths, Stokes explained that mention of a business in Seven Dials had arisen in connection with Lord Meriwell's murder. "Do you know anything of such a business with a link to any of the Meriwells or, by chance, Lord Iffey?"

Puzzled, Wishpole shook his head. "No. I know of all his late lordship's financial dealings, and"—he grimaced faintly—"I suppose, in the circumstances, I can reveal that I am also Lord Iffey's solicitor, so I know of all his business interests as well. It won't come as any surprise to you to hear that both gentlemen are exceedingly conservative in their investments, and I cannot imagine either ever having any association with any endeavor in Seven Dials." He paused, clearly consulting his no-doubt-capacious memory, then added, "Indeed, as far as I am aware, none of the Meriwells, older or younger, have ever had any connection to an enterprise in that area."

They all looked glum.

Wishpole studied their expressions, then somewhat tentatively asked, "Do you have any clues as to the perpetrator yet?"

Barnaby glanced at Stokes and, after receiving an infinitesimal nod, looked at Wishpole and said, "We have four potential suspects, two of whom seem more likely, but at present, we have no proof that links any of the four to a motive strong enough to provoke murder."

"Premeditated murder," Stokes clarified. "The villain came to the house bearing poison for both his lordship's and Miss Meriwell's murder."

Wishpole's brow furrowed as he followed the trail of fact, much as they had earlier. "So," he eventually said, glancing at Stokes, then at

Barnaby and Penelope, "it wasn't my arrival that precipitated Miss Sophie's murder?"

Penelope realized that, due to the timing of Wishpole arriving and Sophie being murdered that same night, the sequence of events might be interpreted in such a way.

"No, indeed," Barnaby assured Wishpole. "The murderer must have intended to use Sophie as a scapegoat from the first."

"Why else"—Penelope spread her hands—"come prepared to kill her in such a way that it might be taken for suicide prompted by guilt?" She fixed her gaze on Wishpole's face. "At this moment, we cannot say that even had his lordship's murder been accepted as due to natural causes, the murderer wouldn't have killed Sophie regardless. He'd come prepared to do so, and for all we know, he always intended to kill her as well and pass off her death as a suicide in the wake of her grandfather's demise."

Hearing her own summation gave her pause.

Distantly, she heard Wishpole thank them for sharing their information and Stokes return the sentiment, then the solicitor left them.

As they settled back in the chairs, their collective focus turned to how best to learn more about "the business in Seven Dials."

Barnaby said, "We need to canvass all our options."

They proceeded to do so, but it quickly became apparent that the most straightforward of the few paths available to them was to ask one of the nephews.

"His lordship was intending to speak with Stephen about the business, remember?" Veronica said. "That suggests Stephen must know something about it."

"And," Penelope added, "Stephen is the suspect we least imagine is the murderer." She looked at the others. "We should ask him."

Stokes sighed. "It goes against the grain, but..."

"Needs must." Barnaby rose, tugged the bellpull, and when Jensen responded, sent him to ask Stephen Meriwell to join them.

Stephen walked in, his expression open and earnest. As he sat in the chair Wishpole had vacated, he assured them, "It may not appear so, but I'm quite cut up over these murders. My uncle was very good to me for all of my life, and Sophie was a dear girl. Almost a sister. I'll help in any way I can."

He leaned forward, hands clasped between his thighs, and looked from one to the other in transparent expectation.

Stokes said, his tone relaxed, "Thank you, Mr. Meriwell. We wanted to clarify a few matters that have come to our attention. If you will, please cast your mind back to when you arrived at Meriwell Hall on Monday afternoon. After greeting the Busseltons, his lordship urged them toward the drawing room, then he turned back and exchanged a few private words with you."

"Oh?" Stephen's frown was one of puzzlement. "I'm not sure that I recall..."

"Our information," Barnaby said, "is that his lordship said words to the effect that he wished to speak with you later, after dinner, in the library, about some business in Seven Dials."

Stephen's face cleared. "Oh. Right. That." He looked a trifle embarrassed. "What with all that's happened since, I'd quite forgotten." He looked from Barnaby to Stokes. "What was it you wanted to know?"

"What business was it that your uncle was referring to?" Stokes asked.

Stephen frowned. "Well, obviously, I don't know. He didn't get a chance to tell me."

Penelope, Barnaby, and Stokes exchanged glances. All of them were being careful to keep Stephen's attention on them, effectively discouraging him from focusing on or even noticing Veronica and David.

Barnaby asked, "Do you have any idea what your uncle might have been referring to? Why he had any interest in a business in Seven Dials?"

Stephen pursed his lips. He looked torn, then he sighed and admitted, "Given Uncle Angus was so angry, I assumed it must be the latest scrape either Arthur or Peter had become embroiled in. Uncle Angus often asked my advice on how to deal with their...peccadilloes, and I assumed this was another such incident." Looking increasingly troubled, Stephen shook his head. "I suppose, now, that I—we—will never know what it was about or which one..." Stephen hung his head and studied his clasped hands. "It doesn't really matter anymore, does it?"

Stokes glanced at Barnaby, a question in his eyes.

Barnaby considered, but could see no point in further explaining and fractionally shook his head.

Stokes uncrossed his legs and rose. "Thank you, Mr. Meriwell. You're free to rejoin the others."

Stephen rose and nodded to Stokes. "Inspector." With a general nod to the others, he walked from the room.

They debated at some length, but eventually felt sufficiently compelled to call in first Arthur, then Peter to ask what each knew of any business in Seven Dials.

When Peter left the library and the door closed behind him, Penelope looked at the others. "Well, if I had to judge by their replies and visible reactions, both were genuinely puzzled, and neither had the faintest idea about any business in Seven Dials."

Stokes grimaced. "Denials aside, we need to know, now more than ever, if any of the Meriwells is or was associated with a business in Seven Dials."

"And," Barnaby added, "we need to learn what that business is."

Dryly, David remarked, "Given it is a business in Seven Dials, I'm sure we're all suspecting that said business will be anything but respectable."

Stokes grunted in agreement.

"For all we know," Penelope said, "it might be Iffey who has the connection. Having such a close and long-term family confidante involved in such an enterprise would incense his lordship every bit as much as if it was one of his nephews."

Veronica nodded. "Given Iffey's long association with Lord Meriwell and her ladyship, he—Lord Meriwell—would see it as a stain on the family name."

Penelope tipped her head, considering. "Regardless, Barnaby's correct. We need to learn not only who has a link to that business but also what the business is." She looked at the others. "We need to confirm that the business, whatever it is, is sufficiently unsavory to provide a motive for murder."

Barnaby nodded. "That, indeed, is the critical point."

After several moments of silence while they all racked their brains for a way to learn what they needed to know, Barnaby sighed and looked at Stokes. "I'm going to send a message to Roscoe. If anyone might have heard of a Meriwell or Lord Iffey being associated with a business in Seven Dials, it will be Roscoe or one of his many informants. If I ask, he'll tell us what he knows or can readily find out."

Stokes pulled a face, but reluctantly nodded. "As a denizen of Scotland Yard, I can't pretend to like having to appeal to London's gambling king, but like you, I can't see any viable alternative. Even if I send some of the Yard's own men into Seven Dials to sniff around, there's little chance they'll turn up anything useful."

"No, indeed." Penelope sighed. "And at this point, even a rumor might help."

Lunchtime had arrived, and at Jensen's suggestion, the investigative team was served a cold collation at the large library table farther down the room.

As they sat around the table and ate, they talked of lighter matters, including Barnaby and Penelope's children and Stokes's daughter, Meg, all of whom David had delivered, and thus he had a genuine interest in their development.

Veronica was amused and intrigued, both by the tales of the children's antics and David's continued professional and personal involvement in the lives of children he'd brought into the world.

But once the platters were empty and, along with their plates, pushed to one end of the table, they turned their minds to the matter at hand.

Penelope opened their deliberations. "With respect to Lord Meriwell's murder, it seems we've reached a point where we have to wait for news. Consequently, I suggest we focus on Sophie's murder." She looked around the table. "To begin with, how did the high-strength laudanum get into her cocoa?"

Veronica reminded them, "Sally said she saw no one from the moment she left the still room until she set the mug of cocoa on Sophie's desk."

"Exactly," Penelope said. "So the laudanum—the extra dose that killed Sophie—had to have been added after that." She looked at the others. "How? And by whom?"

Stokes stirred. "Obviously, after Sally had gone, someone came to the room, and Sophie let them in."

Barnaby nodded. "Again, that implicates one of the family. One of the nephews, who it seems she viewed as brothers, or Iffey or her ladyship." He looked at Penelope and arched his brow. "As she was already in her nightgown, I can't imagine her letting anyone else in."

"Actually," David said, "Sophie was rather…insecure. She certainly wouldn't have allowed any of the Busseltons in, and I seriously doubt she would have allowed Iffey in, either. Or if she did, she would have been watching him closely the entire time he was in her room." He paused, then went on, "I can imagine her being comfortable enough with her cousins to freely invite them in. I gather she was on good and quite relaxed terms with all three. As you mentioned"—he looked at Barnaby —"she treated them more like brothers."

"Yes," Veronica said. "She would have allowed Stephen, Arthur, Peter, or her ladyship in and not thought anything of it. She's known all four since she was a young child and had no reason to distrust any of them."

"All right," Penelope said. "So we believe one of the three nephews, employing the same sleight of hand he used to poison his lordship's wine glass, slipped the high-strength laudanum into Sophie's cocoa." She envisioned the scene, then, frowning, glanced at Veronica. "Sally said Sophie was 'writing as usual,' implying that it wasn't the note she was writing but some writing she did every night…" Behind her spectacle lenses, Penelope's eyes widened. "Did Sophie have a diary?"

Veronica nodded. "Yes, she did. She wrote in it every night. She was quite religious about that, and almost certainly, that was what she was doing when Sally left the cocoa."

Buoyed, Penelope looked at Barnaby and Stokes. "I suggest that Veronica and I should take ourselves upstairs and search for Sophie's diary." She glanced at David. "Perhaps, David, you should come, too, to lend us authority if needed."

Stokes nodded encouragingly. "I think that's a wise move. Sophie's diary might be a treasure trove—who knows what she might have overheard and recorded?" He looked at Barnaby. "As for us, I need to check with O'Donnell and Morgan and see if they've turned up anything useful, then I believe we should go and ask the staff if any of them happened to see anyone in the vicinity of Sophie's room after Sally had left." He glanced at Penelope. "After ten o'clock, wasn't it?"

Penelope nodded. "That's right."

"It might be a long shot," Barnaby said, rising from the table, "but one never knows what someone might have noticed and not thought important."

They all got to their feet and, feeling more positive for having something they could actively do, dispersed about their tasks.

However, when they assembled again over the tea tray in the library, all wore glum or frowning faces.

After taking her first sip of tea, Penelope reported, "Sophie's diary is nowhere to be found. Sally and the upstairs maid both confirmed that Sophie always kept her current journal in the right-hand drawer of her desk, but it's not there now."

Stokes grunted. "Underscoring, yet again, that the villain is a member of the family. Who else would have known she had a diary and kept it up to date?"

"More," Penelope said darkly, "the disappearance tells us that the diary holds something the murderer doesn't want us to know."

"In which case," Stokes glumly concluded, "it'll be ashes by now." He paused, then amended, "Or at least, soon. And damn it, we aren't in any position to prevent that."

"At least," Barnaby consoled, "we can alert the staff to be on the lookout for any sign of an unexpected fire and to report any such sighting immediately." He glanced around their circle. "Whoever he is, he's having to rush around and hide or destroy possible connections. The more he's forced to act, the greater the likelihood that he'll slip up somewhere."

Stokes exhaled gustily. "I know that's how it often works, but relying on the murderer making a mistake doesn't leave me feeling all that confident."

Penelope surveyed the frustrated expressions surrounding her. "I take it no staff spotted anyone near Sophie's room at the critical time."

"Not a single sighting," Stokes confirmed, "but it was a long shot. Not many staff are up on the first floor at that time. Gorton would have been, but with his lordship dead, he has no reason to go up. At that time, he was downstairs with the rest of the staff, enjoying a nightcap before heading for bed."

Forcing her mind from their pervasive disgruntlement, Penelope determinedly searched for some way, some path, some avenue that might get them further, but found little inspiration. Finally, she sighed. "All right. So where are we now?"

Barnaby stirred, then offered, "I told Roscoe the matter was urgent—literally a matter of life and death—and asked him to send a reply as soon as he could."

Stokes roused himself to ask, "To here or to the inn?"

"The inn," Barnaby replied. "Given Roscoe's operations and the hours he generally keeps, I'm hoping something will arrive in the wee small hours."

David was frowning. "Who is this Roscoe? I know you said he's London's gambling king, but what does that actually mean, and why would he be willing to help?"

Penelope replied, "To answer the first part of your question, Roscoe owns an enormous number of the higher-class gambling establishments in the capital."

"We're not talking of businesses in the slums," Barnaby said with a smile. "Roscoe's clients are, at the very least, well heeled. He's an extremely wealthy and, when he wants to be, extremely powerful man, but thankfully, he abides by the same codes we do."

"Which is why," Stokes said, "as a senior member of the Metropolitan Police, I cannot be known to deal with the man, yet I will gratefully accept whatever help he can give us."

David and Veronica regarded Barnaby, Penelope, and Stokes with curiosity in their eyes.

"I sense a story," David said.

Penelope inclined her head. "Your instincts are sound, but the story of Roscoe is not one we're at liberty to divulge. Suffice it to say that, despite any and all appearances to the contrary, Roscoe very definitely works on the side of the angels."

That description made David and Veronica look even more intrigued.

"If Roscoe knows anything," Barnaby said, "he'll tell us."

"Until then," Stokes added, "other than passing a message to the gardeners, the maids, and the footmen to keep an eye out for Sophie's diary or any unexpected blaze, I can't see that we can accomplish anything more here today."

Reluctant though they were to admit what amounted to a minor defeat, all agreed.

Ten minutes later, with the last of the tea cakes consumed, accompanied by David and Veronica, Stokes went upstairs to call on Lady Meriwell and, no doubt, Lord Iffey and explain that while waiting for critical information to arrive, they would retire to the inn, but would return to the Hall as soon as they knew more.

Meanwhile, Barnaby and Penelope went to check on their suspects.

From Jensen, they learned that the company had retreated to the side lawn, where afternoon tea had been served under the spreading branches of two old oaks.

After emerging onto the terrace, Barnaby and Penelope lingered there and observed from a distance. With the tea dispensed and consumed and cups, saucers, and plates stacked ready to be fetched, Mr. and Mrs. Busselton had remained comfortably seated in lawn chairs under the trees' shade and were watching the younger members of the company, who were engaged in a rather desultory game of croquet.

Stephen and Persimone were pitting their skills against those of Peregrine and Peter, while Arthur stood on the sidelines, with his arms crossed over his chest and a brooding expression on his face.

Penelope scanned the players, then refocused on the elder Busseltons. "Mrs. Busselton appears to have taken charge, albeit in a helpful fashion. Mr. Busselton is watching the players with some degree of hope, but Mrs. Busselton…" Penelope narrowed her eyes. "To me, she still appears watchful and even wary."

Barnaby didn't argue but asked his observant spouse, "She's not yet convinced of Stephen's character?"

Penelope pushed up her glasses. "I would say not."

CHAPTER 10

*B*arnaby was greatly relieved when Roscoe lived up to his—
Barnaby's—expectations.

Just as the investigators were finishing breakfast in the inn's private parlor, a courier arrived, bearing a reply from London's gambling king—a reply the courier informed them he'd been well paid to deliver poste-haste.

Holding back his eagerness to read the missive, Barnaby thanked the man and arranged for him to be fed and his horse cared for. "It's possible we'll require your services to take back a reply."

The courier dipped his head. "Any friend of his nibs is someone I'll gladly help."

Barnaby hid a smile and hoped the courier didn't realize who Stokes worked for. Leaving the man in the inn's main room, Barnaby retreated, message in hand, to the parlor.

He was met by eager eyes and impatient expressions.

Grinning, he shut the door, walked to the table, dropped into his chair, and without further ado, broke the seal and unfolded Roscoe's missive.

Penelope jabbed his upper arm. "Read it aloud."

Barnaby duly reported, "Roscoe writes that he doesn't know which Meriwell—or indeed, if any Meriwell—is involved in our 'business in Seven Dials.' However, he has two pieces of information that might prove helpful. First, he suspects he knows which business is being referred to. Apparently, in the underworld, the description 'business in Seven Dials' has come to mean an enterprise called the House of Dreams, and in Roscoe's opinion, exposure of a Meriwell being linked to the place would cause a massive scandal of the level that would definitely qualify as a motive for murder."

"Well," Stokes said, "that's something at least. We now have our likely motive for his lordship's murder."

"And"—Barnaby had been scanning ahead, and his tone suggested mounting joy—"you'll like Roscoe's second piece of information even more. He's heard a rumor that Curtis has been investigating the business —quietly, as is Curtis's wont—and Roscoe suggests that if any Meriwell is involved in the House of Dreams, then Curtis might well know."

Curtis was the highly respected owner and head of the Curtis Inquiry Agency. Barnaby and Stokes had crossed his path several times in the past and, indeed, counted him as an ally of sorts.

Her expression lightening, Penelope sat back. "Even if Curtis was investigating for some other purpose, he's so thorough, he will surely know of all those involved."

Barnaby nodded. "Just as well I kept the courier. I'll get him a fresh horse and send him back hotfoot with a message for Curtis."

Stokes's eyes had narrowed in thought. "Better yet, as it's Curtis, we can make our request official. Rather than the courier, I'll send O'Donnell. Curtis is nothing if not law-abiding—he'll give us all the information he can, and O'Donnell is experienced enough to evaluate it and investigate further at that end if needed, before bringing us the news."

"And just from what Roscoe wrote," Penelope said, "given Lord Meriwell's obsession with the family name and keeping the family reputation untarnished, one can readily see that the news delivered by our unknown man—who might actually be Curtis—that one of his lordship's nephews or his closest friend were involved in such an enterprise would have triggered his temper and sent him into a towering rage."

"Indeed." Stokes nodded at Barnaby. "We have our motive. Now, we need to learn which of our four suspects is involved in such a disreputable business."

Stokes pushed to his feet, went to the door, opened it, and bellowed for his sergeant.

～

They took the path through the wood to Meriwell Hall and entered via the side door. Once in the front hall, with determined stride, Penelope led the way to the library.

As soon as they were inside and the door was shut, she headed for the desk. "Given that we have to wait—again—for news from London, then I believe it's reasonable to assume that it might have been Lord Meriwell for whom Curtis was investigating so quietly."

"That"—Barnaby sank into one of the chairs behind the desk—"seems an eminently justifiable conclusion."

Penelope smiled at him.

"I therefore suggest," he went on, returning her smile, "that we reinterview Jensen and see if we can verify that Curtis is, indeed, our mystery man."

Stokes was already reaching for the bellpull.

When Jensen arrived, the three were sitting behind the desk, and Stokes waved the butler to a chair. "Jensen, we believe we might have established the identity of the man who called on your master on the afternoon of his death."

"Indeed, sir." Uncomfortable about sitting in the presence of his betters, the butler dithered, but eventually perched on the edge of the chair's seat. "How may I help?"

"Please take your time," Barnaby said, "and give us as detailed a description as you can of the man who called."

"Well, he was of somewhat above average height," Jensen began. "Taller than the average, but not as tall as the inspector. A solidly built man with a rather round head. Brown hair, straight, and what I would call a determined-featured face. Strong in body and strong in mind, if you know what I mean."

Penelope smiled. "We do." She glanced at Barnaby and Stokes. "That does sound like the man we're thinking of."

"Oh." Jensen's eyes brightened. "One thing I hadn't thought to mention. He wore a low-crowned hat. Not something I've seen before, but it was of excellent make and quality."

Barnaby shared a look with Stokes. "That settles it. The man was Curtis."

Stokes inclined his head. "Not many others wear hats like that."

Barnaby refocused on Jensen. "Our acquaintance, Curtis, works in London. Did Lord Meriwell go up to town often?"

Jensen nodded. "He went up at least once a month and stayed at his club."

Stokes had his notebook open. "White's?"

"Yes."

"Business, was it?" Stokes asked.

Jensen hesitated, then replied, "He always described it as a combination of business and pleasure in the sense of catching up with friends."

Barnaby caught Stokes's eye, and when Stokes shook his head, turned to Jensen. "Thank you, Jensen. We won't keep you from your duties any longer."

Jensen rose, bowed, and departed.

The instant the door shut, Barnaby leaned back and angled his chair to look at his co-investigators. "If Lord Meriwell heard anything—even just a rumor—to make him wonder if perhaps one of his nephews or his closest friend were involved in some unsavory business, then it's likely he heard it in London. And subsequently, at some point, he hired Curtis, who would arguably be the best man for the job, to conduct a discreet investigation."

Penelope nodded. "Given his lordship's obsession, he wouldn't have been able to let the matter rest. He would have been driven to learn the truth, one way or another."

Stokes rumbled in agreement.

Penelope scooted back her chair and eyed the desk. "Now we know the name of the business and that it was Curtis his lordship hired to investigate, surely we have a legitimate reason to search his lordship's correspondence." She arched her brows at Stokes. "Who knows? Curtis might even have submitted a written report."

Stokes smiled at her attempt to lead him. "You know as well as I do that in such a case, Curtis almost certainly offered a verbal report."

Barnaby nodded. "That was why he called here. To tell his lordship what he'd learned."

Penelope frowned at the desk. "Still, there may be something pertinent in a letter. We won't know unless we look."

Stokes gave up trying to hide his grin. "Yes, all right. Now we know what we're looking for, it's appropriate that we search his lordship's papers. But we'll do this properly, by the rule book. We'll go upstairs"—he pushed back his chair and got to his feet—"and ask Lady Meriwell's permission to search her late husband's desk for any mention of the

House of Dreams or the man we know as Curtis, who reported to his lordship on the afternoon of his death."

Stokes waved Penelope to the door, and she leapt to her feet and led the way.

Of course, Lord Iffey was sitting beside her ladyship in her private sitting room.

Stokes, Penelope, and Barnaby shared a glance as they approached the elderly couple, but when Stokes halted before Lady Meriwell, he made no suggestion that Iffey leave.

Barnaby inferred that they were to observe his lordship for his reaction to Stokes's disclosures.

Stokes explained that they'd received information from London that had identified a business his lordship had shown an interest in and also given them the name of the man who had called and spoken with his lordship on the afternoon of his death. "If you would give us"—he indicated Barnaby and Penelope more than himself—"permission to search your late husband's papers, those he kept in the desk in the library, to see if we can find any mention of either the business or the man he hired, it might get us further."

Penelope added, "Given we have the names of both, we won't need to read every document. We'll simply scan each sheet for mention of either name."

Her ladyship smiled weakly. "Yes, of course, dear." She shifted her washed-out gaze to Stokes. "Please do whatever you must, Inspector. All I ask is that you find who killed Angus and my darling Sophie and bring them to justice."

Stokes bowed. "We will do our level best, ma'am."

"Indeed." Penelope stepped back, preparing to leave.

Iffey gruffly said, "I just hope you're close to learning who was behind Angus's and Sophie's deaths."

Penelope and Barnaby inclined their heads. Stokes nodded politely, and they left the room.

As they headed—in Penelope's case with overt eagerness—for the main stairs, she murmured just loudly enough for Stokes and Barnaby to hear, "I really don't think Iffey is our man. Until his comment at the end, his entire attention was locked on her ladyship."

Barnaby nodded. "I agree. He's focused on her to the exclusion of all else, and despite all, I can't see him bumping off his old friend Angus, knowing how much it would distress her ladyship. That's his lodestone, his measure of what he should do. If any action would make her unhappy, he wouldn't do it." They started down the stairs, and Barnaby added, "And he didn't react in any way to the news that we know who the man who reported to Lord Meriwell is."

Stokes sighed. "I agree. I simply can't see him doing any of it—and especially not with poison."

"Good point," Barnaby said.

They reached the front hall and made for the library.

Between them, they methodically searched the desk. Penelope was the expert at scanning documents, and Stokes and Barnaby searched, organized, and collated while she did.

Yet in the end, when she laid down the last sheet of paper and met Barnaby's eyes, all they'd gained was further frustration.

"Nothing," she declared in a dead, defeated tone. "Not one single mention of the House of Dreams or of Curtis."

She sighed and looked at the piles of papers stacked upon the desk. "The only thing we've established is that Lord Meriwell was not the most organized of men."

Accepting that they would have to wait for word from Curtis, Penelope and Barnaby elected to join the guests and family about the luncheon table, which had been set up in the conservatory, while Stokes returned to the inn to consult with Morgan.

Penelope approved of David's having taken Veronica out for the day in his curricle; according to Jensen, they'd planned to stop at an inn for lunch before returning to Meriwell Hall in the afternoon. Unless Penelope missed her guess, there was a romance pending there; she just wished she could give more time to actively fostering it, but at present, duty called.

She and Barnaby took their seats at the round table, with Lady Meriwell, Lord Iffey, all three Meriwell nephews, and the four Busseltons. The seating arrangement was informal, so Penelope and Barnaby claimed the places beside Lord Iffey, which left them facing the Busselton elders and Persimone Busselton, with Stephen beside her. Peregrine eagerly took the chair beside Barnaby, leaving Arthur and Peter to fill the remaining places, more or less opposite her ladyship.

The circular table allowed Penelope a clear view of most faces. As the company served themselves from the platters Jensen and the footmen had delivered, she took note of the expression, tone of voice, and overall composure displayed by those present. Most appeared to be attempting to behave as if this was a normal house party luncheon and were achieving that goal with varying degrees of success. Then again, this was a group of which two previous members had died by poison almost certainly administered by one of those currently at the table; small wonder that people felt unsettled.

Nevertheless, as Penelope had said to Stokes, the gathering provided an opportunity for her and Barnaby to observe whether the mounting tension was affecting any of their three major suspects in a telling and possibly revealing way.

While addressing a small serving of sliced ham, cheese, and fruit, she wondered if there might be an opening for her or Barnaby to toss a figurative spanner at the murderer and see who ducked.

She slid a sidelong glance at her spouse.

His gaze was on his plate, but he sensed her attention and met her eyes. He read the question there, hesitated, then faintly shook his head. *Not yet.*

She inwardly sighed. Patience was not her strong suit, and she had agreed to wait and see if any of the company broached the subject of the investigation first. They had to be curious as to how the investigators were faring, especially given that she and Barnaby had the leisure to join this gathering.

Finally, George Busselton put her out of her misery. He dabbed his lips with his napkin, then tentatively asked, "Has there been any progress, Mr. Adair? Anything you can share with us?"

Instantly, every eye but Penelope's fixed on Barnaby. He took his time setting down his cutlery and touching his napkin to his lips—giving Penelope plenty of time to assess the degree of anxiety exhibited by all there over his possible reply—then with an expression of benignity, in an even tone, he replied, "I believe the inspector won't mind if I report that there's been something of a breakthrough."

The interest around the table escalated by several degrees.

In measured fashion, Barnaby continued, "We discovered that Lord Meriwell had contacted an inquiry agent in London and, we believe, had requested a report about a particular business there." More for effect than anything else, Barnaby paused as if he was carefully considering his next words.

Intently, Penelope scanned the faces around the table, paying particular attention to Arthur and Peter, although she dutifully kept Stephen in her sights as well.

Then Barnaby went on, "Due to the sequence of happenings that appear to have arisen consequent to the agent reporting to his lordship, we believe there is a connection between the particular business enterprise—or at least his lordship's inquiry into it—and his lordship's murder."

"Good heavens!" Mrs. Busselton appeared more curious than shocked.

George Busselton looked taken aback and quite confounded. "A business venture is behind this?" His expression suggested he was imagining some sort of skullduggery enacted by strangers from outside the house.

A brief glance at Lady Meriwell and Lord Iffey informed Penelope that her ladyship continued to look rather lost, while Iffey's attention, as it had throughout, remained unwaveringly fixed on her ladyship.

Persimone and Peregrine Busselton seemed eaten by curiosity and quite desperate to learn more.

In contrast and to Penelope's chagrin, all three Meriwell nephews looked...*arrested* was the word that sprang to her mind. As if each of them couldn't make up his mind whether to be worried—more deeply worried—or not.

Imperturbably, Barnaby concluded, "We're awaiting further information." With a mild smile for the company, he added, "We're hopeful it will arrive soon."

For a moment more, everyone stared, then they looked down at their plates and pretended to give their attention to their meals.

Beside Penelope, Lord Iffey reached out and patted Lady Meriwell's hand. "It will all work out, my dear. Worry not. Our investigators know what they're doing."

On hearing those words, Penelope swallowed a disgruntled snort. In terms of eliciting some telltale reaction that would allow them to distinguish between their prime suspects, their ploy had failed dismally.

Indeed, Barnaby's revelations had put a dampener on conversation, which sagged to effectively none.

∼

After the by-then-largely-silent gathering in the conservatory broke up, Penelope and Barnaby returned to the library. They walked in to find David and Veronica had returned from their outing and, together with Stokes, were waiting to see whether Barnaby and Penelope had learned anything of note.

While she and Barnaby made their way to the armchairs where the others sat, Stokes opened proceedings with the news that Morgan, who'd been spending his time gaining the confidence of various groups of staff —that being the baby-faced constable's particular talent—had nothing of value to report. "He's convinced the staff are entirely innocent of any degree of complicity, and at this point, no one knows anything about the missing glass, either."

Having noted the color in Veronica's cheeks and that David was exuding an aura of satisfaction, Penelope hid her hopeful delight and, instead, slumped into one of the armchairs and blew out an irritated breath. "Barnaby played our little scene perfectly. Unfortunately, we didn't get the result for which we'd hoped."

Elegantly sinking into the armchair alongside hers, Barnaby dryly observed, "We did succeed in confusing George Busselton with our mention of a business being involved."

Penelope sighed and described what she'd seen in the faces around the table, dwelling most on the reactions of their three remaining suspects. "Sadly, increasingly worrying about what might come next— which is how all three of them reacted to our news—is perfectly explainable without them being the murderer. If we theorize that one of them is our villain, then as far as the other two know, we might be barking up some tree of a business that they have a connection with that, for some reason unknown to them, we see as incriminating." To David and Veronica, she explained, "We only said that it was a business in London, not that it was one in Seven Dials, so the innocent two wouldn't be certain they are not, somehow, implicated."

Stokes tapped a finger on the chair's arm. "Yet for our murderer... well, at the very least, the pair of you just tightened our screws."

David looked from Stokes to Barnaby. "I know we're inclined to drop Iffey from the suspect list, but his words to her ladyship are hardly an exoneration. He could be hiding some terrible secret from her ladyship as well as from everyone else."

Barnaby grimaced and inclined his head. "Unfortunately, that's true.

On the basis of everything we know to this point, Iffey remains an outside chance as our murderer."

Penelope sighed deeply. "So we're still waiting."

Penelope and the others had only just resignedly and somewhat morosely concluded that they could think of nothing else they could do to further the investigation when Jensen tapped on the door and, at Barnaby's command, entered.

His expression uncertain, Jensen approached, halted, and reported, "The gardeners were searching the borders around the house for the missing wine glass—which we still haven't found—but they came across a small brown bottle in the bushes along the family wing." Jensen focused on Barnaby. "The gardeners didn't know if the bottle would be of interest. I thought it best to ask."

Penelope leapt to her feet, and David rose, as did Veronica.

"I'd better take a look," David said. "If by chance the bottle contained prussic acid, then even handling the outside might be dangerous."

Jensen was quick to reassure them, "The gardeners wondered about that, and they swear they haven't touched the bottle."

"Good." David gathered Veronica with a glance.

About to head for the door, Penelope arched a brow at Barnaby and Stokes.

Stokes waved her on. "Go—we'll wait here in case there's any news."

For a second, she wavered—by news, Stokes meant the information from Curtis, and that would be the vital clue they needed to make sense of this case—but the lure of immediate action won out. She nodded and briskly led the way to the door.

In the front hall, she waved Jensen into the lead, and she, David, and Veronica followed the butler through the house, out of the side door, and around one wing of the house. Along that façade, a straight gravel path ran about ten feet from the house, and a thickly planted border filled the space between the path and the wall.

Halfway along the wing, a quartet of gardeners were clustered on the lawn.

As Penelope and the others approached, one of the gardeners—the oldest, judging by his grizzled appearance—stepped away from the group, crossed the path, and halted beside a leafy bush.

Penelope and the others neared, and she smiled at him. "What have you found?"

He ducked his head to her. "We was searching for the glass, but we found a bottle instead." He jabbed a finger at the bush. "In there, trapped in the branches. We weren't sure whether we should fetch it out."

David, who had halted beside Penelope, crouched to peer into the bush. "Just as well you didn't." He glanced up at Penelope, then pulled a handkerchief from his pocket. He shook it out over his hand, then reached into the bush and drew out a small brown bottle shaped more like a vial.

David held the bottle up to the light. "Empty. And the stopper's gone." Tipping the bottle, he squinted at the base of the label, then grunted and rose. "It's from a different London apothecary, another large emporium."

Penelope sighed. "So it's untraceable."

As David carefully wrapped the bottle in his handkerchief, he and Veronica nodded.

David paused, then he closed his hand around the bottle and held his fist for Penelope and Veronica to see.

The vial was completely hidden in his palm.

"A risky maneuver," David said, "but if the stopper was removed just before he got to the dining room, then all it would have taken was a single pass of his hand over the wine glass, and the deed would have been done."

Penelope nodded. "Yes. I see." She paused, contemplating the likely scene. "Not all that hard. Not if one had made up one's mind to do it."

"Indeed," David agreed.

Penelope noticed that Veronica was looking upward, studying the windows above.

When Penelope followed her gaze, Veronica raised her arm and pointed. "That's Sophie's room."

Penelope looked, then lowered her gaze to the bush in which the bottle had been found. The bush was almost directly below Sophie's window. Penelope huffed. "Obviously, we're supposed to deduce that Sophie poisoned her grandfather and flung the vial out of her window to get rid of it. Hah!" Her derisive tone effectively conveyed what she thought of that.

David regarded the wrapped vial. "This is still potentially dangerous. I'd prefer to dispose of it." He looked at Penelope. "But will Stokes need it for evidence, do you think?"

Penelope frowned at the bottle. "You've seen it, I've seen it, and Veronica's seen it. It's effectively untraceable. I can't see that keeping it will be of much use."

"Good." David turned to Jensen and the gardeners, who had been silently watching. He held up the handkerchief-wrapped vial. "Do you have somewhere you gather broken glass? If I break this there, any remaining poison will quickly evaporate, and any residue will vanish in the next rain and be of no further risk to anyone."

Between them, Jensen and the gardeners directed David, Penelope, and Veronica to an area between the rear of the kitchen garden and the stables.

"You'll see the pile," Jensen assured them. "It's quite sizeable."

With the gardeners resuming their search for the missing glass and Jensen returning indoors, Penelope and Veronica trailed David as he strode off across the lawn.

They found the six-foot-high pile of broken crockery and glassware behind the kitchen garden wall. Judging by the style of wares represented amid the detritus, the pile looked to have been continually added to over the past decade and more.

David hunted around and found two good-sized rocks. Crouching by the edge of the pile, he unwrapped the brown vial and carefully sat it on the flatter rock. After shaking out and setting aside his handkerchief, he used the other, larger rock to gently crack the vial, then he crushed and ground it to a powder.

While Veronica watched him, Penelope aimlessly wandered around the pile, noting the various patterns of crockery and glassware the house had at some point used. There was quite a mixture of styles and shapes...

She halted, blinked, then a wide smile split her face. "Aha!" Her smile grew. "Well, well, well."

She hiked up her skirts and clambered halfway up the shifting pile. She was on the side shaded by the kitchen-garden wall, opposite where David was working.

Alerted by her words and the grating of crockery, Veronica came around the heap. "What are you doing?"

Balancing awkwardly on the shifting pieces, Penelope bent over and used the hem of her skirt to grip and wriggle and eventually free the object that had caught her attention.

Carefully, still teetering, she held up her find. "This was sticking out in a rather odd way. I'm willing to wager a considerable amount that it's our missing wine glass."

She was holding the glass by its base. While the edge of the bowl was cracked and chipped, most of the glass was intact, and the bottom of the bowl was stained with the dregs of what appeared to be red wine.

Gingerly, she turned and made her way down the pile.

David had heard and came to join them. He reached out and gripped her elbow and steadied her down and off the shifting pile.

Once she was on firm ground, he wrapped his handkerchief around the stem so she could use that to hold the glass. Carefully, she gripped the protected section and released her skirt, then she, David, and Veronica examined the glass.

Veronica observed, "That does look like one of the set of glasses currently being used in the dining room."

Penelope raised her gaze to the house. "Let's see what Jensen thinks."

They found the butler in his pantry, and the way his eyes widened the instant he saw the glass answered their first question.

"Have any other glasses from this particular set recently been broken and thrown away?" Penelope asked. "Say over the past three months?"

His lips tight, Jensen shook his head. "Definitely not, ma'am. Other than the glass that went missing after his lordship died, that set is still complete."

She nodded. "Excellent. This is, therefore, our missing glass and no other."

Jensen was frowning. "I don't understand why we didn't find it earlier. I gave orders for the crockery-and-glass pile to be searched."

She smiled reassuringly. "You didn't find it then because it wasn't, at that time, there."

Jensen's face cleared. "Someone put it there after we'd searched."

"Almost certainly, which only underlines that our murderer knows this house all too well." She looked at David and Veronica. "Thank you, Jensen. I believe you may call off the search. We'll be in the library if there are any unexpected discoveries."

∽

Penelope took great delight in showing off her find to a suitably appreciative Barnaby and Stokes.

"Pure luck, of course," she admitted as she carefully set the glass, still banded by David's handkerchief, on the hearthstone.

"But good eyes," Stokes teasingly said, with a laughing glance at Penelope's thick-lensed spectacles.

She pulled a face at him, then sat in what had become her armchair. "All we've found today underscores that our murderer is someone who knows this house and its workings intimately and also that our murderer was intent on making Sophie their scapegoat."

Stokes nodded. "So we're looking at Arthur, Peter, or Stephen, with Iffey a very outside chance. And while we might have our prejudices over which one is our villain, in reality, we have no firm evidence on which to make that judgment."

"Yet," Barnaby appended. "I have every confidence that, Curtis being Curtis, his information will open our eyes."

"Or at the very least," Penelope said, "point us toward one of our suspects as the most likely."

Barnaby asked about the brown bottle, and Penelope and David confirmed what it had contained, and Penelope explained their decision to dispose of it.

Stokes grimaced, but accepted their reasoning. "If it comes to it, your testimonies will suffice."

David had been studying the wine glass sitting on the hearth. "I daresay there's enough residue there that an analysis might be of some use." He arched a brow at Stokes. "Should I arrange it?"

Stokes thought, then nodded. "Please. Given the bottle's gone, I feel a need to gather any proof that will help to anchor our case."

David smiled understandingly. "I'll take the glass, then, and see to it."

Penelope had been reviewing the situation. "We've found the missing glass, the missing mug turned up, and we have the bottle of laudanum and have located and disposed of the vial of cyanide." She looked at the others. "What we've yet to find is Sophie's diary."

Stokes's gaze rested on her. "Barnaby and I were discussing our potential case, and we really need to make a push to learn more about the nephews."

"We haven't delved into their characters," Barnaby explained. "Not beyond what we've seen for ourselves. As we're increasingly certain our murderer is one of the three, then while we're waiting for Curtis to give us more information, getting a better idea of their personalities will help shore up our eventual case."

"It might even help us define which one of the three is the villain." Stokes smiled winningly at Penelope. "We were wondering if you and Veronica might go and have a cozy chat with Lady Meriwell. If, as we're told, the nephews have been haunting the house for much of their lives, then her ladyship is likely to have a reasonably accurate view of their natures."

Penelope studied Stokes, then looked at Barnaby. Then she pushed her spectacles higher and nodded. "All right." She glanced at the clock, then at Veronica. "If we go now, perhaps we might share afternoon tea with her ladyship."

CHAPTER 11

$\mathcal{L}$ady Meriwell welcomed Penelope and Veronica into her sitting room and, of her own volition, invited them to partake of afternoon tea with her and the ever-present Lord Iffey.

When Penelope and Veronica readily accepted, her ladyship dispatched Iffey to ring for a maid, saying, "I'm so glad you've come up to see me. I feel quite the failed hostess, but I just can't bring myself to face the Busseltons. I'm mortified that through no fault of theirs, their family has been caught up in our drama, and while they cannot have anything to do with either death, they are stuck here, with the rest of us, while your friend, the inspector, sorts this out."

"I'm sure the Busseltons understand." Penelope sank into the chair Lady Meriwell had waved her to, facing the sofa on which her ladyship was sitting. "The situation can hardly be taken to be any reflection on you."

Sinking onto an adjacent love seat, Veronica murmured supportively, and Iffey, returning from having requested tea for four, gruffly stated, "Just so. No one will be blaming you for anything, my dear."

Lady Meriwell smiled fondly at him as he resumed his seat on the sofa alongside her. "But Iffey, dear, you've been hiding up here with me all this time and avoiding the Busseltons as well, so you can hardly claim to know what they think."

Caught out, his lordship grumbled something along the lines of "stands to reason."

Intent on steering the conversation away from the Busseltons, Penelope ventured, "I wonder, your ladyship, if you could clarify for me how matters stood within the Meriwell family. The relationships between your late husband and his younger relatives are potentially pivotal to our case, and we understand that there were underlying tensions between his lordship and at least some of his nephews."

"Well, yes, one might say that." Lady Meriwell paused as if uncomfortable and debating what to say, then she glanced at Iffey. "I truly do want to be helpful, Mrs. Adair, but..." She gestured vaguely. "Family, you understand? It's hard to know what's appropriate in these rather strange circumstances."

It was an appeal, one to which Iffey—to Penelope's pleased surprise —responded with sound common sense. "After all that's happened, Clementina, and with both Angus and Sophie to see avenged, I can't imagine anyone would disapprove of you giving Mrs. Adair as accurate a grasp as possible of how things are—or were—within the family." Iffey looked at Penelope. "Very important to old Angus, you know—the Meriwell family."

Penelope nodded. "We realized that."

At mention of her late husband's obsession, her ladyship straightened, and her chin rose. "Indeed. Family was everything to Angus, most especially preserving the family name. Making sure the family was never brought into disrepute. I believe I explained to you that it was dealing with his younger brother, Claude, that started Angus down that path. For years, Angus lived in constant fear of Claude plunging the family into the mire."

Beside her, Iffey was nodding. "Even while he was at school. From his earliest years, Claude was a bad 'un."

The maid tapped and entered, bearing the tea tray, and they paused while Lady Meriwell dispensed cups, and they sipped and sampled the shortbread biscuits.

Penelope was relieved when her ladyship returned to the subject without prompting.

"And then there were the boys—Claude's sons." Lady Meriwell grimaced. "Their mother was gently bred, but a weak sort. Claude rode roughshod over her, poor dear, and she passed away when the boys were quite young—as I recall, Peter was still in leading strings. There was no family on her side, so naturally, from that time on, we—Angus and I— made an effort to have the boys spend time here, with us. To give them a proper family life, something Claude paid scant attention to. I know Angus hoped that, by taking a hand in guiding Claude's sons, he could ensure they didn't follow in their father's footsteps."

Iffey put in, "Angus was determined to shape his nephews into more worthy men than their father."

"And then," her ladyship continued, "Claude died."

"In a curricle race!" Iffey gave vent to a disgusted snort. "Reckless to the last."

"How old were his sons then?" Penelope asked.

Lady Meriwell frowned. "I think…yes, Stephen was twelve, so Arthur must have been ten and Peter just eight years old. After that," she went on, "the boys were here whenever they weren't in school or staying with friends. This became their home. Our own son, Robert, was much older, of course, and he'd already married and left with Elizabeth, his wife, to do good works in Africa. That left Angus with Claude's three sons to bring up and mold into respectable gentlemen." Her ladyship sighed. "As matters panned out, while he succeeded in that with Stephen, Arthur and Peter seem to have reverted to type—meaning their father's type."

Iffey nodded. "Stephen was always a sound sort—he seemed to take after Angus more than Claude. Stephen's the sort you can always rely on to do the right thing, you know?"

Penelope nodded. "So Stephen and his lordship got along well, while with Arthur and Peter…" She left the implied question dangling.

With another snort, Iffey picked up her invitation. "Angus fought a losing battle with those two. They're Claude's sons through and through —feckless and uncaring of anyone but themselves."

Her ladyship's lips pinched, then she offered, "Once they'd gone on the town, Arthur and Peter never came here but that they wanted something—usually money—from Angus. In contrast, Stephen often came down just to spend a few days. He's always been a pleasant visitor, easy to please, and"—she glanced at Iffey—"I don't believe he ever asked Angus for so much as a penny."

"As far as I know, that's right," Iffey said. He glanced at Penelope from under his bushy eyebrows. "It's hardly surprising that Stephen is— was—Angus's favorite of the three. And with Robert gone"—he glanced swiftly at her ladyship—"and Jacob, too, then it'll be Stephen who steps into Angus's shoes, and by my reckoning, Angus would have been hugely relieved by that."

Her ladyship nodded. "At least he had one Meriwell male to take on the mantle of defender of the family name."

Iffey huffed. "At one point, Angus nurtured the hope that Sophie and Stephen might make a match of it—keeping any potential issue with Sophie within the family, so to speak—but that didn't go anywhere."

Penelope felt her eyes fly wide, but before she could voice any questions, her ladyship responded with a fatalistic air, "Well, it wasn't ever likely to go anywhere, was it?" Lady Meriwell shook her head. "I tried to explain to Angus that marrying her cousin Stephen simply didn't align with Sophie's great aim to take the ton by storm." She sighed, and her eyes filled with tears. "Poor darling." Her lip quivered. "Thanks to this foul murderer, she'll never see any ballrooms at all."

Abruptly, her ladyship swung her gaze to Penelope, and her eyes burned fiercely. "You must find who killed her—who took away her dreams, however silly and fantastical those were."

Holding her ladyship's gaze, Penelope inclined her head. "We will do our very best."

And she now had new facts and insights to ponder, including a heretofore unknown link between Stephen and Sophie.

In between talking, they'd finished the tea and biscuits and set down their cups and saucers. Penelope gathered Veronica with a glance, and they were about to stand when Penelope remembered her other reason for being there. She caught her ladyship's gaze. "We understand Sophie kept a detailed diary. We looked for it—"

"Oh—I have it." Lady Meriwell hurried to explain, "I wanted a keepsake of my granddaughter, so I had Pinchwell fetch it for me." Her ladyship glanced at the door that, presumably, led to her bedroom. "I haven't had the heart to open it yet."

Penelope could barely believe her luck, but... "When did you send Pinchwell for it?"

Her ladyship blinked. "It was later that morning. After we found Sophie dead." She studied Penelope's face. "Was that all right? I hope it wasn't the wrong thing to do."

"No, no," Penelope reassured her. "As long as you have it, all's well. But I would like to borrow it for a few days, if I may? Knowing what young ladies entrust to their diaries, then reading what Sophie wrote in hers will give me a better idea of what sort of person she was and why she might have been killed."

"Yes, of course." Lady Meriwell looked at Veronica. "If I could trouble you to fetch it, dear? It's on the far bedside table."

Veronica nodded and went to the bedroom door.

Lady Meriwell returned her attention to Penelope. "If you would let me have it back before you leave?" She glanced at Iffey and smiled wanly. "Perhaps by then, I'll have mustered the strength to read it."

Veronica returned and handed a bound journal to Penelope.

She took it, holding it between both hands, and half bowed to Lady Meriwell. "Thank you. I'll make sure to return it before we leave."

Her ladyship inclined her head in farewell, and Lord Iffey rose and escorted Penelope and Veronica to the door.

"Wanted to ask," Iffey gruffly said as they paused before the door, "about when the bodies can be buried." He glanced back at her ladyship, now sitting on the sofa and staring at the window with sorrow clearly etched on her face. "The news has spread to the village, and the vicar called earlier. I put him off, saying Clemmie wasn't up to seeing him yet, but the funerals will have to be faced. So"—he refastened his gaze on Penelope's face—"when do you think the bodies might be released, heh?"

Penelope thought, then replied, "I can't say, but I will tell Stokes that her ladyship needs to know."

Iffey nodded. "Good enough."

With that, he opened the door and held it for them, and with her prize clutched between her hands, Penelope made for the library.

She could barely wait to show off their find to Barnaby and Stokes. "It was Pinchwell—Lady Meriwell's dresser—who took it."

"When?" Barnaby asked.

"Later on the morning that Sophie was found." Veronica took the chair beside David. "Her ladyship wanted the diary as a keepsake."

"So." Stokes leaned forward and fixed Penelope with his gaze. "What did you learn about Lord Meriwell's relationships with his nephews?"

Between them, Penelope and Veronica faithfully recounted all they'd learned from Lady Meriwell and Lord Iffey regarding Lord Meriwell and his nephews.

"Having his lordship there was actually quite helpful," Penelope said. "His memories of how his good friend Angus felt about his three nephews were, in some respects, more insightful than what her ladyship told us."

"Oh," Veronica said. "And his lordship asked—more or less on behalf of her ladyship—as to when the bodies will be released so the funerals can be arranged." Veronica caught Stokes's gaze. "Penelope told him you would let them know."

Stokes looked at David. "Any reason I can't release the bodies for burial?"

David shook his head. "I've examined both sufficiently well to write my report for the coroner."

"Right, then." Stokes rose. "No time like the present. I'll go up and tell her ladyship."

The others murmured encouragement, all except Penelope, who was already flicking through the first pages of the diary.

Smiling slightly, Stokes shook his head at her and headed for the door.

After studying his already-absorbed wife for several seconds, Barnaby remarked, "While we can see you're eager to read all that Sophie wrote, I feel compelled to point out that, as it wasn't the murderer who removed the diary, there's no reason to suppose that there will be anything incriminating within its pages."

Penelope stilled, then she looked up and met Barnaby's eyes. Her own slowly narrowed, then she humphed and returned her attention to the journal in her lap. "I'll read it regardless. You never know what I might find that sheds light, however obliquely, on this mare's nest of an investigation."

That evening, after enjoying a highly satisfactory dinner in the inn's private parlor with Barnaby, Stokes, David, and Veronica, then seeing the latter couple off on the woodland path to Meriwell Hall, Penelope settled in the chair by the fire in the parlor and gave her attention to Sophie's journal.

Barnaby and Stokes sat at the table and prepared to amuse themselves with a game of piquet, an older game they'd developed a liking for—something about pitting their wits against each other.

Penelope left them to it and dove into the diary.

She'd already discovered that, as most young ladies' diaries did, Sophie's current journal commenced on the first day of the year. In some respects, that was useful; it meant Penelope was plowing through only the last five months of Sophie's life. Nonetheless, as Sophie was a keen diarist, filling multiple pages every night, recounting the events of her daily life and touching on her hopes and dreams, there was plenty to digest, and moving forward through the months would take time.

Manfully, Penelope resisted the urge to leaf ahead and was soon glad she had. Starting from early in the new year, Sophie's entries detailed what, to Penelope's experienced understanding, appeared to be a subtle yet distinctly determined pursuit of Sophie by her cousin Stephen.

That, Penelope reasoned, must have been the outcome of Lord Meriwell's notion—no doubt shared with his favorite nephew, Stephen—that Stephen marrying Sophie would be an excellent idea.

From what Sophie had written, she'd actively considered the proposition of becoming Stephen's wife, weighing up the pros and cons with a maturity with which Penelope hadn't previously credited her but which, the further Penelope read, Sophie had, indeed, possessed. In the end, after much deliberation, Sophie had elected to place her trust in love; she'd been determined to make her mark in London and search out a gentleman who could command her affections, and she was very clear in her own mind that she was not in love with Stephen. Or he, with her.

Sophie's decision embodied a straightforward wish for her future, one Penelope could only applaud. Reading further, she found herself wishing Sophie hadn't died, for the diary brought to life a sensible and pragmatic young woman who had lurked behind her melodramatic exterior.

Increasingly, Penelope concluded that Sophie's flirting with hysteria had been—as Lady Meriwell had stated—merely Sophie's way of getting what she wanted, especially when battling her grandfather's arguments and his notions of how she should live her life.

Penelope found herself sympathizing with the murdered girl.

And growing increasingly determined to see Sophie's murderer hang.

Engrossed, she continued reading through Sophie's descriptions of a series of attempts she had made to communicate her decision that she saw no future for herself with Stephen, culminating in a last bid for utter and unassailable clarity, when she'd written Stephen a letter clearly, concisely, and reasonably stating her position and putting a definitive end to any hopes he—no doubt supported by Lord Meriwell—had continued to entertain.

Penelope sighed and turned the page—and nearly dropped the diary.

She seized it with both hands, then flipped back a page, then forward again, feeling her eyes widen as she realized what she was seeing. "Good Lord!"

Barnaby and Stokes glanced sharply her way. Both took in her expression and swung to face her.

"What is it?" Barnaby demanded.

Almost bouncing with elation, Penelope surged to her feet, holding the diary, opened to the critical page, before her. "I *knew* there was something odd about that supposed suicide note." She crossed to the table and triumphantly laid the opened diary between the men. "And here it is." She jabbed a finger at the page, and both men leaned closer to read.

Barnaby realized the implication first. "Stephen was wooing Sophie?"

"Yes! Didn't we mention…" Her words trailed off as she realized they hadn't. Quickly, she explained, "Iffey mentioned it this afternoon. It seems that, earlier this year, Lord Meriwell had formed the notion that it would be a good idea for Stephen to marry Sophie, thus keeping her odd behavior within the family, so to speak. According to Sophie's diary, Stephen was willing, and Sophie didn't immediately refuse. She considered his suit quite carefully and surprisingly sensibly before deciding that such a match wouldn't suit her. Of course, egged on no doubt by his lordship and presumably seeking to please, Stephen persisted, although I would say he didn't apply any undue pressure. Not of any sort."

She paused, then said, "From what Sophie has written of Stephen's behavior, I would say that he, too, wasn't truly enamored of Lord Meriwell's scheme. However, Stephen persisted to the point that Sophie believed she needed to put her refusal to him in writing, which she did."

Penelope pointed to the open diary. "And voila! Before you, gentlemen, is a draft of the letter she subsequently sent Stephen, and you will note that the words that would have appeared as a single, last line in her missive read, 'I'm so very sorry.' And she signed the letter 'Sophie.'"

Stokes was nodding. "Her suicide note was the last page of the letter she sent Stephen."

"Yes!" Penelope said. "Exactly!"

"Well," Stokes said as he closed the diary, "at least we now know where the damned thing comes from and that it isn't a suicide note at all, which confirms our belief that Sophie was murdered. Unfortunately"—he raised his gaze to Penelope's face—"even if the letter was sent to Stephen, that doesn't necessarily mean that he was the one who left it by Sophie's bed."

Penelope nodded. "I would wager both Arthur and Peter—no matter that they don't get along with Stephen—call at his lodgings from time to time, even if only to see if they can extract some cash."

"Indeed," Stokes said. "So either could have found the letter and taken it—"

"And"—Penelope wrinkled her nose in disgust—"used the last page to implicate Stephen." Her shoulders sagged, and she grimaced ferociously. "Damn it! We *still* can't tell which of them is our murderer!"

~

Over breakfast the next morning, Barnaby, Penelope, and Stokes reviewed what they felt they could legitimately define as fact backed by actual solid evidence.

Barnaby pointed out, "Despite that the so-called suicide note being part of a letter to Stephen fails to distinguish between the Meriwell nephews, it does, fairly definitely, rule out Iffey as a suspect."

Penelope crunched her toast and, after swallowing, said, "I seriously doubt that Stephen would entertain Iffey in his rooms, and I can't see Iffey calling on Stephen out of the blue."

Stokes wasn't quite so convinced. "While I can imagine a scenario that might have moved Iffey to call on Stephen at his home, I admit that's a long shot. It's far more likely that one of the other two filched the letter. It seems like just the sort of thing they might do, thinking to gain some advantage later."

Barnaby inclined his head. "There's certainly no love lost between the three."

Stokes sipped his coffee, then lowered the mug and looked from Penelope to Barnaby. "So are we in agreement that, as the case now stands, the evidence points decisively toward one of the three nephews being our murderer?"

Barnaby and Penelope nodded.

Then Penelope tipped her head. "Regarding the antagonism between the three, I got the impression that the feeling is higher—of a different order—between Stephen and the other two. I wouldn't say Arthur and Peter are friends, but they're not as set against each other as each seems against Stephen."

Barnaby inclined his head. "I concur, but I'm not sure that observation gets us any further, at least not at this point."

Penelope grimaced.

Stokes straightened. "As we're still waiting on word from London, I suggest we see what more we can learn about our three prime suspects—and yes, I agree that Arthur and Peter are the more serious contenders." He looked at Penelope. "You learned about their earlier years from Iffey and her ladyship, but we need to know more about them as adults."

Penelope frowned. "I stayed up reading Sophie's diary all the way through. Sadly, she didn't comment much about her cousins."

"We don't even know where in London they live," Barnaby pointed out. "That might be revealing." He looked at Stokes. "We should ask Wishpole—he's almost certain to know."

"Good idea." Stokes jotted in his notebook. "And we should also see what else he knows of the three—or at least what else he will tell us. We might be able to get a better handle on how pressing their motives might be."

"Or whether there are any other motives we've yet to learn about," Penelope added, "and whether any are especially compelling in terms of the murderer acting when he did."

"We should also ask about the terms of the will," Barnaby said, "and how the bequests change now that Sophie—previously the major beneficiary—is also dead."

Stokes pushed back his chair and rose, bringing Barnaby and Penelope to their feet. Stokes met their eyes. "We need to make some decisive headway soon. I've agreed to release the bodies tomorrow, and after that, I can't see that our presence here is likely to get us any further."

They returned to Meriwell Hall to find David and Veronica waiting for them in the library.

After they'd claimed their usual armchairs, Penelope shared what she'd learned from the diary, then handed the journal to Veronica and asked her to return it to Lady Meriwell with Penelope's thanks.

"But isn't it evidence?" Veronica glanced at Stokes.

"Of a sort," Stokes conceded. "But if the diary's safely with her ladyship, we'll know where to lay our hands on it if we need it. And sadly, as Penelope said, the existence of that entry suggesting that the suicide note was the last page of a letter to Stephen Meriwell doesn't help in distinguishing which of the three nephews left it beside Sophie's bed."

Veronica grimaced, but nodded. "I'll go up and see her ladyship later."

David added, "We've already checked in with Lady Meriwell this morning. She said she's hoping to talk to the local vicar today, about arranging a joint funeral for Lord Meriwell and Sophie."

Penelope observed, "That will be a sad day for this household."

"It will be especially hard on her ladyship," Veronica said. "She asked, and I've agreed to stay on, at least until the funerals are over."

David glanced at Veronica, then diffidently said, "I'm afraid I need to return to London this evening. I can't put off my other patients any longer. As it is, I've been lucky none of my currently expecting ladies are approaching their confinements."

Stokes sighed. "I can only hope that we'll have some news from Curtis during the day—some clue that will point definitively to our murderer."

"As the evidence now stands," Barnaby reiterated, "we have nothing that distinguishes which of the three nephews is our murderer. All we can state is that, almost certainly, one of them is the villain of this piece."

"We thought to ask Wishpole," Penelope said, reminding Stokes and Barnaby of their agreed next step, "about what he knows of the three— where they live and his opinions of their characters—and also for an explanation of how the bequests and inheritances now stand."

Barnaby nodded. "In light of Sophie's murder, we need to know how those have changed." He looked at David. "I take it Wishpole is still here?"

David and Veronica nodded. "I believe," Veronica said, "that he intends to remain until after the funerals."

"No doubt he'll read the will to the beneficiaries after the wake," Stokes said. "No sense in him traveling back to London only to return within a few days."

"Especially not at his age," Penelope added.

"From what I gathered," David said, "like us, he's hoping to see the murderer exposed, caught, and justice done. He was Lord Meriwell's solicitor for decades and feels the losses as much as anyone."

"That's reassuring." Stokes rose. "It gives him good reason to allow us to pick his brains."

Stokes tugged the bellpull, and when Jensen arrived, sent him to ask Wishpole to join them.

When the door closed behind Jensen, Penelope looked at David and Veronica. "How are the Busseltons faring?"

With a wry smile, David reported, "The younger two continue to be avidly curious about the investigative process. They've been asking leading questions of me and Veronica whenever they get the chance."

"Meaning," Veronica put in with a smile, "whenever they find us out of sight of their parents."

"Indeed." David's smile widened. "The elder Busseltons' attitude has firmed into what I would describe as bracing themselves for whatever might come, even though neither has any idea of what that might be."

"Both are concerned," Veronica went on, "understandably so, at the prospect that 'whatever might come' will bring adverse repercussions for their family, purely by association—by them being here when the murders occurred."

Penelope grimaced. "One can hardly discount such anxiety." She paused, then observed, "Protecting family, especially a family's good name, has been something of a theme in this case."

Barnaby inclined his head. "Lord Meriwell's devotion to protecting the family name is almost certainly what got him killed."

Stokes nodded. "Because of the killer's certain knowledge that his lordship would act, strongly and decisively, against whoever is behind the looming family scandal." He looked at the others. "Meaning the scandal this business in Seven Dials—the House of Dreams—apparently represents."

The door opened, and Jensen ushered Wishpole in.

They all rose, and while Barnaby and Stokes fetched another armchair to enlarge their circle, Penelope and Veronica greeted Wishpole with welcoming smiles and urged him to the chair closest to the fire.

The elderly yet still determinedly dapper solicitor returned their smiles with a rather wan smile of his own and, leaning heavily on his cane, allowed Penelope to assist him into the comfortable chair.

The investigators resumed their seats, and once Wishpole had settled, Barnaby commenced with "I believe we can rely on your discretion over what we're about to reveal."

Wishpole's eyes widened, and his brows rose. "Of course, sir. That goes without saying."

Barnaby inclined his head in acceptance, paused to marshal his thoughts, then said, "Information has come to light that indicates that the murderer of both Lord Meriwell and Sophie Meriwell is one of his lordship's nephews. As of this moment, the evidence we have does not allow us to identify which of the three is our villain, but we're expecting to receive information from London shortly that will be, we hope, definitive and conclusive. In the meantime, while we await that critical information, we thought to widen our knowledge of the three men and hoped to pick your brain regarding what you know of them."

"For instance," Stokes said, "do you know where they live?"

Wishpole nodded. "Stephen maintains lodgings in Jermyn Street. Arthur has rooms in James Street, off Haymarket, while Peter has rooms in an establishment on Chandos Street, north of the Strand."

Stokes was busily jotting, so Barnaby asked, "If possible, can you give us your opinion of the characters of the three men?"

Wishpole thought, then wrinkled his nose. "As I will most likely find myself acting for at least two of them, I would really rather not say."

Regardless, his dryly contemptuous tone conveyed his general opinion.

Penelope asked, "Is it possible for you to tell us whether any of the three are, to your knowledge, under duress of any kind? Are they subject to any pressure that might push them to murder?"

Wishpole frowned. "I fear I am not well acquainted with any of the three. And what little I do know of their...pressures—for instance, Arthur wanting his lordship's horse and Peter being in debt—I learned from Lord Meriwell rather than directly and so have no actual knowledge of the matters."

The investigators shared resigned looks, then Barnaby said, "Turning from the personal, we wished to ask if you could explain in more detail the legacies that will accrue to each of the three men under his lordship's will."

"And," Penelope added, "whether and in what way Sophie's subsequent death has changed any of those inheritances."

Wishpole studied them for several silent seconds, his gaze passing over their faces before fastening on the empty hearth. The slight frown that knitted his lined brow stated he was thinking, most likely weighing up their request against his duty to the family.

None of them spoke or even twitched. They waited, hoping...

Eventually, Wishpole raised his gaze from the hearth and fixed it on Barnaby and Stokes. "As is customary, his lordship's last testament will be read to the family after the funeral. However, from my knowledge of the family and my consequent deductions, I have arrived at much the same conclusion as you, and I'm concerned that the villain might find some way to slip free of the law's net. As you have confirmed, the evidence is sparse and, sadly, unspecific. Given Lord Meriwell's instruction that I arrive here prepared to legally alter his will, I can only conclude that he was intent on seeing the villain of this piece struck out and deprived of any inheritance. As my first and dominant duty remains to his lordship and, beyond him, to her ladyship and the principal heir, then I believe that, at this time and in this situation, it's appropriate that I assist you by explaining as much as legal restraint allows."

Stokes inclined his head. "Thank you, sir."

Everyone else looked encouraging.

Wishpole drew breath and admitted, "Like you, on the basis of what I know as fact, I cannot distinguish which of the three—Stephen, Arthur, or Peter—is the murderer. I might have opinions based on observations of the three men's characters, but they are not facts. So"—Wishpole blew out a breath—"let me start by telling you how matters stood before Miss Sophie's untimely death."

Penelope kept her gaze firmly fixed on Wishpole's face. For a legal eagle, his face was unusually expressive; it was easy to discern what he disliked or disapproved of and equally easy to gauge what had gained his approbation.

Wishpole continued, "Under Lord Meriwell's will, all three nephews stood to gain to a greater or lesser degree. First, Arthur Meriwell has been left the stallion that I understand he's been hounding his lordship over for the past few years. Peter Meriwell will receive an amount sufficient to meet what his lordship believed was the sum of Peter's immediate debts. Stephen Meriwell has been left a somewhat larger amount. Most of Lord Meriwell's unentailed wealth—which includes this house and the estate that supports it and all monies in the Funds—go to Lady Meriwell during her lifetime, and otherwise, had Miss Sophie lived, to her. Sophie was by far and away the largest beneficiary."

Puzzled by what seemed to be a glaring omission, Penelope asked, "What about the title and the entailed estate? From what I gathered from the Busseltons, Stephen expects to inherit those."

Wishpole sat back and steepled his fingers before his face. "I believe Stephen and many others expect that he will ultimately inherit both, but first, he will need to establish that Jacob Meriwell, Robert Meriwell's son and Lord Meriwell's grandson, is deceased. I am aware that the family believe that to be the case, but beliefs are not facts, and the court will insist on proof of that claim. Stephen will have to produce substantive proof of Jacob's death or else move to have Jacob formally declared dead and then wait for a rather large number of years to pass before petitioning the courts to grant the inheritance."

Mildly, Wishpole met Stokes's gaze. "To my certain knowledge, no formal declaration of the assumed death of Jacob Meriwell has yet been made."

Barnaby was frowning. "Are you saying that Jacob's death was never confirmed? That there's no actual evidence of it?"

"Just so." Wishpole paused, then added, "I am aware that Lord Meriwell led others to believe that his grandson had followed his parents to Africa and, subsequently, died there, but if there ever was any actual evidence to support that assertion, I have never seen it, and his lordship has—again, to my certain knowledge—never presented any such evidence of Jacob's death to any court."

"So essentially," David said, "there is no death certificate for Jacob Meriwell."

When Wishpole nodded, David explained to the others, "That means that legally, he's still alive."

"Indeed." After a moment, Wishpole continued, "And to clarify, the physical estate tied to the title of Lord Meriwell, Baron Meriwell of Alderley, is a ruined castle in a barren field in the Midlands, along with twenty acres of surrounding land. As inheritances go, the title is worth more socially than the entailed estate is worth financially."

Frowns deepened as they wrapped their minds around those facts.

"I see," Stokes eventually said. "So as things stand, Stephen might be in line for the title, but to actually inherit it, he will have to provide proof to the court that his second cousin, Jacob, is actually dead."

"Correct." Wishpole looked at Penelope. "Now, to the point you raised, dear lady, about how Sophie's death alters the inheritances, there is, effectively, no change to the direct bequests to her ladyship and the three nephews. However, as to Sophie's portion, which is the bulk of the unentailed estate beyond its use by Lady Meriwell during her lifetime, that will revert to Lord Meriwell's senior direct descendant, meaning whoever legally claims the title."

David confirmed, "The unentailed estate doesn't get split between the nephews?"

"No. It does not." Wishpole paused, then added, "That might have provided a significant motive for any of the three, of course, but no. The bequests and inheritances will not play out in that way."

"So," Barnaby summed up, "as matters stand now, post Sophie's death, the title, entailed estate, and the bulk of the unentailed estate go to..."

Wishpole filled in, "Jacob Meriwell if he's alive or Stephen Meriwell if Jacob is proved dead."

Stokes was almost scowling. "So you're saying that neither Arthur nor Peter benefit from Sophie's death, but Stephen potentially might."

"And by quite a significant amount," Barnaby said.

Wishpole looked from one to the other, then nodded. "That's the situation in a nutshell."

Penelope pulled a rueful face. "While it's tempting to conclude that given Stephen stands to gain so much, *he* must be the murderer, we cannot discount that, despite benefiting significantly less from his lordship's death, Arthur or Peter could have been sufficiently desperate to kill his lordship for their inheritance—for the horse or the money to pay off pressing debts. And then they killed Sophie purely as a way to cover their tracks." She paused, and her brows rose. "And perhaps they used Sophie's letter to Stephen in the hope that Stephen would be taken up for both crimes."

Suddenly struck, she looked at Wishpole. "If Stephen was convicted of his lordship's and Sophie's murders and Jacob Meriwell is proved to be dead, who inherits the majority of the Meriwell estate then?"

Wishpole blinked at her, then slowly replied, "Arthur."

The five investigators exchanged a questioning—speculating—glance.

"That," Stokes said, "is convoluted, but it just might fit."

After a moment, Barnaby said, "Correct me if I'm wrong, but I believe we can now feel confident that Lord Meriwell discovering the association of one of his nephews with the House of Dreams in Seven Dials, combined with that nephew's certain knowledge that his lordship would act to disown the guilty party, was what prompted the guilty nephew to murder his lordship."

The others around the circle, including Wishpole, nodded.

"However," Barnaby went on, "as of yet, we cannot tell if Sophie's murder was purely an attempt to provide the authorities with a convenient scapegoat or if it was also motivated by a desire to gain more financially from the Meriwell estate."

They all thought that through, then Stokes groaned and fell back in his chair. "All of which means that we *still* can't tell which of the three nephews is the murderer."

CHAPTER 12

enelope had little appetite for the cold collation Jensen
provided for the investigators in the library. Wishpole
remained to take his luncheon with them, and she listened as the others
chatted about inconsequential subjects while slaking their appetites.

They finished eating and pushed away their plates and were disaffect-
edly looking at each other, waiting for someone to suggest what they
might do next, when Jensen returned with the footmen to clear the table.

Leaving Thomas and Jeremy to gather the crockery, Jensen paused by
Penelope's chair. When, curious, she looked his way, he said, "If you
would, ma'am, Mrs. Hutchinson would like a word."

Penelope blinked. "Yes, of course." What on earth the housekeeper
would want with her, she couldn't imagine.

Before she could inquire, Jensen half bowed. "If you could come to
Mrs. Hutchinson's sitting room, ma'am, I suspect that might be wisest."

Curiouser and curiouser. Penelope exchanged a mystified look with
Barnaby and Stokes, then nodded to Jensen. He drew out her chair, and
she rose and glanced at Veronica. "Perhaps Nurse Haskell could show me
the way?"

Veronica all but leapt to her feet and joined Penelope as she made for
the door.

Jensen held it for them.

Penelope noted his relieved expression and inwardly wondered all the
more.

~

Veronica led the way past the green-baize-covered door to the housekeeper's room. She tapped on the door frame, then pushed the partially open door wide, ushered Penelope through, and followed.

At their entrance, Mrs. Hutchinson rose from the chair behind her small desk, and a maid—the upstairs maid, Jenny—leapt up from a stool on the housekeeper's right.

Both women bobbed curtsies, then Mrs. Hutchinson waved Penelope and Veronica to a pair of simple armchairs set facing the desk. "Thank you for coming, ma'am. Miss Haskell."

They sat, and Mrs. Hutchinson resumed her seat and waved Jenny to her perch.

Intrigued, Penelope prompted, "How can I help?"

Mrs. Hutchinson looked at Jenny. When the girl, eyes huge, looked helplessly back, Mrs. Hutchinson sighed and said, "Jenny works above stairs, and one of her duties is to change the sheets on the family's beds. She was busy doing that on Wednesday afternoon."

Penelope clarified, "The afternoon after Miss Sophie died?"

Mrs. Hutchinson's lips tightened, and she nodded. "Death or no death, we still had to change the sheets." When Penelope dipped her head in understanding, the housekeeper continued, "The linen closet on the first floor is off the gallery, across the stairwell from the corridor leading to the family's rooms, including Miss Sophie's chamber."

Mrs. Hutchinson looked at Jenny and, with a hint of exasperation, said, "There, now. You tell the rest."

Staring at Penelope, Jenny swallowed, gripped her hands tightly in her lap, and offered, "The door was open, and I was sorting through the sheets." She paused, then said, "I had to leave the door open, or I wouldn't have been able to see. It's right dim in that spot. I was there, in along the shelves of sheets and towels, when I heard a noise. Not close and not loud, but like a door closing. I'd thought as I was the only one up there, so I looked out, and I saw Mr. Stephen walk away from Miss Sophie's door."

Penelope considered that, then confirmed, "This was the afternoon following the morning when Miss Sophie was found dead."

Jenny nodded. "About three in the afternoon, ma'am. I always change the sheets on Wednesdays, you see, but what with the ruckus in the morning, I was running late."

"Yes, I see." Penelope knew that households of the ilk of Meriwell Hall's, managed by competent housekeepers like Mrs. Hutchinson, tended to run like clockwork. Regimentation was the only way to ensure all the work got done. "Could you see if Mr. Meriwell was carrying anything?" He couldn't have had the diary, because Pinchwell had removed it earlier in the day.

"He didn't have anything in his hands, ma'am." Jenny paused, then added, "And I didn't get the impression he'd put anything in his pockets, either." The maid met Penelope's gaze. "I could tell because he was walking up the corridor straight toward me, and the light from the cupola was beaming that way, onto him."

Penelope really didn't think Stephen was their murderer, yet still, she asked, "Did he see you?"

"Oh no, ma'am," Jenny assured her. "The linen closet's tucked away in the shadows, and of course, I didn't want to intrude on the family, so I stayed still, and I'm sure he didn't see me at all."

Penelope accepted that as most likely accurate. "Could you see his expression? Was the light good enough for that?"

"Yes, ma'am. When he got to the end of the corridor and stepped into the gallery, the light from above fell full on his face."

"So how did he look?"

Jenny squinted, apparently imagining the sight and searching for words, then offered, "Puzzled. A bit worried-like." She focused on Penelope and added, "Like he couldn't figure something out and was anxious about it."

"I see." Penelope paused, but could think of nothing more to ask. She focused on Jenny, then glanced at Mrs. Hutchinson. "Thank you both. That might well help us. You were right to think that we'd want to know."

Both women smiled in relief.

Penelope glanced at Veronica.

Veronica met her gaze, and together they rose and, with gracious nods to the housekeeper and maid, left the pair to their day and headed back to the library.

With Veronica on her heels, Penelope reentered the library to find four faces turning their way, each sporting an expression of hope mingling with curiosity.

She sighed, went forward, and dropped into her now-usual armchair. "Jenny, the upstairs maid, saw Stephen leaving Sophie's room on the afternoon Sophie died. He was empty-handed and looked puzzled."

"In Jenny's words," Veronica added as she sank into the chair beside David, "'he looked as if he couldn't figure something out and was anxious about it.'"

Barnaby arched his brows. "Had he been looking for the diary? Or something else?"

Penelope frowned. "If he'd been after some keepsake, then I can't imagine why he would have looked puzzled. There were plenty of little knickknacks there, pieces that might serve as mementos."

Stokes inclined his head. "So it seems more likely that he'd been looking for the diary and couldn't think where it might have gone."

"Or," Penelope added, "who might have taken it. You would imagine he would have known of Sophie's habit. Perhaps he wondered what she'd written about his pursuit of her. He wouldn't want the Busseltons to learn about that."

"True," Barnaby said. "And by all accounts, of the three nephews, he'd spent more time with Sophie."

Wishpole looked faintly confused. "What's this about Stephen pursuing Sophie?"

Barnaby explained that Lord Meriwell had encouraged a match between Sophie and Stephen. "Thinking to keep Sophie's behavior within the family, so to speak."

"And from what Sophie wrote in her diary," Penelope said, "Stephen was diligent in endeavoring to win her to his—or rather his uncle's—cause, but Sophie declined. She had other ideas about finding a husband."

"Ah." Wishpole nodded. "That does sound like the sort of scheme his lordship would have hatched, and he'd mentioned how set Sophie was on taking the ton by storm." His expression grew somber. "Poor girl."

Wishpole's ensuing glumness was infectious; they all seemed to slump dejectedly in their chairs.

Penelope looked around the circle and sighed. "It seems quite unfair that while clues like Stephen looking for the diary, the suicide letter that wasn't, the vial of cyanide, and the missing glass are now falling into our laps, none of them point anywhere useful, much less definitively. I mean" —she gestured—"it's not as if we're imagining Stephen as our murderer."

Stokes grunted. "Arthur or Peter. Theoretically, Stephen is still a suspect, but my money's on one of the younger pair."

"Unless," Barnaby said, "there's something major we've yet to stumble on, Stephen has by far the weakest motive. He might stand to inherit a reasonable sum of money and, ultimately, might inherit the title and entailed estate—and now Sophie's portion as well—yet there's zero evidence that he actually needs those things, much less that he needs them desperately enough to murder to get them."

Penelope grimaced. "And as for Stephen's standing, financial and character-wise, we have the testimony of Lord Meriwell himself. His lordship would never have encouraged a match with Sophie if he didn't know Stephen to be a sound and decent man."

"Plus," Veronica pointed out, "we have Mr. Busselton willing to countenance an offer for his daughter's hand."

Penelope nodded. "Even though, regarding Stephen, Mrs. Busselton, Persimone, and Peregrine are still on the fence, none have raised any factual objection." She paused, then observed, "I have to say that, for myself, in all we've seen while here, I haven't noticed any behavior on Stephen's part that would make me question his honesty or integrity."

Veronica offered, "He's always seemed the steady, reliable, sensible, even staid nephew."

Wishpole concurred. "My experience is that Stephen is the conservative sort, while the other two are unpredictable and wild."

Barnaby glanced at the clock on the mantelpiece. "Meanwhile, we're running out of time. It's already two o'clock."

Stokes, too, glanced at the clock, then growled. "If O'Donnell doesn't bring us news from Curtis soon, I'm going to be very displeased."

As if summoned by his superior's words, O'Donnell arrived in the library less than ten minutes later.

The sergeant stuck his head around the door and, spotting them, came in and carefully closed the door behind him.

Noting O'Donnell's eager expression as he crossed toward them, expectation gripped Barnaby, and together with his co-investigators, he sat up, alert and waiting to hear what the sergeant had to report.

O'Donnell halted before the armchairs and dipped his head respectfully to the company, then fixed his gaze on Stokes. "The gent you sent me to speak with wasn't of a mind to entrust what he had to say to me. Instead, he's come himself and is waiting at the inn."

Barnaby exchanged a surprised glance with Stokes and Penelope. For Curtis to put aside whatever he was doing in London and come into Surrey purely to give them information…that had to mean something.

Seeing the questions in their faces, O'Donnell added, "He didn't want to come to the house in case someone here recognized him. He said that was something you wouldn't want, so he's waiting at the inn." O'Donnell added, "Once I told him about the murders, I didn't need to say anything more to convince him to help us, but he says you need to hear what he knows directly from him—just as it was with Lord Meriwell himself."

Barnaby met Stokes's eyes, then Penelope's. None of them knew what to make of that.

Stokes gestured. "If he insists…" He rose, and the rest of them quickly got to their feet, except for Wishpole.

Noting the attitude of straining at the leash that seemed to have infected them all, Barnaby warned, "We can't race off. We need to look like we're just strolling back to the inn."

Stokes nodded. "I don't understand why Curtis is playing least in sight, but he's wily enough to have good reason. We don't want to tip our murderer off and send him running."

"Not when we're finally about to learn which of the nephews he is." Penelope summoned an airy and completely false smile, walked to Veronica, and linked her arm with hers. "We'll lead the way. Just a gentle stroll through the wood."

Barnaby grinned and, with David, fell in behind the ladies.

Stokes paused beside Wishpole. "If you would, sir, it would be helpful to have someone remain within sight of our suspects while we hare off to learn our murderer's identity."

Wishpole met Stokes's gray gaze and smiled faintly. "I will repair to wherever the bulk of the company are and keep an eye on proceedings."

Stokes grinned, inclined his head, and strode after the others.

Of course, once Penelope and Veronica reached the wood and the trees' shadows enveloped them, they increased their pace and were striding briskly by the time they got to the inn.

Nevertheless, they walked calmly through the door as if they were merely returning to their temporary residence.

With his palm at the back of Penelope's waist, Barnaby nudged her toward their private parlor, and smoothly, she steered Veronica in that direction.

He paused just inside the door, allowing Stokes and David to amble past him, then he scanned those in the inn's taproom and spotted Curtis nursing a pint of ale at a table in one corner.

Curtis had, of course, seen them and was watching Barnaby.

Without making any show of it, he tipped his head toward the parlor, then turned and followed the others.

He entered the parlor behind David and held the door open, and seconds later, Curtis walked in, carrying his signature low-crowned hat as well as his half-full glass of ale.

Stokes had diverted to give orders for drinks at the bar, and he followed the experienced inquiry agent into the room.

Barnaby shut the door and waved toward the table, to which David had pulled up an extra chair. "Curtis, you know my wife, myself, and Stokes. This is Dr. David Sanderson and Miss Veronica Haskell."

David reached across the table and offered Curtis his hand. "I'm the Meriwell family's physician."

Curtis gripped and shook and arched his brows. "Quite some way from Harley Street."

David smiled. "In my line of work, I'm often called to country houses, and this was a true emergency."

"So it seems." Curtis exchanged polite and faintly curious nods with Veronica.

David glanced at her and explained, "Miss Haskell is a nurse. She'd accepted a position here at my instigation, which is how she came to be mixed up in this strange affair."

"Ah." Curtis set down his glass and pulled out the chair beside Penelope. "Strange, indeed." He sat, set his hat on the table, waited while Stokes and Barnaby claimed seats, then said, "This is probably the strangest case I've come across in all my years."

A tap on the door heralded the serving girl with a tray of glasses and two jugs, one of ale, the other of cider. The company remained silent while she placed the tray on the table, and when Barnaby assured her they needed nothing more, she bobbed and left.

The instant the door closed, as one, the investigators focused on Curtis.

Entirely unnecessarily, Stokes informed him, "We're agog to hear what you can tell us about the House of Dreams."

Curtis snorted and reached for his ale. "More like the House of Nightmares."

He waited, sipping and eyeing them as Barnaby poured two glasses of cider for the ladies and David filled three glasses from the jug of ale.

Once everyone was supplied, Curtis looked at Penelope and Veronica and, in his deep voice, rumbled, "My apologies, ladies, but the business of the House of Dreams is highly unsavory."

Penelope inclined her head, acknowledging the warning. "Don't mind our ears. We need to learn what this is about more than we need to preserve any rosy-eyed view of the world."

Veronica murmured, "Indeed."

Curtis studied Penelope for a moment, then looked into his glass. "Think of the worst debauchery you can imagine, then think of something worse. Significantly worse. Something skin-crawlingly bad. What goes on in the House of Dreams is about the lowest ebb of humanity I can think of or care to know exists. That's what the House of Dreams dishes up to those brainless enough and wealthy enough to be lured through its doors."

"Lured?" Barnaby frowned.

Curtis nodded. "By invitation only, because, unsurprisingly, the owners don't make the bulk of their quite spectacular profits from payments for the entertainment they offer. They rake in the money from what enjoying that entertainment exposes the idiot punters to."

Stokes's eyes widened in understanding. "Blackmail."

Curtis's expression grew grim. "That's their real game."

"So," Penelope said, "one of the Meriwells was foolish enough to accept the lure and is now being blackmailed."

Curtis met her gaze levelly. "Don't get ahead of me." He paused, then said, "I'd better tell this tale from the start. If I don't, you'll just get confused."

"Starting at the beginning is usually wise," Barnaby drily observed.

Curtis grunted, paused to marshal his thoughts, took another sip of his ale, then commenced. "Lord Meriwell contacted me about four weeks ago. He came to my office in the City. Turned up out of the blue and hired me to verify the truth of a rumor that had come to his ears, namely that a member of his family—he assumed one of his nephews—was frequenting a place known as the House of Dreams in Seven Dials. If the rumor proved true, he wanted me to ascertain the identity of the nephew involved."

The heavy-set inquiry agent shrugged. "Seemed straightforward enough."

"And?" Stokes prompted.

"It took quite a lot of exceedingly careful digging," Curtis went on. "More than I'd expected, truth be told. I had to first learn who to speak with, then find those people and discover how to get them to talk. It took me and my crew weeks, which is not the norm for inquiries of that sort. The layers of secrecy surrounding the House of Dreams and its operations are numerous and extensive. However, eventually, we had verification enough, solid enough, to satisfy his lordship's request. We could say absolutely that the rumor was true—that a Meriwell was frequenting the House of Dreams—and we knew his identity."

Curtis grimaced and tugged one ear lobe. "The thing was, the information went further than I'd anticipated, and a good bit deeper than I knew his lordship was expecting. It turned out that the Meriwell involved was not frequenting the place as a punter. Instead, he's one of the founding joint-owners, and more, he's the owner primarily involved in luring the most profitable punters through their doors."

For the first time in a long while, Penelope was truly shocked. "A Meriwell—one of his lordship's nephews—was acting as a...a *shill*?" She couldn't keep the scandalized tone from her voice; she was sincerely horrified. "For a place as awful as that?"

Curtis's expression showed he understood her reaction; indeed, that he shared it. "Exactly. And once I learned that, I knew I had to be very sure—incontrovertibly certain—when I reported to his lordship as to which nephew it was."

"It was only one of them?" Stokes asked.

Curtis nodded. "But in this case, one was more than horror enough." He paused, then went on, "I decided to do the surveillance personally so I'd be able to tell his lordship that I'd seen who it was with my own eyes. I knew he'd find it difficult to accept—knew that I'd need every piece of rock-solid evidence I could lay my hands on."

He glanced at Barnaby and Stokes, and both nodded in understanding.

Curtis continued, "By then, I had more than enough solid documented evidence about the place and the business and how it was run and about the other four joint-owners. They were easy enough to get information on —they're crooks to their eyeballs, and I know how crooks work, and I know who they deal with. The Meriwell involved was a harder nut to crack. If he has a bank account, I've yet to find it. He always seemed to deal in cash, so there was no discernible, provable connection between himself and the ongoing business. I daresay his name appears on certain deeds and agreements with the other joint-owners—in fact, given this Meriwell's current situation, such documents have to exist—but they are guarded too well for even me and the more light-fingered of my crew to access."

He glanced at Stokes. "You'll need warrants, a squad of experienced men, and a safe-cracker to get hold of them, but they'll be there, somewhere."

Grimly, Stokes nodded.

Curtis went on, "The one piece of the jigsaw I was lacking was irrefutable evidence—something seen with my own eyes—that would identify which Meriwell it was. I couldn't risk going into the place myself —too likely someone there would recognize me—and besides, I wasn't about to serve myself up as prey to the likes of the joint-owners." He paused, then head tipping, went on, "In the end, it actually wasn't all that difficult. I set up as an old codger sleeping rough in the alley across the lane from the House of Dreams. The man—our Meriwell—was so over-weeningly confident, he was totally unaware that he was being watched as he ushered his latest prey through the doors of the House of Dreams."

Curtis paused, then added, "I watched for six nights and saw him take three different young gentlemen inside, each time patently playing the role of experienced elder introducing a less-experienced man into the ways of the world. And every morning, by the time I quit my post just before dawn, although Meriwell had left the place, the newcomer he'd brought in the evening before hadn't."

Stokes grimaced. "I see."

Barnaby stirred. "So which Meriwell was it?"

Stokes straightened. "Arthur or Peter?"

Curtis gazed at them. "That was it, you see. It wasn't either of the younger pair. The Meriwell involved in the House of Dreams is Stephen Meriwell."

"Oh." Penelope felt as if all the pieces of the puzzle—the clues they'd gathered—whirled kaleidoscope-like around her head, then stopped and fell into her brain, forming a completely new pattern. "That's why you needed to be so sure. And that's where he gets his funds from." She looked at Stokes and Barnaby. "We never heard from what business Stephen derives his income, which has to be at least reasonable given his clothes and his lodgings."

The others were staring and gaping at Curtis and, now, at her.

She looked at Curtis. "I want to say you're joking, but I know you aren't." She adjusted her spectacles and declared, "The pieces all fit, far too well to be anything but the truth."

Curtis dipped his head to her. "On the evidence, Stephen Meriwell is a past master at pulling the wool over people's eyes. That's why he excels in his role of shill for the House of Dreams—young gentlemen from wealthy, well-born families meet him and think he's just like them, only a few years older and wiser. He knows the ropes—the ropes they'd like to learn—and they swallow the stories and assurances he feeds them, and then he reels them in, and they follow him through the doors of the House of Dreams. By the time they wake up and learn the truth about him, it's too late. They're caught on the House's hook and can never dare tell anyone what he's truly like, much less what he's doing."

Curtis looked at Stokes. "The House of Dreams has been a blight on London society for the past ten years, and it's been able to remain undisturbed by the authorities because of the people it has in its clutches. Too many young men from the best families."

Stokes returned Curtis's regard, his own gray eyes steely. "Earlier, you said you had evidence to implicate the four other joint-owners and that Meriwell was also a joint-owner."

Curtis nodded. "Stephen Meriwell was one of the founding five joint-owners. He might even have been the instigator behind the scheme. He and the four others—I can give you their names later, as they're all underworld 'businessmen' you'll be happy to get your teeth into—established the House of Dreams. From the first, it was designed to be exclusive and to generate most of its profits from blackmail. However, Stephen himself had no money, which is why he needed the other four to bankroll the business. The other four contributed their share as well as a quarter each of Stephen's share—each share was a fifth each, so not inconsiderable, even in Seven Dials. I was told that the agreement struck was that Stephen would contribute his services in luring lucrative punters through the doors for ten years, and after that time, he would repay the other four for the monies they'd effectively loaned him, but on the basis of repaying them in total a fifth of the current value of the business."

Barnaby's eyes widened. "Ah. I take it that the business, having grown steadily through the years, is now worth much more than it was at the beginning."

Curtis smiled thinly. "Just so." He looked at the others. "The ten years was up late last year. The other four served Stephen with notices of monies due. I've been told they were quite taken aback when he told them he didn't have the wherewithal to pay them. They knew how much profit he'd taken from the business—they shared the profits equally, after all—and they didn't understand and couldn't believe that all that cash had gone."

"Because they don't live within the ton," Barnaby wryly put in.

Curtis dipped his head. "Exactly. Stephen had squandered the lot. So instead, he asked for the 'loan,' as it were, to be extended for another ten years."

"They refused." Penelope's eyes gleamed. "Of course they did— they'd be getting nervous about dealing with someone that profligate. And so they told Stephen he had to find the money, and that was why he tried to court first Sophie and, when that didn't work, Persimone Busselton."

"I don't know about any courtships," Curtis said, "but from different sources entirely, I know that three of the four other joint-owners were counting on that cash. They need Stephen to pay them, and they need that to happen soon, and they've told him as much and made it very plain."

"So," Stokes said, "Stephen's time has run out, and he has to find cash —a significant amount of cash—soon."

Curtis nodded. "More cash, all at once, than he's likely ever contemplated, and he's been given a month to come up with his dues. Either pay up or, in three of the four cases, prove that he'll be able to pay by the end of the year."

"That's why he came prepared with the poisons," Penelope said. "Not just one poison but two poisons. The cyanide for his uncle, to be followed by high-strength laudanum for Sophie." She looked around the table. "Stephen was always going to murder both Lord Meriwell *and* Sophie. He needed money—or the promise of it—and he needed much more than his lordship was planning to leave him."

His lips grimly set, Barnaby nodded. "He needed Sophie's portion as well."

"And," Stokes put in, "most likely, he's assuming that, with Jacob Meriwell presumed dead, he'll be able to skip through the legal hoops and claim everything."

"More," Barnaby said, "he won't even need to actually clear those hoops to lay his hands on the money he requires. With Lord Meriwell dead, and Sophie as well, and Jacob Meriwell presumed to be so, moneylenders will be lining up to loan Stephen money on the basis of his expectations."

"I hesitate to point this out," David said, "but surely we now have to question whether Jacob Meriwell actually went to Africa at all. Was he Stephen's first victim?"

The others stared at him as that sank in.

Aghast, Veronica raised her hands to her face. "This is simply *horrible*." She met David's eyes. "Can you imagine what his lordship must have felt, learning that the one nephew he thought he could count on was…well, even more dreadful than his father?"

Barnaby nodded. "That Stephen posed even more of a threat to the family name than Claude ever had."

Penelope huffed and crossed her arms. "*I'm* still struggling to get my brain around the fact that it's Stephen who's the villain. His lordship must have been staggered by the news."

Curtis nodded. "He was. It took me over an hour to convince him, but once I had, he grew angry and determined."

"He gave you that letter for Wishpole," Barnaby said.

"Yes. And by the time I left," Curtis said, "he was absolutely determined to put an end to Mr. Stephen Meriwell and the House of Dreams. If I understood his lordship correctly, disowning Stephen was just the first step. I believe he would have summoned the authorities—turned Stephen in—as a way to throw up a social bulwark of sorts to protect the rest of the family."

Stokes nodded. "That could have been his plan, and I daresay it might have worked to stem the backlash against the family."

"Hmm." Penelope, too, nodded. "In that regard, the fact that the Busseltons had also been hoodwinked would have worked in his lordship's favor. It wasn't just the Meriwell family Stephen had tricked."

Stokes pulled out his notebook—in deference to Curtis, until then left in his pocket—and looked at Curtis. "This House of Dreams. What's the address?"

Curtis rattled it off. Stokes wrote down the information, then closed his notebook. "Once we're squared away here, I'll arrange to have a squad of the Met's best pay a visit."

Barnaby refocused on Curtis. "During your meeting with his lordship, was there a particular piece of evidence that convinced him it was Stephen and not Arthur or Peter?"

"Aye," Curtis said. "In part, it was seeing Stephen with my own eyes and being able to describe him. I'd never met the man—or his brothers—but the family resemblance was clear enough, and when I described the man who lured young gentlemen into the House of Dreams as having lighter-colored, not quite blond, pale-brown hair, I could see his lordship started to believe. But the final nail in Stephen's coffin was these." Curtis pulled out a small stack of papers from his pocket.

He handed them to Stokes. "I kept these as insurance. Don't ask me how I came by them, but as you can see, they're invoices of sorts for supplies to the House of Dreams, and Stephen's signed them as having received the goods. He doesn't normally do that, but he must have been left in charge of the place for a few months. The invoices are several years old and were stuffed in a drawer in his bureau. He'd probably forgotten they were there." Curtis tipped his head at the papers. "Once his lordship saw those, that was it. He believed completely and utterly. And as I said, he started to get angry."

Having received the invoices from Stokes and glanced over them, Barnaby passed them to Penelope. She studied them, then shook her head and handed them to David. "I know we kept Stephen on our list of suspects, but that was more because we couldn't cross him off, not because we actually thought it might be him!" She pulled a face at Barnaby. "I feel so wrong-footed!"

He gave her a rueful look, then switched his attention to Curtis. "Other than giving you the letter for Wishpole, did Lord Meriwell tell you anything more of his plans regarding Stephen?"

"Only that he intended to disown him, and that would be just the beginning." Curtis grimaced. "His lordship was out for blood, it seemed." He paused, then added, "I think that once he started to believe, too many things fell into place—like where Stephen got his money from through all these years. His lordship muttered that he'd always wondered about that, but of course, being a gentleman, had never asked."

Curtis looked at Barnaby. "When I left Lord Meriwell, he was rather grimly silent. He'd given me the letter for Wishpole, and like I said, I think he was working out more pieces of the puzzle by the minute. Just as I reached the door, he mumbled something that sounded like 'Good Lord! So that's why he wants to offer for her!'"

"Oh my goodness, yes!" Penelope's eyes widened. She looked at the others. "The man is an absolute *fiend*. He wants to marry Persimone Busselton so he can get his hands on her dowry, but that would merely be his first step. Later, he could—and assuredly would have—let George

Busselton, MP, know what 'business' Stephen, by then Busselton's son-in-law, was engaged in, what business paid the bills of the house he by then would have been sharing with Persimone, his wife."

"George Busselton would have paid and paid and paid," Stokes said, "to keep such a scandal out of the newspapers."

"To keep his son, Peregrine, free of the taint." Barnaby felt equally horror-struck as he met Penelope's eyes. "That's diabolical. Persimone's dowry, and George's position, and Hermione's as well, and then there's Peregrine! It's a never-ending cascade of blackmail."

Stokes growled, "There's no doubt at all that Stephen Meriwell is exceedingly clever in choosing his victims."

Curtis nodded. "That's what made him such an excellent shill. He has a remarkable talent for appearing to be a sincerely sound and solidly respectable gentleman. By the time his victims realize the truth of him, it's too late to escape his clutches."

"True evil," David said. "It's as if he has no bounds."

"It's what Veronica said earlier," Penelope said. "Stephen is *far* worse than Claude ever was."

Barnaby shifted. "Stephen is Claude with much greater ambition."

They all sat and pondered, then Stokes shifted, grimaced, and finally, raised his gaze and looked around the table. "Be that as it may—and it seriously pains me to say this—even with Curtis's evidence linking Stephen to the House of Dreams, when it comes to his lordship's murder and to Sophie's murder, we have no incontrovertible evidence that it was Stephen who committed the deeds. Yes, he could have poisoned both—we've established that much—but so could Arthur and Peter. *We* know that Stephen killed his uncle, and with his lordship mentioning the House of Dreams to Stephen when he arrived, Stephen had good reason to act immediately and end his uncle's life."

"And with that murder accomplished," Barnaby said, his tone coldly judgmental, "he moved to his next victim and murdered Sophie, too, using her character against her in order to paint her death as a suicide driven by guilt over her killing his lordship."

David's lip curled. "The depths to which Stephen has sunk—deliberately and willingly—are almost beyond comprehension."

Penelope stirred, then looked around the table. "We now know, with absolute certainty, who our murderer is. So"—her eyes bright, she challenged everyone there—"how are we going to bring the fiend to justice?"

Slowly, Stokes shook his head. "I honestly don't know." He glanced inquiringly at Penelope with the air of one hoping she might have an answer.

She smiled intently and, surprisingly mildly, suggested he call for a tea tray. "We need sustenance to feed our brains."

The tea tray was duly ordered and arrived. They ate, drank, and discussed.

As Penelope had expected, after every option was thoroughly explored, they all agreed that, in this strange and difficult situation, there was really only one way forward.

"Right, then." She pushed her spectacles higher on her nose and announced, "We have to stage a denouement and pray he panics and gives himself away."

CHAPTER 13

*W*ith the rest of their company, including Curtis, O'Donnell, and Morgan, Penelope walked briskly back to Meriwell Hall.

The afternoon was well advanced; it was nearing four o'clock when they emerged onto the rear lawn and headed for the house.

Stokes dispatched Morgan to haunt the stable in case Stephen slipped through their net and made a dash for it; the Channel coast wasn't that far away. The rest of them gained the terrace and paused, surveying the foursome playing on the croquet lawn and the others sitting and watching the game from beneath the spreading branches of the nearby oaks.

David tipped his head toward the latter group. "Go," he said to Stokes, Barnaby, and Penelope. "Veronica, O'Donnell, Curtis, and I will set our stage."

"In the drawing room," Penelope instructed. "It's better suited to our purpose."

Veronica nodded and looked at David. "We'll set up there."

The group split, with David, Veronica, O'Donnell, and Curtis entering the house through the side door while Stokes, Barnaby, and Penelope descended to the lawn and strolled toward the figures reclining in the chairs beneath the oaks.

They'd agreed that to give their denouement every chance of success, they should request Lady Meriwell's permission and her assistance to gather all involved for their performance.

Penelope fought to keep her gaze from the croquet players, especially Stephen Meriwell. She and her co-investigators recognized the need to obscure their purpose and were focused on behaving as if they were about to admit defeat and retreat to the capital. Consequently, she, Barnaby, and Stokes had to affect a dispirited air. All three had played such charades before, pretending to be flummoxed even though they knew who their villain was, but all of them were very aware that this time, they were attempting to deceive a master of deception.

Stephen Meriwell was assuredly that; even now, as Penelope surreptitiously studied him from the corner of her eye, she couldn't detect any mark of his evil deeds in the façade he displayed to the world.

The croquet game had been rather desultory and, today, involved Arthur and Persimone playing against Peregrine and Peter. The contest paused as Stokes, Barnaby, and Penelope approached, and all four players halted and straightened, resting their mallet heads on the grass, the better to discern what was afoot.

Wishpole and Lord Iffey were seated in cane armchairs to one side of the lawn and appeared to have been idly chatting; they broke off their exchange and gazed questioningly at Stokes, Barnaby, and Penelope as they drew near.

George Busselton and Stephen were standing a few yards beyond the cane armchairs in which Lady Meriwell and Mrs. Busselton were relaxing. Deploying his customary veil of genial respectability, Stephen had been chatting with his hoped-for father-in-law with an attitude of sophisticated confidence, but together with Busselton, Stephen fell silent the better to hear what Stokes, Barnaby, and Penelope had come to report.

Other than running a sharp eye over the three of them, Stephen showed no sign of excessive interest, and as Penelope, Barnaby, and Stokes were taking pains to appear dejected and the very opposite of hopeful or expectant, she felt passingly confident that Stephen's lack of nervousness, much less trepidation, was genuine; he had no idea they had him in their sights.

Excellent.

As they'd planned, they halted before the older ladies, and Barnaby stepped to the fore and bowed to Lady Meriwell. "Your ladyship." He nodded to Mrs. Busselton, then returned his gaze to Lady Meriwell and rather formally said, "Inspector Stokes, my wife, and I thought that, prior to us leaving for London, we should give you and the company here an accounting of where the investigation stands."

Her ladyship looked faintly troubled. "Oh, I see. You're leaving."

Penelope stepped in to reassure her, "The investigation will continue, but it seems we've exhausted the local information, and that being so, it's difficult to justify remaining at Meriwell Hall."

Iffey had got to his feet and came stumping up to stand behind her ladyship's chair. From under beetling brows, he scowled at Stokes. "Giving up, are you?"

Stokes managed to look believably irritated. "No, my lord. As Mrs. Adair intimated, the investigation will remain open, and further inquiries will be made, but at this time, we lack definitive proof as to who killed Lord Meriwell and Miss Meriwell." Stokes looked disgusted to have to admit that. "Consequently, we're unable to make an arrest at this time, but we sincerely hope that situation will change. The Metropolitan Police are not in the habit of giving up."

Penelope was quietly impressed by how much truth Stokes had crammed into those sentences while appearing to be defending their failure to identify the murderer.

Lady Meriwell had been looking back and forth between Stokes and Iffey. Now, she raised a hand. "Help me up, Iffey. Of course we wish to hear whatever the inspector and Mr. and Mrs. Adair have to tell us." Her ladyship gripped Iffey's arm and allowed him to assist her out of the chair, then she inclined her head graciously to Stokes, Barnaby, and Penelope. "I, for one, would like to hear what you have discovered so far." She glanced around. "If the others wish to be informed as well…"

Penelope could have kissed the older lady, for of course, all those present responded with alacrity to that invitation. How could they not? They were all equally curious.

Her ladyship read the answer to her implied question in the faces about her and in the way the players abandoned their mallets. She returned her gaze to Penelope. "In that case, I think the drawing room might be best, don't you, Mrs. Adair?"

Penelope inclined her head. "I expect everyone will feel more comfortable there."

She'd been prepared to steer the company that way, but her ladyship suggesting it was much better. Less likely to highlight that Penelope and her co-investigators were intent on controlling all aspects of the gathering.

Mrs. Busselton was quick to agree and gathered her brood with a single commanding glance; no doubt she was looking forward to her family being released and able to return to their home. Not that she had to encourage Persimone or Peregrine to fall in as the group set off across the lawn; the younger Busseltons were openly curious and eager to learn what the investigators were about to reveal, however humdrum that might be. The pair followed their mother, her ladyship, and Iffey, drawing Arthur and Peter Meriwell with them.

Stokes, Barnaby, and Penelope stood back and allowed the company to go before them. Wishpole came to join them. His wise gray eyes had seen more than most of the ways of men and police inspectors. Of all those present, he seemed most aware that Stokes, Barnaby, and Penelope were not as lacking in direction as they were striving to appear. But Wishpole merely nodded to them and paused beside Penelope, waving to Stephen and George Busselton to go ahead.

Busselton strolled behind his children and Arthur and Peter, with Stephen keeping pace alongside. Stephen was walking with his hands clasped behind his back, his head tilted deferentially toward Busselton, his posture indicating that he was paying close attention to the wisdom the elder Busselton was imparting. From the few words Penelope caught, the advice related to Stephen taking his seat in the House of Lords.

Jumping the gun a trifle, but if Stephen was thinking along such lines, it seemed likely he considered himself safe.

Once Stephen had passed, Penelope smiled intently and linked her arm in Wishpole's, and with Barnaby on her other side and Stokes flanking Wishpole, the four of them brought up the rear of the small procession.

They followed the others into the house and through the front hall to the drawing room.

Just before the drawing room door, Penelope slipped her arm from Wishpole's and urged him to go in, murmuring sotto voce, "David Sanderson will show you where to sit."

Briefly, Wishpole studied her, then glanced fleetingly at Stokes and Barnaby before facing forward and walking slowly into the room.

Through the doorway, Penelope scanned the disposition of the company, noting with approval that David and Veronica had adhered to the agreed arrangement. The fireplace lay directly opposite the door, and on the long sofa to its left sat three Busseltons—Mrs. Busselton, flanked by her children, with Peregrine closer to the hearth. Mr. Busselton sat in an armchair alongside the end of the sofa occupied by his daughter, and Wishpole had been guided to an armchair beside the MP.

To the right of the fireplace, opposite the sofa, Lady Meriwell and Lord Iffey sat on a love seat with Iffey nearer the hearth. On her ladyship's other side, three smaller armchairs had been arranged in a line, and the Meriwell nephews had been directed to those.

Penelope wasn't surprised to see that Stephen had claimed the position on her ladyship's left; she hid a satisfied smile.

David and Veronica occupied straight-backed chairs set a yard behind the love seat, the position intended to indicate that they were not directly involved in the performance that was about to ensue.

As Penelope had directed, the low table that normally filled the space between the sofa and the love seat had been removed, clearing the way for the three principal investigators to walk directly up the room to their chosen stage before the fireplace.

A low hum of conversation, laced with an element of speculation, blanketed the company.

Her gaze returning to Stephen, who, with his expression open and earnest, was speaking with his aunt, Penelope murmured, "He's definitely a cool customer."

From behind her, Stokes growled, "He genuinely seems entirely unconcerned."

"However," Barnaby countered, "we know he's a consummate actor." A soupçon of predatory expectation threaded through his voice. "It's going to be interesting to see how he reacts when we draw back the veil and reveal his true character."

We can only hope. Penelope drew in a deep breath and led the way into the room.

Stokes followed her up the long room to the fireplace, and Barnaby brought up the rear. As they'd arranged, Stokes took position at center stage, in front of the fireplace, facing down the room. Penelope flanked him on his left, standing closer to where David was sitting. If Stephen bolted for the long window to the terrace on that side of the fireplace, David would be there to block any escape.

In claiming his position on Stokes's right, Barnaby, too, had a long window to the terrace beyond him. As he settled facing the room, Jensen closed the double doors, and Barnaby allowed his gaze to, apparently idly, sweep over the company seated before them.

Arthur was gnawing at a fingernail and looking worried and distinctly wary.

Peter was constantly shifting position as if he couldn't find a comfortable pose.

Both appeared a great deal more guilty than Stephen, who calmly viewed the three principal investigators with an open, expectant expression.

Just waiting to hear what we're going to say before we go away.

Barnaby suppressed a snort and, with a comprehensive glance, took in the concerned expressions on Lady Meriwell's and Lord Iffey's faces. They were anxious over what might or might not be revealed and were prepared to be disappointed rather than being worried on their own accounts.

Judging by the elder Busseltons' expressions, they were patently hopeful that this gathering would be the last of its sort they would have to attend and that they would be free to leave shortly after its conclusion. In contrast, the younger Busseltons appeared keen to hear all the investigators deigned to share and were avidly curious as to what might transpire.

All in all, everyone was reacting exactly as Barnaby, Penelope, and Stokes had foreseen.

Barnaby glanced at Stokes.

Stokes caught his eye, fractionally dipped his head, then faced the room and stepped slightly forward, instantly capturing everyone's attention. "Thank you for your cooperation and your help to date with this case."

Other than Barnaby, Penelope, and Stokes, no one saw the drawing room doors open and O'Donnell and Curtis slip into the room. Silently, they shut the doors and took up positions on either side, with Curtis assuming a stance that, despite his civilian garb, declared him just another of Stokes's men.

"We have now confirmed," Stokes continued, "beyond all doubt, beyond all question, that both Lord Meriwell and Miss Sophie Meriwell were murdered. They were poisoned, and the details are as follows."

Succinctly, with a dry delivery that owed much to having long experience in reciting evidence in court, Stokes described how his lordship was poisoned with cyanide dropped by sleight of hand into his wine glass as the company gathered in the dining room.

That was more than most had known before, and palpable unease spread as the realization took hold that—without doubt or question—the murderer still sat among them.

Imperturbably, in the same even tone, Stokes continued, revealing that his lordship's wine glass had subsequently gone missing. Without naming names, he commented, "Given the movements of the company and the staff, only certain of those present could have hidden the glass, and its later retrieval from the broken-glass heap only reinforced our thoughts on who could be responsible. Specifically, who our murderer might be."

Stokes paused to sweep the company with his gaze, then went on, "When it came to Sophie Meriwell's murder, the mechanism was remarkably similar. She was given an overdose of high-strength laudanum that could only have been put into her mug of cocoa by someone she allowed into her room after the maid had delivered the nighttime drink. Again, a degree of sleight of hand had to have been employed. We are, consequently, confident that the murderer of both his lordship and his granddaughter are one and the same person." He paused, eyeing the now-rapt company. "We are looking for only one murderer."

Judging by the expressions Barnaby saw as he glanced around the gathering, the steady recitation of fact following fact had succeeded in drawing everyone in, capturing all in a net of unwilling fascination. The two who had died had been people they knew, and the manner and method of their deaths held a certain macabre attraction.

An attraction Stokes fed by moving on to outline possible motives for the murders, which, unsurprising to anyone, centered on inheritances expected from his lordship's will. A recounting of the bare facts made Arthur and Peter squirm, but Stephen looked, if anything, mildly amused by his brothers' discomfort.

Indeed, Barnaby thought, Stephen looked distinctly smug.

Stokes progressed to recounting their clues, which made the younger Busseltons sit up even straighter. Mention of the man who had called at the house prior to the Busseltons' arrival caused Stephen to blink, his expression blanking, but that was a reaction his brothers shared. Stokes explained how the man's visit had precipitated his lordship's ire on that fateful evening—that, they'd all noticed at the time—and then stated that they'd been forced to send to London for further information regarding the unknown man in an attempt to discover what he had disclosed to Lord Meriwell.

The expression on Stephen's face was almost bland, but his eyes were shifting, his brow faintly furrowing as he wondered who else knew of his misdeeds—who else knew enough to be a threat to him and, without doubt, how he could silence them.

Stokes returned to the missing glass and its discovery in the broken-glass heap, plus the discovery of the vial that had contained the cyanide in the bushes bordering the family wing. "Increasingly, we grew sure that the murderer is a member of the family. Everything points to someone who knows this house well and who stands to gain from his lordship's will."

With his gaze resting on the three nephews, Stokes listed again the legacies each would receive due to his lordship's death. Both Arthur and Peter had paled and were doing excellent imitations of rabbits trapped before a fox, but Stephen remained outwardly undisturbed; he knew everyone there thought he was well-to-do and didn't really need the money his lordship had left him.

As far as anyone knew, he was certainly not desperate for his legacy in the way Arthur and Peter demonstrably and provably were. Indeed, neither Arthur nor Peter protested the obvious conclusion Stokes was leading the company to draw, namely that one of them was the murderer.

Watching the nephews closely, Penelope hoped Stokes knew better than to press too hard; both Arthur and Peter were as tense as bowstrings. They—the investigators—didn't need the pair to break and throw their careful plans into disarray.

In contrast, Stokes's direction had reassured Stephen. He was starting to relax again.

He was almost smiling when, without warning, Stokes shifted their line of attack to the business in Seven Dials.

Stephen's features blanked, and he visibly stilled.

Stokes explained how his lordship had been overheard telling Stephen that his lordship wanted to speak with him privately about the business in Seven Dials. "Stephen denied any knowledge of such a business, and it was suggested by several sources that the business might have links to Arthur or Peter, but both denied it, convincingly so."

Stokes looked at the younger pair.

Penelope could almost see their burgeoning relief.

Stokes went on, "No one seemed to know to what the phrase 'the business in Seven Dials' referred. Mr. Wishpole had never heard of it. It wasn't and never had been a part of or connected to the Meriwell estate. The reference was a puzzle that took time and the assistance of members of Mr. Adair's information network in London to solve."

Penelope saw Stephen stiffen. His expression grew discernibly wary.

"The first piece of news to reach us was inconclusive," Stokes said, and Stephen's tension eased a fraction. "But," Stokes continued, "the information led us to the man Lord Meriwell had hired to look into the matter. We learned that, most likely through friends he met at his club in London, Lord Meriwell had heard a rumor linking a Meriwell with a most unsavory business in Seven Dials. Subsequently, his lordship hired a man known as the most-discreet inquiry agent in London to ferret out the truth and, if a Meriwell was, in fact, involved in that business, to identify which Meriwell it was."

At the edge of her vision, Penelope saw Curtis's lips curve slightly at that "most-discreet" description. However, the focus of her attention remained on Stephen, who now looked a trifle wild-eyed.

Stokes didn't give Stephen time to regroup. "We learned from Curtis, of the Curtis Inquiry Agency, that the 'business in Seven Dials' that his lordship had hired the firm to investigate was called the House of Dreams." Stokes glanced at the Busselton ladies and tipped his head their way. "For our purposes, we only need to note that the House of Dreams was a brothel that catered to the worst of human nature and, more, that the principal source of profit for the business was not the so-called entertainment it offered but extortion and blackmail of those unwary enough to be lured through its doors." Stokes didn't pause but hammered his points home. "The agency discovered that the rumor his lordship had heard was accurate. Further, that a Meriwell was a joint-owner of the business and, indeed, had been one of its founders and that the business has been operational for at least ten years."

Stephen's eyes had flared, and he'd gone preternaturally still.

Relentlessly, Stokes continued, "It took Curtis and his associates some time to be sure of the identity of the Meriwell involved, but once they were, Curtis realized that to convince his lordship of the truth, incontrovertible evidence would be needed."

The entire company were hanging on Stokes's words, waiting for the revelation that had to be coming.

Stokes glanced at Arthur and Peter, who appeared as puzzled and intrigued as anyone. "Curtis watched the House of Dreams for a week and saw the Meriwell involved lead young, wealthy, inexperienced gentlemen through its doors. Essentially, he saw the Meriwell involved deliver up young men to the never-ending blackmail practiced by the five owners of the place." Stokes drew in a breath and switched his gaze to Stephen's now-white face. "The Meriwell Curtis saw was Stephen."

Stephen reared back as if struck. "No." His gaze darted around the room, then locked on George Busselton, and Stephen attempted a reassuring smile. "This is nonsense." Stephen looked at Stokes. "Everyone knows—"

"That you're the reliable, steady, respectable Meriwell nephew?" Stokes's expression was harsh. "We know that's what you led everyone to believe, the charade you played and played exceedingly well, but that persona was and is a façade."

Arthur and Peter had swiveled to stare at Stephen as if they'd never truly seen him before.

"Curtis knew that your uncle, Lord Meriwell, would have trouble accepting the truth, and when Curtis came to make his report, he came prepared not just with the evidence of his own eyes but with documentary proof of your involvement in the business. By the time Curtis left, more than an hour later, your uncle believed him, and what's more, Curtis carried a letter that he delivered to Mr. Wishpole in which his lordship stated that he required Wishpole's immediate attendance in order to change his will." Stokes held Stephen's gaze. "Lord Meriwell was about to disown you, Stephen. You might not have known that, but in telling you he wished to speak with you privately about 'the business in Seven Dials,' your uncle sealed his fate."

His expression cold and accusatory, Barnaby stepped forward, drawing Stephen's attention. "You'd come prepared with a vial of cyanide and a bottle of high-strength laudanum because you'd already decided to use the opportunity of visiting here with the Busseltons, the family into which you intended to marry, to murder both your uncle and his granddaughter. What better cover?" Barnaby spread his hands in appeal to the company. "Who would imagine a man intent on convincing an MP and his wife to allow him to marry their daughter would cold-bloodedly commit murder—twice—during the visit?"

Barnaby trapped Stephen's dark and narrowing gaze. "The reason you had to act now, more or less immediately, was that your four joint-owners are insisting that you pay them for your share of the business, essentially repaying an intra-business loan they'd extended to you when the House of Dreams was first established. But you don't have the money. They gave you an ultimatum, a date by which you had to pay up or convince them that you could and shortly would. To do that, you needed not just your inheritance from your uncle but also Sophie's portion as well."

Her arms folded, Penelope stated, "You had to kill them both. So you did. First his lordship, and then you killed Sophie and used the last page of a letter she'd sent you, gently and considerately declining your offer of marriage, to make it appear that she'd killed his lordship and then, driven by guilt, committed suicide." Penelope stared into Stephen's ashen face. "That was utterly despicable."

Stephen couldn't seem to drag his gaze from Penelope's dark eyes, but slowly, he shook his head. He swallowed and croaked, "No. You have it all wrong." The words freed him, and wildly, he looked at the Busseltons. "You know I'm not like that."

But George and Hermione Busselton were staring at Stephen in abject horror as if he was their most hideous nightmare made flesh.

"At the dining table that first evening," Barnaby went on, "it was you at whom his lordship was glaring. It was you to whom Sophie sent the letter, part of which you used to bolster the case that she'd committed suicide. And it was you she allowed into her room on the night she died. While she was writing in her diary, you tipped a large dose of high-strength laudanum into her cocoa, knowing that, with her previous experience of the drug, she was unlikely to balk at the more bitter taste."

"More," Penelope said, "the next day, you remembered the diary, and uncertain about what Sophie might have written, you returned to her room that afternoon to remove it. But it had already vanished. Unbeknown to you, her ladyship had taken possession of the diary as a keepsake, but she loaned it to me, and I read it cover to cover."

Penelope leaned a touch closer, staring into Stephen's face, her own a mask of loathing. "You were right to worry. Among other revelations, Sophie had written a draft of the letter she sent to you declining your offer of marriage—another way you'd thought to achieve sufficient funds to pacify your creditors. The note you left by her bed was the last page of that letter. In it, she apologizes so sweetly—not for murdering your uncle, as you thought to make us all believe, but for any hurt she might have visited on your feelings."

Penelope flung up her hand, appealing to the universe. "She was just a young girl on the cusp of her life, and you cold-bloodedly sacrificed her to save your own financial skin!"

"And for that," Stokes intoned, "and all your other crimes, you will hang."

"You don't know what you're saying." Stephen started to rise, his gaze scanning the room for any avenue of escape.

Penelope adjusted her spectacles and recrossed her arms. "We do, actually."

Stephen stared at her and, shaking his head, stepped back, around his chair.

"And," Stokes pressed, his expression harshly determined, "we now have enough hard facts to prove it."

Stephen broke, but not toward the door or windows. He swung around and lunged at Veronica, hauling her out of the chair and onto her feet. With one arm around her waist, he anchored her in front of him.

Both Stokes and David leapt forward, but Stephen raised a hand, and a knife gleamed in his fist. "Stay back!"

Everyone was now on their feet. The Busseltons huddled in front of the sofa, while Lady Meriwell clung to Lord Iffey, and Wishpole hovered beside them.

Arthur and Peter had sprung up and swung to face Stephen. Their faces were grim, but no more than anyone else did they know what to do for the best.

"Don't be stupid," Stokes said, drawing Stephen's wild-eyed attention. "Put the knife down and let Miss Haskell go."

From the corner of her eye, Penelope saw David, who was standing facing Veronica and plainly restraining himself from attacking Stephen, catch Veronica's shocked gaze and mouth, "Faint."

Barely moving her head, Veronica nodded.

"Let me tell you how this is going to go." Stephen was holding the knife extended before him and waving it from side to side. "You're all going to stay here and allow me and Nurse Haskell to go to the stable. Once they give me a horse, I'll leave her there. Unharmed. Once I'm on a horse, I'll be away. The coast is close enough. I'll take myself off, and none of you will ever see me again." He swung the knife back and forth. "All right?"

"No, you blithering idiot!" Iffey roared. "It's damned well *not* all right!"

Stephen startled.

Veronica seized the moment and "fainted," letting her dead weight slip and slide through Stephen's restraining arm.

Trying to juggle her dragged him off balance.

Stokes launched himself over the love seat at Stephen.

David lunged for Stephen as well.

Desperately backpedaling, Stephen let Veronica go.

David changed trajectory and, leaving Stephen to Stokes, swooped on Veronica, hauled her up against him, and drew her away from the action.

Stokes had seized Stephen's wrist, grappling for the knife.

Abruptly, Stephen let go of the knife and, gritting his teeth, shoved Stokes, now off balance, back into Barnaby.

Stephen swung and raced for the door.

Curtis was standing on one side of the double doors, and O'Donnell was on the other.

Both squared up, ready to seize Stephen.

The doors were flung wide.

Jensen marched in and announced, "Lord Meriwell."

For a second, everyone froze—Stokes, Barnaby, Stephen, Arthur, Peter, and all—their minds scrambling to make sense of that announcement.

Then a tall, lean, dark-haired man stepped into the room and halted, a faint frown forming on his face as he looked around, patently trying to make sense of what was happening.

In the same instant, staring at him, everyone realized who he was; his features were unmistakable.

Driven by desperation, Stephen recovered first and surged toward the door.

"Stop him!" Stokes yelled.

Jensen stepped into Stephen's path, but Stephen seized the butler and ruthlessly flung him aside.

Curtis and O'Donnell were still blocked by the doors.

The only man between Stephen Meriwell and the front hall was the newcomer—Jacob, Lord Meriwell.

What happened next was so swift and smooth, Penelope barely believed her eyes.

Jacob saw Stephen barreling toward him. He stepped to the side, out of Stephen's path, then at just the right moment, Jacob extended one booted foot, tripping Stephen, then Jacob pivoted and pushed Stephen on —into the door frame.

Stephen's head connected with a solid *thunk*. Slowly, he slid to the floor and stayed there.

O'Donnell and Curtis had, by then, managed to push their way around the doors.

Curtis looked down at Stephen and nodded approvingly. "Nice move."

O'Donnell sighed and reached down to haul Stephen up. Obligingly,

Curtis seized Stephen's other arm, and they hoisted Stephen, groggy but at least partially conscious, to hang between them.

Stokes stalked up with a pair of handcuffs, and in short order, Stephen's wrists were secured.

Stokes stated, "Stephen Meriwell, I'm arresting you for the murder of your uncle, Lord Meriwell, and his granddaughter, Miss Sophie Meriwell. You will be taken to London and thrown into a cell and will shortly be charged with both murders."

Stokes paused, but Stephen didn't even try to raise his head. Stokes nodded to O'Donnell. "Take him to the stable. Morgan will be there, waiting. The pair of you can take the coach and ferry our murderer to the Yard."

O'Donnell shook Stephen like a doll. "It'll be our pleasure, guv."

With Barnaby, Penelope walked up as Curtis caught Stokes's gaze. "I'll be off, too." Curtis nodded to Barnaby and Penelope. "No doubt I'll see you sometime in town."

They nodded back. "Thank you for your help." Penelope looped her arm with Barnaby's. "We appreciate it."

Stokes turned to Curtis. "I'll call on you to get a copy of the report you made to Lord Meriwell."

Curtis grunted. "No need to call. I'll send a copy around." With a wave, he followed O'Donnell, who was dragging Stephen Meriwell into the front hall.

Stokes swung to face the tall, dark-haired man who had so efficiently captured the fleeing murderer.

To Penelope's eyes, Jacob—assuming that was who he truly was— was significantly more handsome than his male relatives. However, he was now frowning and looking from Stokes to Barnaby and Penelope as if about to demand to be told who they were and what they thought they were doing.

Before he could speak, Wishpole came up, a huge smile wreathing his face. "Jacob, my boy. It does my old eyes such good to see you." Wishpole glanced at Stokes, Barnaby, and Penelope. "And before you ask, yes, this gentleman is, indeed, Jacob Meriwell, the late Lord Meriwell's only surviving grandchild."

Jacob's frown deepened, and he looked at Stokes. "Only surviving. Did I hear you correctly? Did Stephen murder Sophie?"

Wishpole replied, "Sadly, yes. That was after I sent for you, informing you of your grandfather's death. His death, too, I regret to say, proved to have been at Stephen's hands."

Jacob exhaled. "I should never have stayed away so long."

To Stokes, Barnaby, and Penelope, Wishpole explained, "I always knew where Jacob was. He was nineteen when he left here, but even at that age, he wasn't irresponsible enough to simply disappear. He always kept me apprised of his address, and I notified him immediately after I learned of his lordship's death. However, I wasn't sure how long it would take him to respond or even if he would come."

Jacob sent Wishpole a look of fond exasperation. "I'm only near Doncaster. Of course I came."

Thinking to nip any developing guilt in the bud, Penelope said, "Incidentally, it is in no way on your head that Stephen acted as he did. Had you returned to Meriwell Hall earlier, you might simply have become another of his victims. To his admittedly warped mind, he had no other recourse. He needed the Meriwell wealth and was determined to have it."

Stokes nodded and caught Jacob's eye. "She's right. Your presence might have changed the order of things, but you wouldn't have prevented what happened."

Lady Meriwell swept up and, without any by-your-leave, tugged Jacob to face her. Her gaze fairly devoured his features. "My God! It truly is you. Oh, my dear boy!" And with that, she launched herself into his arms and promptly burst into tears.

Wisely leaving Jacob, assisted by Wishpole and Iffey, who stumped up, to deal with her ladyship and her exclamations, Penelope, Barnaby, and Stokes turned toward David and Veronica, only to find the elder Busseltons putting themselves firmly in their path.

George Busselton seized Stokes's hand and shook it vigorously. "Thank you, Inspector! You did excellent work there." Smiling broadly, Busselton released Stokes and offered Barnaby his hand. "I'm deeply impressed, Mr. Adair." He dipped his head Penelope's way. "And Mrs. Adair, too—your contribution was decisive. That was a terrible riddle there. Solving it is quite the feather in your caps."

Hermione Busselton graciously inclined her head to the three of them and boldly stated what her husband had either not yet seen or not been willing to put into words. "Through your actions in exposing Stephen Meriwell, you've saved our family from making what would have been a disastrous mistake." She sent a sharp look at her spouse. "Had Persimone or I been more easily pleased, we might even now be allied with a man—

I will never again call him a gentleman—who would have squandered Persimone's portion and then come to us to bail him out under threat of making his situation and our apparent complicity in it public, and I shudder, simply *shudder*, to think of how he might eventually have led Peregrine astray." She shook her head. "Truly, it doesn't bear thinking about."

As it was obvious that Mrs. Busselton had already thought through all the potential ramifications and, indeed, foreseen them accurately, Penelope felt that all that was required was to smile and graciously accept the couple's heartfelt thanks.

She and Barnaby left Stokes speaking with Mr. Busselton regarding the funding of the police and continued toward Veronica and David, who had drawn back to stand near one of the long windows.

On the way, they glanced at the knot of people who had formed around Jacob Meriwell. Not only his grandmother—who looked unlikely to let go of Jacob's arm anytime soon—and Iffey and Wishpole were clustered about him but also Arthur, Peter, Persimone, and Peregrine, all avidly listening to what, Penelope assumed, was an accounting of how Jacob had spent his recent years.

Penelope studied the group, then leaned closer to Barnaby and whispered, "From the look in Persimone's eyes, Jacob Meriwell is much more her style than Stephen ever was."

Barnaby huffed. "Matchmaking? Even here?"

Looking to where Veronica and David had their heads together, for all the world giving the impression—to those with eyes to see—of hoping to hear wedding bells in their immediate future, Penelope smiled and lightly shrugged. "Why not? Murder and mayhem have a habit of focusing the mind on what's most important in life."

Barnaby thought, then inclined his head. "I have to admit there's wisdom in that."

Penelope grinned. Despite all the frustrations along the way, now that they'd come to the end of this case, she was, she discovered, peculiarly satisfied with the way matters had fallen out. This hadn't been their first successful denouement, but at that moment, she was willing to accord it the title of "most rewarding."

EPILOGUE

MAY 13, 1840. ST. NICHOLAS'S CHURCH, SURREY.

*A*ll of the visitors save only Veronica and Wishpole had left Meriwell Hall on the evening of Stephen Meriwell's arrest.

The prodigal grandson, Jacob, had remained as well, and when Penelope, Barnaby, Stokes, and David returned five days later for the joint funeral of Angus, Lord Meriwell, and Sophie Meriwell, Veronica informed them that Jacob, shortly to be recognized as his grandfather's successor to the title and the combined Meriwell estate, was likely to return permanently from the Midlands, where he'd established and been managing a highly successful manufacturing business.

"Apparently," Veronica said as she and Penelope, flanked by David, Barnaby, and Stokes, strolled between the stones in the graveyard, "Jacob feels that the time is right to establish a similar business somewhere in Surrey or Sussex. He and Wishpole have been as thick as thieves, discussing various prospects." She smiled. "It's as if Jacob returning has given Wishpole new life, just as it has for her ladyship. His being here has helped both, and Lord Iffey, too, cope with Lord Meriwell's death. All are still sad, but they're coming around. Jacob's giving them something to live for."

Penelope nodded. "Out of tragedy, good may come."

Indeed, that was one reason Penelope had felt compelled to attend the funeral. To her mind, it was fitting to see those murdered laid to rest with all due care and affection and also to be reassured that life would, nevertheless, continue for those left behind. In this case, it seemed that the future looked quite positive.

They paused not far from the church door and watched the large and varied congregation stream out into the mild sunshine. The burial services would be private, held later and attended only by the males of the family.

The Busseltons were present, and the older pair came up to exchange greetings.

From what Penelope gleaned, Mrs. Busselton, at least, was still counting her blessings.

Even Mr. Busselton had taken a lesson from their recent experience. "You may be sure," he confided to Penelope and Barnaby, "that henceforth, I will be very much less trusting about situations that seem too good to be true."

Overhearing the comment, Mrs. Busselton looked pleased. "When we left here last week, we went straight home to Guildford and were gratified to have the new Lord Meriwell visit a few days later. He brought word of the funeral and was kind enough to thank us for our support of his grandmother through such a trying time." Mrs. Busselton nodded with obvious approval. "It was very prettily done."

"Veronica mentioned that Jacob's presence has greatly eased Lady Meriwell's heart," Penelope put in.

"Indeed, I imagine that's so," Mrs. Busselton replied. "Jacob told us a little of his endeavors in the Midlands, and I must say, it was refreshing to hear of a young gentleman of his wealth and standing so willing to involve himself in bettering the lives of those less fortunate. Not in any ramshackle, self-aggrandizing way but in a considered, thoughtful, productive manner. He clearly has a passion for improving the conditions of his workers, and he's adamant that the return he gets is worth the investment."

It was patently obvious that in Mrs. Busselton, Jacob had found a supporter.

"Hmm, yes." Mr. Busselton didn't look quite as enthused. "His politics might be a trifle radical, you know, but I daresay that's the old generation speaking of the new, and in the end, one has to bow to progress."

Mrs. Busselton smiled on her spouse. "I wouldn't have thought I would ever say it but"—her gaze shifted to the group standing just outside the church door—"our stay at Meriwell Hall has definitely brought some benefits."

Following Mrs. Busselton's gaze, Penelope saw Persimone and Peregrine talking earnestly with Jacob. The trio seemed quite absorbed.

Mrs. Busselton lowered her voice to confide, "If Peregrine must look up to a more experienced gentleman, then I'll be well pleased if he chooses to emulate Jacob Meriwell."

Penelope bit back a laughing comment that her ladyship's rosy-eyed view of Jacob all but mirrored her spouse's earlier assessment of Stephen, but in truth, from what Penelope had seen and heard, Jacob was, indeed, a young gentleman with his feet planted firmly on the ground, and by taking his direction from his late parents, he was very much following the path of the angels.

What caught Penelope's interest now was the look in Persimone's eyes as she darted glances Jacob's way and the rather hopeful and encouraging looks Jacob sent in return.

Hmm. More wedding bells, perhaps?

There were few events that brought Penelope more pleasure than the celebration of a happy union, and she sensed that a marriage between Jacob and Persimone might work very well.

Penelope's gaze wandered farther, and she saw Lady Meriwell and Lord Iffey, arm in arm as they walked slowly down the path. Just watching them stroll together, glancing at each other and smiling as they went, conveyed a sense of them moving forward in life side by side, supporting each other and being there for the other, as Iffey had certainly been for decades.

Penelope had to wonder if there might be a small ceremony there, too. In time.

But for now…she considered the sight of Jacob Meriwell chatting with several of the local gentry. Persimone held to her position beside him, and the hope in her face was easy to read.

Before she and the others had left Meriwell Hall, Penelope had taken shrewd note of Jacob's reaction to his grandfather's death and, even more, to the shocking news that his younger sister, too, had met her end at the hands of Jacob's cousin. To Penelope's eyes, Jacob had been genuinely grieved, even though Lady Meriwell had let fall that the connection between brother and sister, with ten years in age between them, had never been all that strong. Jacob's feelings for his grandfather had clearly been deeper, and the untimely death of his grandsire had affected him at a more profound level, yet Jacob was young, and more than anything else, he was the sort who picked themselves up and forged on.

Yet after the salutary tale of Stephen Meriwell—who Penelope freely admitted had hoodwinked even her—she'd felt the need for caution. Over the intervening days, she'd turned her researching skills on Jacob Meriwell and had learned considerably more about his doings over the years since he'd left Meriwell Hall.

Viewing again the way Persimone looked at Jacob and the way he looked at her, Penelope decided it behooved her to share her findings with the Busseltons. Barnaby had drifted from her side and, with Stokes, was talking with Wishpole. Her mind made up, she turned to the Busseltons, who had remained beside her, and after drawing them somewhat apart from the chattering horde still filling the churchyard, she told them of the facts she'd ascertained regarding Jacob Meriwell and his life over recent years.

The Busseltons were suitably impressed and also distinctly grateful.

"Thank you, my dear." Mrs. Busselton briefly closed her hand about Penelope's wrist. "That was kind of you to share that information." She, too, glanced toward her daughter and the new Lord Meriwell. "I suppose it's obvious we harbor hopes in that direction, but if I've learned anything of Persimone, watching from the sidelines is the best approach. That said, it would be something of a coup to snap up the new Lord Meriwell before he ever sets foot in the ton."

Penelope heartily concurred and, leaving the Busseltons dreaming, she seized the moment to approach Lady Meriwell and Lord Iffey, who were standing a few yards away and, momentarily, were free of others.

After complimenting her ladyship on the flowers in the church, Penelope airily remarked, "I do hope you will find some degree of happiness in the years to come."

Lady Meriwell's eyes were laughing as she met Penelope's gaze. "My dear, you are known to be quite observant, so I daresay it will come as no surprise to you that Iffey and I plan to tie the knot at some point."

"Once Clemmie is out of mourning, of course," Iffey hurried to assure Penelope.

"Indeed. I have no wish to wear gray at my next wedding." Her ladyship smiled at Iffey, and Penelope felt her own heart warm at the love that glowed in her ladyship's old eyes. "Even at our age," her ladyship went on, "even after all this time, it will be nice to be able to be open about things."

"Definitely," Iffey declared.

With a sincerely delighted smile, Penelope wished the ageing pair well, then finally managed to catch up with Veronica and David. Penelope had already learned that the couple planned to marry, which she considered an excellent development.

When she brazenly asked when she might expect to receive a wedding invitation, Veronica laughed, then shot a questioning glance at David. "We were thinking of early autumn. September, perhaps?"

"To some extent, our timing will be dictated by when I can get colleagues to cover my patients for me." David smiled, and the depth of his happiness shone in his eyes. "Physician to the ton must be one of the few professions where getting married requires such organizational contortions."

Veronica laughed. "Of course, once we're married, the organizing will fall to me."

Penelope had learned of the couple's plan to work side by side in David's practice, and as one of David's patients, she wholeheartedly supported the notion.

After several minutes of catching up with news of shared acquaintances and assured that all in Veronica and David's soon-to-be-joint life was progressing as it should, Penelope parted from the pair. David would return with Veronica to Meriwell Hall to pick up her cases before driving them both to London in his curricle.

Ambling along the edge of the crowd, Penelope tried to spot her husband or, failing him, Stokes. She'd last seen the pair talking with Wishpole. She skirted clusters of people, peering this way and that, then spotted Wishpole standing to one side.

He was currently speaking with Arthur and Peter Meriwell.

Something about their gestures and Wishpole's expression and the tenor of his responses gave Penelope pause. She hung back, concealed amid the crowd, and when Arthur and Peter finally took their leave of the old solicitor and walked away, she went forward, looped her arm in Wishpole's, and asked, "What on earth was that about?"

Wishpole's eyes twinkled. "I could claim client confidentiality, but in this case, I can't see that it matters. First, of course, the legacies received from his lordship's estate have greatly eased the financial pressures on Arthur and Peter, enough to allow both to pause and reflect. You'll be pleased to learn that their elder brother's rather spectacular fall from grace has, it seems, pulled the younger two up short. Both, I gather, have spent some time dwelling on the follies of their pasts and their prospects for the future, such as they currently are. The upshot of that is that both—

independently—decided to pull up their socks, and wonder of wonders, they came together and discussed their options, and then they came to see me."

The solicitor's eyes twinkled even more definitely as his gaze met Penelope's. "They've asked, and I've agreed to assist them to find suitable positions in the civil service—positions they are actually capable of filling. Both had perfectly adequate educations, and neither is a dunce. They might not have been using their brains all that much in recent years, but they are not incapable of doing so. And most tellingly, neither wish me to inform Jacob of their plans, nor do they wish to ask him for any support whatsoever." He paused, then added, "I think both feel somewhat responsible for their uncle's death and, even more, Sophie's. Guilt as such would be misplaced, but it seems that the lingering impact of the past week might well be the making of Arthur and Peter, and I, for one, am prepared to be grateful."

"Indeed!" Penelope was suitably taken aback. "I never would have expected such common sense from them."

"Well, my dear." Wishpole patted her hand as it lay on his sleeve. "It's early days yet. No doubt, we shall see."

Penelope remained chatting with Wishpole about his view of Jacob and his novel ideas. The solicitor's opinions proved to be much in line with hers. Eventually parting from him, she set off once more to track down her husband.

She finally located him and Stokes. Or more accurately, having finished chatting with various people, they were searching for and found her. She smiled at them delightedly and took Barnaby's arm. "Gentlemen, I have to admit that I feel particularly satisfied with the results of our endeavors on multiple fronts. I predict that, in counterpoint to this joint funeral, we'll soon have three weddings to attend." With relish, she declared, "Life goes on."

Amused, Stokes murmured agreement.

Barnaby smiled at her. "And on that note, I believe we can, with all due complacency, head home."

"Indeed." Her face wreathed in a smile, Penelope gestured expansively. "Home to our waiting families and all the joys they bring." She met Barnaby's cerulean-blue eyes and more quietly admitted, "I did miss them."

She meant Oliver and Phillip, and she saw understanding and fellow-parental feeling in Barnaby's face.

Without further discussion, they turned their steps toward their waiting carriage.

Mulling over all she felt and why, Penelope said, "If you analyze this case, it was all about legacies, first to last. Not merely legacies in the physical sense—the inheritances and bequests—but even more than those, this case was driven by legacies of character."

Stokes grunted. "Stephen being the same as his father, only much worse in that Stephen was a master of deception on top of all his other faults."

"And Angus Meriwell and Sophie Meriwell were both obsessed by the aspect that featured most highly in their minds, by the thing that mattered most to them." Penelope looked up and elucidated, "Family reputation for Angus and the social whirl for Sophie. In their single-mindedness, Sophie and Angus were much alike."

Barnaby added, "Robert, Jacob and Sophie's father, seems to have been in a different mold, possibly taking after Clementina. He appears to have cared about others every bit as much as he cared for himself, and in that sense, Jacob seems a chip off Robert's block."

Penelope nodded. "Exactly. Indeed, Jacob seems to be following in the footsteps of his parents—committed to working for the betterment of all, albeit in a different way, in a different country."

They walked on, then Barnaby observed, "I rather think that if Angus had lived to deal with Stephen's perfidy and Jacob had subsequently returned, while Angus would initially have been rocked back on his heels, ultimately, he would have been immensely proud of the man Jacob has become."

"Yes." Penelope squeezed Barnaby's arm and grinned. "Aside from all else, Jacob's personality, achievements, and endeavors reflect so very well on the Meriwell name!"

"Hah!" Stokes said, and Barnaby chuckled.

Smiling, too, Stokes stated, "This was, indeed, a case of legacies. Yet always, in the end, life—and families—endure and go on."

Dear Reader,

When I commenced writing this manuscript, I realized that the title simply had to be *The Meriwell Legacy*. Not only were all the prime suspects in line for a meaningful inheritance from Lord Meriwell's estate, but inherited character traits played a major role in the interactions between the Meriwell family members as well as providing much of their motivations.

I've only just realized that's it's been *six whole years* since the release of the last Casebook of Barnaby Adair mystery! I suppose that, because the characters are more or less constantly alive in my mind, the interval doesn't seem anywhere near as long as that to me. Regardless, I truly enjoyed getting back to these characters and their lives, and am keen to spend the next few years following their further adventures.

I hope you enjoyed the latest installment.

My next release will be another investigative jaunt with Barnaby, Penelope, and Stokes, as they scramble to identify the true villain who killed a much-detested viscount in order to save Barnaby's long-time friend, Charlie Hastings, from being accused of the crime.

More information about earlier volumes in THE CASEBOOK OF BARNABY ADAIR series—*Where the Heart Leads, The Peculiar Case of Lord Finsbury's Diamonds, The Masterful Mr. Montague, The Curious Case of Lady Latimer's Shoes, Loving Rose: The Redemption of Malcolm Sinclair, The Confounding Case of the Carisbrook Emeralds*, and *The Murder at Mandeville Hall*—can be found following, along with details of my other recent releases.

Barnaby, Penelope, Stokes, Griselda, and their families and friends continue to thrive. I hope they and their adventures solving mysteries and exposing villains will continue to entertain you in the future just as much as they do me.

Enjoy!

Stephanie.

For alerts as new books are released, plus information on upcoming books, exclusive sweepstakes and sneak peeks into upcoming novels, sign up for Stephanie's Private Email Newsletter http://www.stephanielaurens. com/newsletter-signup/

Or if you don't have time to chat and want a quick email alert, sign up and follow me at BookBub https://www.bookbub.com/authors/stephanie-laurens

The ultimate source for detailed information on all Stephanie's published books, including covers, descriptions, and excerpts, is Stephanie's Website www.stephanielaurens.com

You can also follow Stephanie via her Amazon Author Page at http://tinyurl.com/zc3e9mp

Goodreads members can follow Stephanie via her author page https://www.goodreads.com/author/show/9241.Stephanie_Laurens

You can email Stephanie at stephanie@stephanielaurens.com

Or find her on Facebook https://www.facebook.com/AuthorStephanieLaurens/

COMING NEXT:

DEAD BESIDE THE THAMES
Casebook of Barnaby Adair #9
To be released in October, 2024.

Despite a certain restlessness, Charlie Hastings tells himself he is content with his uneventful life as a fashionable gentleman in London. The last thing he expects is for Inspector Stokes to knock on his door and inform him that he is the prime suspect in the murder of Viscount Sedbury, a dislikable sort who Charlie had run afoul of only days before. But murder is to ton gossip as honey is to bears, and within hours, Charlie and Stokes find themselves working with Barnaby and Penelope to determine who actually did the deed. Unexpectedly, they are joined by Sedbury's nearest and dearest, who also feature as prime suspects, in a race to protect Charlie's and the family members' reputations in the only possible way— by finding the real murderer.

Available for pre-order by August, 2024

. . .

RECENTLY RELEASED:

A FAMILY OF HIS OWN
Cynster Next Generation Novel #15

#1 New York Times *bestselling author Stephanie Laurens returns to the quintessential question of what family means to a Cynster in this tale of the last unmarried member of the Cynster Next Generation and the final mission that opens his eyes.*

Toby Cynster is not amused when informed that his new mission is to be his last in the shadowy service of Drake, Marquess of Winchelsea. Courtesy of Toby being the last unmarried Cynster of his generation and the consequent martial obsession of his female relatives, he will be given no more excuses to avoid society and, instead, expected to devote himself to finding a suitable bride. But Toby sees no point in marrying—thanks to his siblings, he has plenty of nephews and nieces with whom to play favorite uncle, and he has no thoughts of establishing a family of his own.

But then the mission takes an unexpected turn, leaving Toby to escort the irritatingly fascinating Diana Locke plus the three young children of a dying Englishman from Vienna to England.

Diana is no more enthused about their journey than Toby, but needs must, and forever practical, she bows to events and makes the best of things for her godchildren's sakes. She's determined to see them to safety in England and does her best to ignore her nonsensical and annoying awareness of Toby.

But then their journey becomes a flight from deadly pursuit, and their most effective disguise is to pass themselves off as a family—the sort of family Toby had been certain he would never want. Through a succession of fraught adventures, Toby, Diana, and the children lean on each other and grow and mature while furthering their ultimate aim of reaching England safely, and along the way, Toby and Diana both learn what having a family actually means to them, individually and together, and each discovers the until-then-missing foundation stone of their future lives.

A classic historical adventure romance that sprawls across Europe to end in the leafy depths of the English countryside. A Cynster Next Generation novel. A full-length historical romance of 108,000 words.

PREVIOUSLY RELEASED IN THE CASEBOOK OF BARNABY ADAIR NOVELS:

Read about Penelope's and Barnaby's romance, plus that of Stokes and Griselda, in
**The first volume in
The Casebook of Barnaby Adair mystery-romances
WHERE THE HEART LEADS**

Penelope Ashford, Portia Cynster's younger sister, has grown up with every advantage - wealth, position, and beauty. Yet Penelope is anything but a typical ton miss - forceful, willful and blunt to a fault, she has for years devoted her considerable energy and intelligence to directing an institution caring for the forgotten orphans of London's streets.

But now her charges are mysteriously disappearing. Desperate, Penelope turns to the one man she knows who might help her - Barnaby Adair.

Handsome scion of a noble house, Adair has made a name for himself in political and judicial circles. His powers of deduction and observation combined with his pedigree has seen him solve several serious crimes within the ton. Although he makes her irritatingly uncomfortable, Penelope throws caution to the wind and appears on his bachelor doorstep late one night, determined to recruit him to her cause.

Barnaby is intrigued—by her story, and her. Her bold beauty and undeniable brains make a striking contrast to the usual insipid ton misses. And as he's in dire need of an excuse to avoid said insipid misses, he accepts her challenge, never dreaming she and it will consume his every waking hour.

Enlisting the aid of Inspector Basil Stokes of the fledgling Scotland Yard, they infiltrate the streets of London's notorious East End. But as they unravel the mystery of the missing boys, they cross the trail of a criminal embedded in the very organization recently created to protect all Londoners. And that criminal knows of them and their efforts, and is only too ready to threaten all they hold dear, including their new-found knowledge of the intrigues of the human heart.

FURTHER CASES AND THE EVOLUTION OF RELATIONSHIPS CONTINUE IN:

The second volume in
The Casebook of Barnaby Adair mystery-romances
THE PECULIAR CASE OF LORD FINSBURY'S DIAMONDS

#1 New York Times *bestselling author Stephanie Laurens brings you a tale of murder, mystery, passion, and intrigue – and diamonds!*

Penelope Adair, wife and partner of amateur sleuth Barnaby Adair, is so hugely pregnant she cannot even waddle. When Barnaby is summoned to assist Inspector Stokes of Scotland Yard in investigating the violent murder of a gentleman at a house party, Penelope, frustrated that she cannot participate, insists that she and Griselda, Stokes's wife, be duly informed of their husbands' discoveries.

Yet what Barnaby and Stokes uncover only leads to more questions. The murdered gentleman had been thrown out of the house party days before, so why had he come back? And how and why did he come to have the fabulous Finsbury diamond necklace in his pocket, much to Lord Finsbury's consternation. Most peculiar of all, why had the murderer left the necklace, worth a stupendous fortune, on the body?

The conundrums compound as our intrepid investigators attempt to make sense of this baffling case. Meanwhile, the threat of scandal grows ever more tangible for all those attending the house party – and the stakes are highest for Lord Finsbury's daughter and the gentleman who has spent the last decade resurrecting his family fortune so he can aspire to her hand. Working parallel to Barnaby and Stokes, the would-be lovers hunt for a path through the maze of contradictory facts to expose the murderer, disperse the pall of scandal, and claim the love and the shared life they crave.

A pre-Victorian mystery with strong elements of romance. A short novel of 39,000 words.

The third volume in
The Casebook of Barnaby Adair mystery-romances

THE MASTERFUL MR. MONTAGUE

Montague has devoted his life to managing the wealth of London's elite, but at a huge cost: a family of his own. Then the enticing Miss Violet Matcham seeks his help, and in the puzzle she presents him, he finds an intriguing new challenge professionally...and personally.

Violet, devoted lady-companion to the aging Lady Halstead, turns to Montague to reassure her ladyship that her affairs are in order. But the famous Montague is not at all what she'd expected—this man is compelling, decisive, supportive, and strong—everything Violet needs in a champion, a position to which Montague rapidly lays claim.

But then Lady Halstead is murdered and Violet and Montague, aided by Barnaby Adair, Inspector Stokes, Penelope, and Griselda, race to expose a cunning and cold-blooded killer...who stalks closer and closer. Will Montague and Violet learn the shocking truth too late to seize their chance at enduring love?

A pre-Victorian tale of romance and mystery in the classic historical romance style. A novel of 120,000 words.

The fourth volume in
The Casebook of Barnaby Adair mystery-romances
THE CURIOUS CASE OF LADY LATIMER'S SHOES

#1 New York Times *bestselling author Stephanie Laurens brings you a tale of mysterious death, feuding families, star-crossed lovers—and shoes to die for.*

With her husband, amateur-sleuth the Honorable Barnaby Adair, decidedly eccentric fashionable matron Penelope Adair is attending the premier event opening the haut ton's Season when a body is discovered in the gardens. A lady has been struck down with a finial from the terrace balustrade. Her family is present, as are the cream of the haut ton—the shocked hosts turn to Barnaby and Penelope for help.

Barnaby calls in Inspector Basil Stokes and they begin their investigation. Penelope assists by learning all she can about the victim's family, and uncovers a feud between them and the Latimers over the fabulous shoes known as Lady Latimer's shoes, currently exclusive to the Latimers.

The deeper Penelope delves, the more convinced she becomes that the murder is somehow connected to the shoes. She conscripts Griselda, Stokes's wife, and Violet Montague, now Penelope's secretary, and the trio set out to learn all they can about the people involved and most importantly the shoes, a direction vindicated when unexpected witnesses report seeing a lady fleeing the scene—wearing Lady Latimer's shoes.

But nothing is as it seems, and the more Penelope and her friends learn about the shoes, conundrums abound, compounded by a Romeo-and-Juliet romance and escalating social pressure…until at last, the pieces fall into place, and finally understanding what has occurred, the six intrepid investigators race to prevent an even worse tragedy.

A pre-Victorian mystery with strong elements of romance. A novel of 76,000 words.

The fifth volume in
The Casebook of Barnaby Adair mystery-romances
LOVING ROSE: THE REDEMPTION OF MALCOLM SINCLAIR

#1 New York Times bestselling author Stephanie Laurens returns with another thrilling story from the Casebook of Barnaby Adair…

Miraculously spared from death, Malcolm Sinclair erases the notorious man he once was. Reinventing himself as Thomas Glendower, he strives to make amends for his past, yet he never imagines penance might come via a secretive lady he discovers living in his secluded manor.

Rose has a plausible explanation for why she and her children are residing in Thomas's house, but she quickly realizes he's far too intelligent to fool. Revealing the truth is impossibly dangerous, yet day by day, he wins her trust, and then her heart.

But then her enemy closes in, and Rose turns to Thomas as the only man who can protect her and the children. And when she asks for his help, Thomas finally understands his true purpose, and with unwavering commitment, he seeks his redemption in the only way he can—through living the reality of loving Rose.

A pre-Victorian tale of romance and mystery in the classic historical romance style. A novel of 105,000 words.

The sixth volume in
The Casebook of Barnaby Adair mystery-romances

THE CONFOUNDING CASE OF THE CARISBROOK
EMERALDS

#1 New York Times *bestselling author Stephanie Laurens brings you a tale of emerging and also established loves and the many facets of family, interwoven with mystery and murder.*

A young lady accused of theft and the gentleman who elects himself her champion enlist the aid of Stokes, Barnaby, Penelope, and friends in pursuing justice, only to find themselves tangled in a web of inter-family tensions and secrets.

When Miss Cara Di Abaccio is accused of stealing the Carisbrook emeralds by the infamously arrogant Lady Carisbrook and marched out of her guardian's house by Scotland Yard's finest, Hugo Adair, Barnaby Adair's cousin, takes umbrage and descends on Scotland Yard, breathing fire in Cara's defense.

Hugo discovers Inspector Stokes has been assigned to the case, and after surveying the evidence thus far, Stokes calls in his big guns when it comes to dealing with investigations in the ton—namely, the Honorable Barnaby Adair and his wife, Penelope.

Soon convinced of Cara's innocence and—given Hugo's apparent tendre for Cara—the need to clear her name, Penelope and Barnaby join Stokes and his team in pursuing the emeralds and, most importantly, who stole them.

But the deeper our intrepid investigators delve into the Carisbrook household, the more certain they become that all is not as it seems. Lady Carisbrook is a harpy, Franklin Carisbrook is secretive, Julia Carisbrook is overly timid, and Lord Carisbrook, otherwise a genial and honorable gentleman, holds himself distant from his family. More, his lordship attempts to shut down the investigation. And Stokes, Barnaby, and Penelope are convinced the Carisbrooks' staff are not sharing all they know.

Meanwhile, having been appointed Cara's watchdog until the mystery is resolved, Hugo, fascinated by Cara as he's been with no other young lady, seeks to entertain and amuse her...and, increasingly intently, to discover the way to her heart. Consequently, Penelope finds herself juggling the attractions of the investigation against the demands of the Adair family for her to actively encourage the budding romance.

What would her mentors advise? On that, Penelope is crystal clear.

Regardless, aided by Griselda, Violet, and Montague and calling on contacts in business, the underworld, and ton society, Penelope, Barnaby, and Stokes battle to peel back each layer of subterfuge and, step by step, eliminate the innocent and follow the emeralds' trail…

Yet instead of becoming clearer, the veils and shadows shrouding the Carisbrooks only grow murkier…until, abruptly, our investigators find themselves facing an inexplicable death, with a potential murderer whose conviction would shake society to its back teeth.

A historical novel of 78,000 words interweaving mystery, romance, and social intrigue.

The seventh volume in
The Casebook of Barnaby Adair mystery-romances
THE MURDER AT MANDEVILLE HALL

#1 NYT-bestselling author Stephanie Laurens brings you a tale of unexpected romance that blossoms against the backdrop of dastardly murder.

On discovering the lifeless body of an innocent ingénue, a peer attending a country house party joins forces with the lady-amazon sent to fetch the victim safely home in a race to expose the murderer before Stokes, assisted by Barnaby and Penelope, is forced to allow the guests, murderer included, to decamp.

Well-born rakehell and head of an ancient family, Alaric, Lord Carradale, has finally acknowledged reality and is preparing to find a bride. But loyalty to his childhood friend, Percy Mandeville, necessitates attending Percy's annual house party, held at neighboring Mandeville Hall. Yet despite deploying his legendary languid charm, by the second evening of the week-long event, Alaric is bored and restless.

Escaping from the soirée and the Hall, Alaric decides that as soon as he's free, he'll hie to London and find the mild-mannered, biddable lady he believes will ensure a peaceful life. But the following morning, on walking through the Mandeville Hall shrubbery on his way to join the other guests, he comes upon the corpse of a young lady-guest.

Constance Whittaker accepts that no gentleman will ever offer for her —she's too old, too tall, too buxom, too headstrong...too much in myriad ways. Now acting as her grandfather's agent, she arrives at Mandeville Hall to extricate her young cousin, Glynis, who unwisely accepted an invitation to the reputedly licentious house party.

But Glynis cannot be found.

A search is instituted. Venturing into the shrubbery, Constance discovers an outrageously handsome aristocrat crouched beside Glynis's lifeless form. Unsurprisingly, Constance leaps to the obvious conclusion.

Luckily, once the gentleman explains that he'd only just arrived, commonsense reasserts itself. More, as matters unfold and she and Carradale have to battle to get Glynis's death properly investigated, Constance discovers Alaric to be a worthy ally.

Yet even after Inspector Stokes of Scotland Yard arrives and takes charge of the case, along with his consultants, the Honorable Barnaby Adair and his wife, Penelope, the murderer's identity remains shrouded in mystery, and learning why Glynis was killed—all in the few days before the house party's guests will insist on leaving—tests the resolve of all concerned. Flung into each other's company, fiercely independent though Constance is, unsusceptible though Alaric is, neither can deny the connection that grows between them.

Then Constance vanishes.

Can Alaric unearth the one fact that will point to the murderer before the villain rips from the world the lady Alaric now craves for his own?

A historical novel of 75,000 words interweaving romance, mystery, and murder.

ABOUT THE AUTHOR

#1 *New York Times* bestselling author Stephanie Laurens began writing romances as an escape from the dry world of professional science. Her hobby quickly became a career when her first novel was accepted for publication, and with entirely becoming alacrity, she gave up writing about facts in favor of writing fiction.

All Laurens's works to date are historical romances, ranging from medieval times to the mid-1800s, and her settings range from Scotland to India. The majority of her works are set in the period of the British Regency. Laurens has published over 80 works of historical romance, including 40 *New York Times* bestsellers. Laurens has sold more than 20 million print, audio, and e-books globally. All her works are continuously available in print and e-book formats in English worldwide, and have been translated into many other languages. An international bestseller, among other accolades, Laurens has received the Romance Writers of America® prestigious RITA® Award for Best Romance Novella 2008 for *The Fall of Rogue Gerrard.*

Laurens's continuing novels featuring the Cynster family are widely regarded as classics of the historical romance genre. Other series include the *Bastion Club Novels*, the *Black Cobra Quartet*, the *Adventurers Quartet,* and the *Casebook of Barnaby Adair Novels*.

For information on all published novels and on upcoming releases and updates on novels yet to come, visit Stephanie's website: www.stephanielaurens.com

To sign up for Stephanie's Email Newsletter (a private list) for heads-up alerts as new books are released, exclusive sneak peeks into upcoming books, and exclusive sweepstakes contests, follow the prompts at http://www.stephanielaurens.com/newsletter-signup/

To follow Stephanie on BookBub, head to her BookBub Author Page: https://www.bookbub.com/authors/stephanie-laurens

Stephanie lives with her husband and a goofy black labradoodle in the hills outside Melbourne, Australia. When she isn't writing, she's reading, and if she isn't reading, she'll be tending her garden.

www.stephanielaurens.com
stephanie@stephanielaurens.com